# FALL WHE

'Stand still, you Paddy bastard!'

Of course that was the wrong thing to say because after twelve years service to the Crown, twelve years of checking under my car and watching where I go and who I talk to and how I live my life, I was sensitive about things like that and I felt the rage shooting up inside me but there was nothing I could do except stand there like a fool. The girl was running across the road. The gunman was watching both of us. The man with the thin face shouted at him.

'Stop her, for Christ's sake!'

*Richard Crawford was born in 1961 in Lisburn. He now works as a Belfast civil servant and lives in Hillsborough, County Down. Fall When Hit is his first novel.*

# Richard Crawford
# FALL WHEN HIT

Mandarin

**A Mandarin Paperback**

FALL WHEN HIT

First published in Great Britain 1993
by Mandarin Paperbacks
an imprint of Reed Consumer Books Ltd
Michelin House, 81 Fulham Road, London SW3 6RB
and Auckland, Melbourne, Singapore and Toronto

Reprinted 1993

Copyright © 1993 by Richard Crawford

The author has asserted his moral rights

A CIP catalogue record for this book
is available at the British Library

ISBN 07493 1376 5

Typeset by ROM Data Corporation Limited, Cornwall, England
Printed in Great Britain by
BPCC Paperbacks Ltd
Member of BPCC Ltd

For
Detective Constable Kenneth Crawford,
Royal Ulster Constabulary.

Go gentle into that good night.

'Targets will appear at irregular intervals.
Fire one round at each target.
Targets will fall when hit.'

Instructions given during All-Arms Annual
Personal Weapon Test

# FALL
# WHEN
# HIT

Just past Bleary and heading towards Tullyherron on one of those narrow roads with the high hedges and the trees almost meeting over the top, absolutely pitch black except for the travelling pool of light pushed from the headlights, the mind almost numb from the steady beat of the wipers against the rain and the constant whoosh of the wheels on the wet road. I was driving fast, too fast, fifty-five or sixty on the straights with the car square in the middle of the road and the brain tired and drifting.

Slow down.

Of course I was too tired and should have stopped the car for a rest but you always feel you can go on, don't you, just a few miles more with the cold air on full blast and your eyelids pegged open and the car bouncing off the kerb. My mind was thick and soft and blurred, already home, slipping into thoughts of sleep and bed and the warm, heavy duvet. Sleep. I needed sleep. Even the sound of the word was long

1

and warm and luxurious. I rolled it around in my head.

The radio. Yes, try the radio; Tammy Wynette and steel guitars, a lonely sound for the end of a lonely night. Her husband was no good and she wanted to leave, but love was holding her back, twanging her sorrows into the darkness for the few awake to hear. Sorry for your troubles, Tammy. I wondered how many people were listening to her and the soft-spoken DJ at this hour of the morning, not too bloody many I'd imagine.

They had been expecting too much recently and I was going to have to do something, talk to someone: I needed a rest. Five duties in a row and fourteen in the month so far, not counting training during the weekends, and it was too much, it was just far too much. And all right, there was a lot on at the minute and things were tight, they were expecting that bomb for Lurgan in the next few days but I couldn't carry the whole bloody company on my back. I wanted to sleep. To lie all morning and get up at noon. And not have to work, not have to drag myself from bed and shave and dress and try to think about normal life until the next duty.

Headlights, too close to my wing as they whipped past, quick adrenalin surge pumping through me as I over-corrected and hit the kerb again; well, at least it keeps you awake.

Through Balinderry and the brief company of the sleeping houses and the drab, yellow street-lights, then back into the country again and the lonely road rushing past and nothing to watch but the flickering white line, with sleep stroking at me again.

I was half-conscious of their headlights flickering through the trees ahead of me, moving at right angles to the road; far away and pretty but nothing to do with me and then I turned the next bend and suddenly they were there, bursting out of a side road with their beams on full, moving too fast to turn easily and too hard to stop. Fear. Adrenalin. My mind suddenly wide awake and straining for information.

Their car was long and white and it reflected my own headlights back at me and the sudden glare blinded me. My mind shifted into that illusion of slow motion that comes with the fear of death or injury, giving the fore-brain time to gather and evaluate the available data. In a matter of seconds I would hit their car and it seemed there was no way to avoid it. Collision was inevitable. The cars drifted towards each other at a snail's pace. I wrenched at the wheel, tugging it round, standing on the brakes and trying for cadence braking but losing it on the wet road, aiming for the rear of their car as my own car bounced on to the verge. Unimportant details were flooding into my brain, perception sharpened by fear: the orange needle of the speedometer sliding quickly down from sixty to thirty; the sound of my tyres sliding on the wet grass; the face of the other driver, illuminated and paled by my headlights, his eyes wide and frightened.

I might have bounced round behind them, sliding the car towards their rear and hoping they would miss me but the other man had used his instinct when he saw my lights and slammed on his own brakes. Now there was nothing I could do but wait for the impact and it seemed to take whole seconds but suddenly it came, the sickening crunch and the jolt in the same instant. I was thrown forward and the seatbelt locked and the pain caught me across the chest, snapping the breath from my lungs. I closed my eyes, aware of the car spinning, totally helpless and out of control. This is it, I thought, this is it, I'm dead, the end, this is where it all ends. I opened my eyes briefly and the hedge was blurring towards me and then I hit it, broadside on, the car lurching violently to a halt and throwing me sideways against the door.

The car stalled and the silence was sudden and deafening and I lay there for a few seconds with my mind empty, only the sharp pain across my chest and the mad, hollow drumming as my heart strained in my chest. Rain pattered gently on the roof. The cassettes had spilled out across the floor. I eased myself up and grasped at the steering wheel for support and winced at the pain in my ribs, but at least I was alive and my mind was recovered enough to realise it. Thank you, God, I thought.

I hung on the steering wheel, gasping for breath, and, somewhere far away, I heard an engine revving, revving hard. They were behind me. They were trying to get away. They were leaving the scene of the accident. Bastards. I was suddenly angry because it was their fault and my car was wrecked and they were damn well going to pay. Half-remembered stories of insurance claims began to spin through my head, what did I need, I needed their name and address. Their insurance company. What the hell did they think they were at, anyway, tearing out of a side road like that. Bloody madmen. Well, there was no way they were going to get away with it, no way at all. I twisted around and began to scrabble at the door handle. A drunk, I thought, probably a bloody drunk. Bastard.

The door opened and I lurched out and on to the road. The air was cold and sharp and the rain was soft on my face. I could see the red tail-lights from the other car, perhaps thirty metres down the road, stuck in the ditch, judging from the angle, nose down in the mud and no purchase for the wheels and that was why they were revving her so hard. I glanced quickly back at my own car, hard against the hedge and spattered with mud, with one wing crumpled from the impact. This was going to cost someone a fortune, I decided.

It was shortly after five and the light was improving slightly, the first glimmer of dawn sneaking into the eastern sky, and I could just make out two figures moving around the other car. They seemed to be trying to push it back out on to the road. I walked quickly towards them, peering into the gloom, trying to discern details. I was shaking with rage and the after-effect of the adrenalin high, my hands trembling as I strode quickly down the wet road, working out in my head what I would say to them, reviewing all the foulest adjectives I knew and selecting a few choice ones.

At about twenty metres I called out to them, 'Hey, you!' They froze instantly, then one of them seemed to jump back into the car, the interior light flickering briefly as he opened and closed the door. The other moved around between me and the car and I thought they were going to make a run for it so I began to run towards them, shouting again, and I was quite close when the man nearest me swung round with both his hands thrust out in front of him in the classic, combat pistol stance. It was too dark to see a pistol but I knew the posture well enough and something inside me flipped over and fell.

You go through life half-expecting it at any moment, and there are times when you see someone or something and you think, this is it, this is the time, they've got me now. And then it comes to nothing, the man was waiting for his wife, or the car was simply pulling over to ask for directions, and you can release your grip on the pistol in your waistband and let the air out of your lungs and breathe again. But always, in your mind, in the deep animal part of the mind, some part of you expects it, is waiting for it, ready with the appropriate instructions for movement and action.

But now, here it was in front of me, at last, the gunman and the gun, my own personal appointment in Samarra, and I was too full of anger to think, standing there like a fool, waiting for the thump in the chest or the cracking pain in the head. I suppose that's the way it always is, always when the brain is doing something else and the animal is asleep.

He shouted something at me and I didn't hear it

and stood there, unable to move. My mind was racing through all the options and there were none which impressed me at all. He had a gun and I was ten metres away from him and about six or seven from the nearest cover, so no matter which way I moved he could get off four or five aimed shots, and, judging by the way he was holding the thing, he knew how to use it. I stood in the darkness with the rain soaking into my clothes cursing my stupidity. Approaching a strange car at night on a dark road with an unknown number of persons in it and driving without due caution, I had asked for it. And now I had it.

He shouted again, 'Stand still!' and the accent was Midlands, Birmingham maybe; I had been expecting a harsh Belfast accent or a southern brogue, and I thought, what the hell is going on here, then a lot of things seemed to happen at once. The back door of the car flew open and a small figure tumbled out, appearing between me and the gunman, half-falling on to the grassy verge. In the red glow of the tail-lights I caught a glimpse of long hair and a bulky, light-coloured coat but I was paying more attention to the gunman, who had smartly kicked the door closed, catching the struggling figure on the head and shoulder. There was a high-pitched cry of pain and anger. I made to move forward, but the man waved the gun at me.

'Stay where you are!' he shouted.

'I only need a name for the insurance,' I called back.

'Shut up!'

Someone else seemed to have leaned out of the car

and was grappling with the fugitive, but it was difficult to make out details in the darkness with the glow of the lights on the edge of the scene, and I was taking care to watch the man with the gun. Another scream of anger, and I realised that the struggling figure was a girl.

Maybe it's old-fashioned, but in my book you don't treat a girl like that; even those IRA bitches we bring in were treated with the deference due to the fair sex, even though they hardly deserved it. I wanted to do something but the other fellow had the gun and if I moved he would kill me. As I stood there I could feel the rain dribbling down inside my collar and running down my back.

Suddenly someone inside the car screeched in pain and the door opened again and the girl burst out and I thought, well done, love. This time she found a purchase on the wet ground, belting on to the road and away from the car. I saw the blur of her face, white and frightened.

As she ran past the gunman, he slipped for a second, then recovered, still with the pistol aimed at me but obviously in a dilemma about the girl, unsure who was the more important. Another door opened and another man appeared on the far side of the car, staring across the roof, a thin, pale face and dark hair plastered down by the rain. I tried to move forward again, but there was another urgent gesture from the man with the pistol.

'Stand still, you Paddy bastard!'

Of course that was the wrong thing to say because after twelve years' service to the Crown, twelve years of checking under my car and watching where I go and who I talk to and how I live my life, I was sensitive about things like that and I felt the rage shooting up inside me but there was nothing I could do except stand there like a fool. The girl was running across the road. The gunman was watching both of us. The man with the thin face shouted at him.

'Stop her, for Christ's sake!'

Looking back on it, he probably meant restrain her physically but the gunman was dealing with two problems at the same time and when this order came from a superior it released him from his dilemma. His course of action had been decided. He had been ordered to stop her and that was what he would do, and he quickly and professionally shifted his aim from me to the running girl. Events shifted into slow motion again. He had given me the chance I needed and while he tried to pick up on what was a difficult target at any time of the day, let alone in darkness and drizzle, I dropped to one knee and drew my own pistol, slamming right hand into left and pointing the whole body at him. They say that the secret in close quarter combat is the desire, the wish to kill. If you passionately want to kill the target then the instinct will aim the body for you and all you have to do is pull the trigger. The thought ran through my head, 'He's going to kill the girl', and at that moment the animal took over and the animal wanted him dead.

He was quicker than I was and he fired first, the ear-splitting crack of the heavy calibre pistol loud and familiar and the bullet zipping off past me. I lined up on his chest, the biggest target, and then he saw me crouching and began to turn but I squeezed off a round and the revolver banged and jerked and almost at the same instant the gunman clutched at his chest and looked down at the blood pumping from the hole in his jacket. Somebody shouted 'Jesus!' and I fired again, half-blinded by the muzzle flash but I hit him in the chest again and this time he collapsed where he stood, face down on to the wet grass.

The whole thing was very unreal. I couldn't believe that I was shooting at real people. The thin-faced man appeared at the rear of the car, looking at me over the boot, and I swung round and fired at him, as well. I hadn't seen a gun but at that point the animal was still in charge and if the Good Lord Jesus Christ had appeared behind the car I probably would have shot him, too. I fired three shots and was aware of a white, dancing flash at the man's waist, then the rounds were whizzing past my head like angry bees, but I had hit him somewhere because the loud ripping noise stopped suddenly and he lurched over across the boot, holding on to himself and coughing. The submachine-gun clattered on to the ground.

There was silence for a moment, very loud after the sound of the shooting, and my ears were still ringing from the noise. I felt naked and exposed standing right in the centre of the road, only one round left in the gun and I needed a reload, so I spun round and down and slithered across to the opposite ditch, rolling down the soaking grass and fumbling in my pocket for the speedloader, thanking God that

10

I'd remembered to bring it. I remember that I wasn't afraid at all. The only thing in my head was the need to stay alive, the need to win. I was working out how much of a threat was left across the road, whether or not the two men I had fired at would be dead, how many more there were in the car. I fumbled the cylinder open and reloaded with shaking hands, slipping the unused round back into my pocket. The sky was lightening now and I could make out the shapes of the trees and the hedges limiting the horizon.

Suddenly I was aware of someone behind me and I swung round with the revolver at arm's length and the finger resting on the trigger but it was the girl, pale faced and soaked, her hair hanging in damp ringlets round her face.

'Don't shoot!' she cried, recoiling in fear, and I slipped the gun down.

'How many?' I asked her.

'What?'

'In the car. How many?'

'Three.'

'They're all armed?'

'I think so.'

Her accent was polite, perhaps English, well-educated. Even there in the ditch, cold, wet and scared, and part of my mind was telling me how attractive she was. I pointed down the road at my car, the rear lights still on.

'Go down there. Wait for me. All right?'

She nodded once and was away, crawling awkwardly in the ditch, slipping and sliding in the

11

mud. Nice backside, I thought, watching it merge with the shadows.

I turned back to the car, keeping my head as low as I could. The tail-lights glowed evilly in the half-light, and the first, pale daylight was glinting on the wet, rounded surfaces. I could make out the body of the first gunman, slumped by the open rear door, completely and finally still. There was no sign of anyone else. The engine was still running. I could just make out a dark object on the road which might have been the second man's machine-gun. There was no movement inside the car.

I lay still for a few moments and ran various courses of action through my head, the most sensible being to stay where I was until help arrived. The shooting would have been heard and reported and it was only a matter of time before the RUC or the Army arrived. But the anger was still coursing through me and I wanted to settle things with those bastards and I suppose the decision-making apparatus was still a little unbalanced. So I took a deep breath and jumped up and scuttled across the road at a crouch.

Down beside the first man, kneeling on the wet grass with my back against the car and yes, he was definitely dead, the blood forming a black pool on his back. The skin was pale in the half-light of daybreak. I had seen plenty of bullet wounds before, but never any caused by myself and it was a strange and unsettling thing, to see the damage you yourself have caused to another human being.

I glanced into the car through the open rear door.

12

Empty. The smell of stale cigarette smoke drifted out into the clean, damp air. I slid around to the far side of the car, to where the second man had appeared, holding the revolver out in front of me. There was blood on the wing of the car, smeared where he had slid down on to the grass. No sign of a body, although the grass was flattened and marked where it had been dragged away. On the edge of the road the weapon lay where he had dropped it, an Ingram MAC 10, very professional with two magazines taped together ready for an instant change. I reached out and scooped it up, hefting it against my chest, feeling a little more dangerous and a lot more confident.

It looked as though he had been dragged down into the ditch and through a gap in the hedge; I could see dark patches of blood here and there on the grass and the hedge was trampled and damaged. The second man was obviously wounded and a third person had dragged him away, which was good news in itself, but I had to make sure they were out of the area before I could begin to relax. Or dead, I reminded myself.

Through the hedge was a small field and beyond the field another hedge, maybe fifty metres away. There was a gap in the hedge beside a prominent tree and I thought, if I was dragging a wounded man that's where I would make for; not too far away and easy access into the next field, certainly easier than skirting round the hedges looking for a gate. I put my revolver back into the holster, raised the Ingram into my shoulder and fired a long burst in the direction

13

of the tree. The noise was deafening, the long white muzzle flash flickering in front of me and the weapon suddenly clicking into silence as the magazine emptied, but I got the answer I wanted: from the hedge by the gap there was a flicker of light and I heard the sound of the firing just as the answering burst flicked into the hedge around me. I threw myself on to the damp ground, my heart hammering against my ribs. Bastards, I thought. They were away, well away, and out of my reach now.

I pulled myself up to the car and crawled over to the body on the verge. He looked pathetic, face down in the grass with the massive holes in his back. He looked unreal. I had to remind myself that this object had once been a man, a human being, with a mother and a father and maybe kids, hopes and fears and dreams, all ending here in the early morning drizzle. I was surprised at my lack of feeling. I had killed a man, but there was no guilt, no remorse. Not then, anyhow. It had been a straight contest. He had a gun, so had I. He had fired first. He lost. Simple as that.

I reached into the car and switched off the ignition. The silence was somehow clean and fresh, just the rustle of the trees and the soft hiss of the rain. Peaceful. I held out one hand and watched my fingers shaking, sick from the adrenalin surge, coming down now and my body gasping for breath. Then I heard a noise from the road and my body started to move again, adrenalin flooding, until I recognised the sound of my own car. The girl, I realised. She was still at the car.

She had started the engine and was trying to

reverse out of the hedge but the wheels were spinning in the damp grass and throwing up a great spray of mud. I started to walk towards it, not unduly worried but I thought I had better try to calm her down, then all of a sudden the wheels found a grip and the Vauxhall shot backwards on to the road. Bitch is stealing my car, I thought, and I stood in the centre of the road as she spun the car round to face me. She would stop when she saw it was me. She probably wasn't sure who had survived the quick-fire fight. I held up my hand to her in the classic 'pull in and stop' gesture, just like a normal VCP, but she was revving hard and the back end was sliding about as she accelerated towards me and I just managed to jump clear as she tore past, engine screaming, speeding away down the road towards Balinderry.

I picked myself up and stood stupidly in the middle of the road, staring after her, watching the tail-lights until they disappeared round a bend. I was dumbfounded. The bitch, I thought. The bloody bitch. She might at least have thanked me. I let the Ingram clatter on to the wet tarmac and far away I heard the growing whine of approaching sirens.

The interview room was bare and cold and chilly and I was shivering at the table, both hands wrapped around the lukewarm plastic cup with the dregs of the machine-made coffee I hadn't been able to drink. Up in one corner the closed circuit camera stared malevolently at me and the steady unblinking red light below the lens was somehow cold and accusing. Like some vicious old woman stuck up there, I thought; a bitter, twisted, accusing old crone.

The incident was replaying itself constantly in my head, over and over again, all the details locked into my memory. The rain, the glow of their rear lights in the darkness, the feel of my own gun jerking in my hand, the long, dancing muzzle flash from the sub-machine-gun. The gunman clutching at his chest before his life ended.

I had killed a man. There it was, in all its starkness. I had killed a man. I had taken a life, destroyed a fellow human being, a man like me who had slept and risen and eaten breakfast and who was now

16

lying face down in the cold morning dew and would never wake again. And yes, he had fired first, and by all the rules of peace and war I was justified in killing him but it didn't make it easier. I knew him. I had sat by him for almost five minutes until the first policemen arrived. I knew his face, his clothes, his hair. The dirt beneath his fingernails and the sodden desert boots on his feet. The two bloody holes in his back.

This is the way to madness, I told myself. Snap out of it. You've seen it all before. Wise up. Think about something else.

I pushed the plastic cup away from me and leaned back on the hard chair, feeling the cold. My clothes were still damp from the rain and their boiler might be broken down but they might at least have produced a heater, for heaven's sake, it wasn't as if I was a terrorist. I thought about the cold for a few moments and tried to lose the thought that way but it kept creeping back, into the background, looming up like a shadow and I was afraid to think it. English accents, the voice kept saying, English accents.

'Captain Kearns?'

I hadn't noticed the door opening and I jumped, startled.

'Yes.'

'Sorry. Didn't mean to startle you. Tom Martin, Army Legal Services. I'll be handling your case for you.'

He advanced towards me with his hand extended. Stand up, shake hands, sit down. The Sandhurst manners never fail you. I sat back and watched him settle himself in the chair across the table from me, tall and neat in his dark blue pinstripe and paisley tie, the hair parted immaculately on the correct side and the remnants of a summer tan, Barbados, no doubt, he looked the type.

'How do you feel?'

'Pretty shitty, actually.'

'Yes, I can imagine.' He looked at me with what must have been the understanding expression. 'Well, we'll have you out of here in no time at all. Things are a little confused at the moment, they usually are after this kind of thing.'

He was rummaging in his neat modern briefcase, open on the desk in front of him, peering into it the way a dentist peers into a mouth. A lock of hair had fallen across his forehead and shook there as he spoke and I imagined that he would be the type the girls would fall for, urbane and handsome and always in control. I had to stop myself running my hand through my own hair.

'I've taken the liberty of telephoning the school; spoke to a Mr Appleby–he's the headmaster, isn't he? I explained as much of the situation as I was able to, and he seemed very understanding. Said you were to take as much time off as you needed, sent his regards.'

'Decent of him.'

Old Appleby, the twisted old bastard, do anything for a posh accent in pinstripes.

'I've also spoken to your Commanding Officer,' Martin went on, still organising his papers. 'He'll be in touch with you personally as soon as he can; he's sending the adjutant down to see you later today. Oh, and he asked me to tell you that he's putting you in charge of the Battalion pistol team next year.'

I actually laughed a little and felt the morale inch up slightly. Thank God for black service humour. Martin snapped his briefcase closed and placed it carefully on the floor beside him, leaving three neat piles of paper arranged on the table before him. He squared the edges up with tiny movements of his hands.

'Now', he said at last. 'Our priority at this time is to get you out of here and home, to a hot bath and some sleep, I'd imagine.' Jesus Christ, I thought, did I look as bad as all that? 'Things are in hand at the moment, and we should have you away in about an hour or so. Obviously the police have certain formalities to go through and they have requested that you be available for a short while in case they need to talk to you again.'

'They've been talking to me for the last two hours.'

'Just in case. There are routines to follow. Procedures.' He kept his voice soft and light, as if he were talking to a child. 'Besides, it'll give us time to hammer out a general plan of action as regards the legal situation from now on. Prepare to meet the onslaught, as it were.' He was smiling but I wasn't in the mood. I had my own onslaught.

'Onslaught?'

'Well, yes. The press are bound to take an interest in this case and there will be all kinds of rumours and allegations flying about, especially in the current political climate. Shoot to kill, and that sort of thing.

You know what the press are like these days, they'll get their teeth into this and there'll be no holding them back. Never mind the truth when you can boost the circulation. Of course, there'll be no substance to any of it, but that won't stop someone saying it.'

I looked up at the camera and the little red light and all I could see was the man in the grass with the blood oozing through his thin jacket. I tried to drag my attention back to Martin.

'So what do we do?'

'I'll need a statement.'

'Christ, not another one!'

'I won't need it immediately. I have a copy of your police statement and that will do for the meantime. We can get together in the near future and fill in a few details. It's only a formality, really.'

His smile was quick and just a little too practised and in another time and place I might have got on with him but it wasn't working and I could feel irrational anger boiling up inside. I clasped my hands together in my lap and worked at my fingers. The unfortunate thing was that he was fast becoming the straw on the overladen camel's back.

'Do you charge a fee?' I asked him suddenly.

He looked at me in surprise.

'What?'

'Do you charge a fee? Because if you do I'm not interested.'

The smile was wavering, the eyes uncertain. I was just saying it for something to say, I didn't know why. I guessed he was putting it down to the strain.

20

'Good God no, I'm army, same as you. Fixed wage, I'm afraid.'

'Well, that's all right then, isn't it.'

'Yes, I … ah … hope so.'

We stared at each other in silence for a few moments and I tried to put my finger on what it was about him that annoyed me so much and then suddenly I realised that it was the accent, the smooth, rich, home counties accent; confident and assured, landowning family perhaps, a job with the army for a few years before settling into a nice city firm with a neat haircut and a few stories to tell, 'when I was in Northern Ireland' and so forth. Images flashed into my head, darkness and the rain and the gunman clutching at his chest.

'What do you need more detail for?'

'I'm sorry?'

'The statement. You said you needed more detail.'

'Oh, yes.' He glanced down at the papers on the table. 'Well, background, mainly: where you were coming from, what you had been doing–I understand you have been on duty rather a lot recently–your state of mind at the time, that sort–'

'State of mind? What has that got to do with it?'

'Well, probably nothing, but you never know what might come up. I'd just like to make myself *au fait* with the entire situation; have all the information at my fingertips, so to speak. Might come in useful if it ever comes to court.'

'You think this could come to court?'

He sighed heavily. I could see he was becoming irritated and I hadn't meant to do that.

'Look, I'm sorry for all these interruptions. I'm a bit ... on edge, you know. You realise I've never been in this position before and I want to find out as much as I can.'

He smiled thinly.

'I understand. I shouldn't think it would go as far as court proceedings. The DPP would decide there was no case to answer. There is an outside chance that it would get to court, but in that case you would probably be charged with manslaughter and given an absolute discharge.'

I felt something heavy plummet in my stomach. The law was like a massive gun which I had been servicing for years, carrying ammunition to it, cleaning and polishing it, and now suddenly the bloody thing was lumbering round to point at me.

'That really is a very outside chance,' Martin was saying, 'most unlikely to happen. In fact the only scenario I could envisage would be if the public outcry became too vociferous, if the press took too big an interest. Then it might be decided that the best way to clear your name would be to put you through a trial.'

'What are the chances of that happening?'

'Very, very slim, I'd say. Hardly worth bothering about.' He smiled again, with the mouth open. 'Dead terrorist, complete with arms and ammunition? I wouldn't be surprised if they gave you a medal, old son.'

That thought again, that fear rising up in my mind, and anger with it because there was nothing I could do. The thing had happened and I was trapped in it and now here I was facing a trial, with a too-smooth lawyer who didn't really give a damn. I leaned across the table and placed my hand on his forearm.

'Do you know who he was?' I asked him.

'Who?'

'The man I killed this morning,' I said, keeping my voice as steady as I could.

'Well, no, not yet. In any case–'

'Then go and bloody well find out!' I yelled, swinging my arm across the table and sweeping his precious neat piles of paper on to the dusty floor.

He quickly threw himself back in his seat, and I got up and walked to the wall and back again and felt a little better for my outburst. He was watching me, his face pale. I leaned forward and put my arms on the back of the chair.

'Find out who he was,' I said again, quietly, 'because I don't think he was a terrorist.'

He sat silent for a long time, his hands resting on the arms of the chair, his eyes steady and angry. I had challenged his authority and he was annoyed and I was very sorry about it but there were more important matters than his bloody relationship with his client.

'What do you mean, you don't think he was a terrorist?'

'Just that, I don't think he was.'

'Well who was he, then?'

And that was what I didn't like to consider. 'I think he was on our side.'

'Army, you mean?'

'Maybe army, maybe police. Sneaky-beaky of

some kind.'

'And what makes you think that?'

'I don't know, really. Just a feeling. He had an English accent. It was all ... I don't know. Just a feeling.'

The room was very quiet, soundproofed, and the silence reflected in on us. Thick, heavy, guilty silence. I walked back to the wall and leaned against it.

'I assume everything you said in your statement is the truth? There are no other ... details?'

'It's the truth.'

'Well in that case you have nothing to worry about. You acted in accordance with the rules of the yellow card; you opened fire to save the girl's life, quite acceptable in the circumstances. Even if they were some kind of undercover group it was quite blatantly wrong to fire on an unarmed woman.'

His voice was very calm and cold.

'You make it sound very simple.'

'It is very simple.'

'You don't have to live with it.'

'Neither do you. Forget about it. No matter who they were, you acted lawfully and morally, and let's face it, you're still alive. Look on the bright side.'

He slowly gathered up all the papers from the floor, taking his time about it for emphasis, and I watched him from where I stood at the wall. I could imagine him relating the story in his local pub, back home in Suffolk or Hampshire or wherever, leaning on the bar with a pint and a cigar, oh, yes, there was this crazy UDR captain, killed one of our own, too bloody trigger happy but then they all are, aren't

24

they, that's what's wrong with the bloody country.

'I'll be in touch,' he said, snapping the case closed. 'You can get me at HQNI if you need me.' The tone said don't call me, I'll call you. I had thought of trying to apologise but I put it from my head.

'OK,' I said.

After he left I sat in the silence and listened to the little sounds I was making; the creak of the chair, the squeak of my shoes on the floor, the scrape of the table as I leaned on it. I never thought a room could be so empty. My mind was racing round inventing scenarios to explain the English accent but it all came back to the one thing; they were our own people. They weren't terrorists, they were undercover, and now one of them was dead. A mother somewhere in England answering the door and probably already sensing that her son was dead before the sombre, sad-faced uniform broke the news to her. A chair empty next Christmas, and every Christmas to come.

I felt the emotion scalding my throat; I had attended too many funerals, I knew exactly what death by gunshot meant to a family. Too many coffins, too many sad and lonely graveyards. I knew what they would go through, and it was I who had caused it, and the knowledge of it burned me inside.

I think I sat for half an hour, perhaps more; time dragged. I played with the tin foil ashtray, tapping it on the formica table-top. I fiddled with the empty plastic cup. I tried to hum. Anything to occupy my mind. A policewoman popped her head in and asked if I wanted anything and I said yes, I'd love another cup of coffee and she disappeared but I never got the coffee.

Simpson appeared shortly after that. He looked around the door and grinned at me.

'Well well, look what the cat's dragged in,' he said lightly.

I stood up quickly.

'By Christ I'm glad to see you!'

'Having a hard time?'

'Just a bit.'

'Do you good.' He slipped in and closed the door and moved quietly across to the table. 'How are you feeling?'

'I'll survive.'

'You weren't hurt, then?'

'No.'

'That's the main thing.' He pulled out the chair and sat down, patting his pockets for a cigarette packet in the familiar ritual. He was the only detective I knew in the station, a big, burly man with sandy hair and a plain honest face but his eyes were hard and missed nothing. He drank dark rum and went quiet when he'd had too much. Once he had had to deal with the remains of a child dismembered in a car bomb and I knew the memory of it had stayed with him. Sometimes you would find him in the corner with his glass empty and his eyes full, staring at the wall and seeing nothing. Or perhaps seeing too much.

'Who's dealing with your case?' he asked.

'I can't remember their names. Dark-haired man with glasses and a moustache ... Edwards, is it?'

'Jimmy Edwards. Detective Sergeant.'

'That sounds like it.'

26

He nodded wisely as he lit a cigarette, waving the match to and fro to extinguish it.

'Aye. Jimmy's all right,' he said.

'You heard what happened?'

'Aye. You're the talk of the station. You'll not have to buy drink for a while.'

'Any news on who the dead man is yet?'

'No. Nobody has recognised him yet, anyway. Did Jimmy ask you to go through the mug shots?'

'No.'

'That's not like him. He usually has everybody going through the mug shots. He's a great believer in photographs.'

He sat back in the chair and drew contentedly on the cigarette, blowing the smoke into the air above his head. He was casually watching me with that expression that policemen have, the look that makes you feel suddenly guilty no matter how innocent you are. I knew he was waiting for me to say something.

'What about the car, any news on that?'

'Hire car. Rented two days ago.'

'That's unusual.'

'That's what I thought.'

'Look, Phil, I don't think those men were PIRA.'

He looked down at his feet, then back at me.

'What makes you think that?'

'A feeling. Instinct. They were too good for the Provies. Professional. They'd been well trained.'

'Provies can be well trained, you know that.'

'They don't often have English accents.'

'Aye, well that's true enough.'

He crossed his legs, pushing the chair back from

27

the table for more room, and tapped the cigarette gently on the ashtray.

'So who do you think they were?'

'I think they were on our side. Sneaky-beakies.' I was watching his face carefully and there was no reaction.

'Army?'

'Most likely.'

'Then who was the girl?'

'Well, this is the thing, isn't it? Who was the girl?' There was a nervous tremor in my voice which embarrassed me. I hoped he hadn't noticed it.

There was a silence between us for a while and I looked at the floor while he looked at me. Simpson was a farming man. He belonged to the land. A century ago he would have worked a small farm, a peasant, big and strong and simple but with his ideas of truth and justice ingrained like dirt in his hands, good and bad with nothing in between and a skelping for you if you leaned the wrong way. Honest as the day is long. I could picture him in a fading Victorian photograph, the family lined up in front of the low, white walls and himself in the centre like a minor king holding court. Thatch and turf and a wee drop of poteen, that would have been Simpson.

'Nah,' he said at last. 'They wouldn't have been on our side. I know we've some yahoos but I wouldn't think they'd shoot at an unarmed girl.'

'Well, I hope you're right. I wouldn't like to think I'd killed some squaddy.'

'Ah, you'll be all right. Soldiers do it all the time. My oul' man killed more men in the war than you and I have ever fired bullets, and it never did him any harm. Mind you he was pissed most of the time. I was always surprised he could even see the enemy, let alone shoot at them.'

His big, broad face was deadpan and I couldn't help smiling at him. A good man, I thought, a good, honest man.

'Anyway, he started the shooting; if he was one of ours, not that I think he was, but if he was, then it served him right. A lot of these people think they're over here playing games, you know. It's no fucking game, this.'

He eased himself out of the chair and straightened his jacket, sucking in his stomach and sticking out his chest. I stood up too.

'I'd better get on with some work here,' he said. 'I've a pile of paperwork on my desk that's been there this past fortnight, and it's about time I got stuck into it.' He put out his hand and I took it and it was big and strong and comforting. 'I'll see Jimmy for you later on, find out what's happening. I'll let you know before you leave, all right?'

'Yeah, that'd be great, Phil. Thanks for calling in. Tell Patsy I was asking for her.'

He nodded, then turned and slipped out of the door and I was alone again in the dull and droning silence. I felt better for his visit. I felt I had a friend.

He came back half an hour later, slipping in in the same, unobtrusive way. Something in his expression jangled warning bells inside my head.

'Bad news?' I asked.

'Might be,' he said slowly. 'Might be.' He pulled

out the other chair and sat down heavily. He seemed tired.

'What?' I demanded. 'What's wrong?'

He let out a sigh and scratched thoughtfully at his cheek. 'I had a wee chat with Jimmy Edwards. Asked him what the score was about your man. The fellow you shot.'

'And?'

'Well. When the uniformed boys picked you up there was the usual report sent in to Divisional Head-quarters. Your name, registration number of the car, weapons found, that sort of thing. Like your incident reports.'

I nodded. He shifted in his seat.

'Almost immediately we got a signal down on the MSX. Hold everything, including you, until further advised. And apparently the Chief Inspector has had a few phone calls from the very top, because he's going around like a bear with a beehive up his arse.'

My mind was racing but I couldn't take it in.

'So what does it mean?'

'Well, it looks as though you have come across some kind of covert thing. Now that's not to say that the fellow you shot was one of ours.'

'But it looks very like it.'

He nodded slowly.

'Aye,' he said. 'It does look very like it.'

'I see.'

So it was true and he was one of ours and I had killed him. Jesus Christ. I thought of that mother answering the door. God help her, I thought. God help her.

'Jimmy was saying that they got another signal about half an hour ago. Apparently they can let you go shortly. Must have discovered you were in the UDR or something.' From his expression I half expected him to spit on the floor. 'Oh, and they found your car.'

'Where?'

'Just outside Tandragee.'

'What about the girl?'

'No sign of her. The car was abandoned, doors lying open. Driven into a hedge. Apparently they found blood on the front seat; you didn't cut yourself or anything … ?'

'No.'

'Must be hers, then.'

I remembered her face and the way the rain had weighted her hair around her cheeks. Her nice backside. Poor bitch.

'They must have got her after all.'

'Aye,' Simpson agreed.

'But, look, Phil, something isn't right here,' I protested. 'She was English, she had an English accent. She wasn't a Provie. And if they were our own, then what did they want her for? And if they did want her, why not just arrest her? That's what we all have to do, why the hell can't they? What's the point of all this fucking about in the middle of the night when all they have to do is wind up your lot and wind up our lot and send us out to bring her in? A legal arrest, Jesus Christ we're doing it all the time, one more wouldn't hurt. What the hell happened to the rules?'

Silence. I suddenly realised I had been shouting, half out of my chair, hands on the tabletop. Simpson looked up at me with expressionless eyes and I sat down slowly, embarrassed.

'God, sorry, Phil ... I just ... There's something wrong here. Why did they shoot at her?'

He looked down at his tie and brushed a speck of dust from it and heavily cleared his throat.

'I've been ... ah ... having a wee nosey around. Unofficially. Just out of interest, you know, because I was a wee bit curious about that myself.'

'And?'

'Well, I found out who lives up that road. The road they came out of. It doesn't really lead anywhere; ends up in a farmyard. Anyway, there's four houses up there, and the uniformed boys went out this morning to see if there was anyone missing.'

'And was there?'

'There was indeed. One of the houses was only just off the market. Apparently used to belong to an old lady who died and the family sold it off. To a young English girl who said she was a civil servant in Belfast. Quite well off, apparently, nicely spoken, that sort of thing. No one really knew her that well because she hadn't moved in long, about a month, I think.'

'That's her!'

'Might be. Jimmy phoned the NIO to find out if she had gone to work that morning, and they said she was away on three weeks' leave. In Canada, apparently.'

'It's her, bound to be. Thank goodness for that!'

'It might be her. On the other hand, she might be

safely in Canada enjoying the company of her relations.'

'Well, get me a photograph and I'll tell you.'

'Hold on a minute. This is all off the record, and only because I happen to know you. I can't go any further.'

'Why not?'

'Because we've been told to drop it. Lay off. Discontinue enquiries.'

'But where does that leave me?' I protested.

'You're all right, for heaven's sake, they're going to forget about it, aren't they? Nothing's going to happen! That's what you want?'

'Great for me, but what about the girl?'

'What about her?'

'You can't just leave her like that! God knows what they've done to her! I mean, for Christ's sake, they were going to kill her!'

Both our voices were raised now but I was past caring, the two of us leaning at each other across the table.

'Certainly I'm going to leave her! I've got a pension to think about! I can't do anything and I'm not going to try!'

'I never thought I'd hear that kind of thing coming from you!'

'Listen, Garrett, when the Chief Constable's office tells you to lay off something, you lay off it. There's fuck all else you can do. This is the government we're talking about here, it's their game and they pay for the counters. You and I don't matter a damn, and if we get caught up in it then that's just too bad.'

'So we let them kill her?'

That hit him hard for some reason and he paused, anger draining the colour from his face or perhaps it was a memory. I swallowed hard, suddenly worried because Phil was not a man to get on the bad side of.

He looked hard at me for a long moment. 'Forget it, Garrett. Forget it ever happened. That's the best you can do.'

I looked down at the floor and the anger was subsiding in me and sadness was flooding in. He was right, of course he was right, but the course of my life had been altered and it was grossly unfair but there it was, I was involved, tangled, and it wasn't so easy to get out.

'Fuck it,' I said quietly and seriously. 'Fuck it all.'

Simpson reached across and I felt his big hand on my shoulder.

'I have to go. If you need me, you know where to find me. OK?'

'Yeah, OK. Thanks, Phil.'

'No problem. I'll see you.'

The door banged closed again and the room seemed very cold and empty and I sank my hands in my pockets and shivered. I was sick and tired and I wanted to get out of that bloody room. I kept seeing his face, shocked, staring down at the hole in his chest, the sudden hole from which his life was emptying. And I kept seeing her face, pale and wet in the grey dawn, frightened and shaking and alone. Christ, I thought. What a world, what a bloody awful world.

It was still raining when they dropped me off at home and I went into the kitchen and put the kettle on for a cup of tea. The house was grey and cold with the rain spattering disconsolately on the windows and I sat and stared out at the garden for a long time, out of my routine and lost. The kettle boiled and switched itself off. The house was silent. Sometimes you wish you didn't live alone, sometimes you would give anything for someone to talk to.

But life goes on and after a long time sitting there I boiled the kettle again and made a pot of tea and threw some toast in the toaster, out of jam again and must buy two or three jars next time.

I wandered round the house flicking on all the lights and turning on the radio for company, wishing there was a fire in the grate instead of the cold, flaking ashes of last week's blaze. I moved through the rooms seeing all the familiar objects of my life, opening the same doors and touching the same light switches that I had used time and time again for the past three years, things which had become a part of my life, a part of the little pool of existence which was me. Things which encompassed the normality of my life, all changed now forever. For now I opened doors as a killer, now I used the light switches as a killer, now I was changed and different and my normal places were strange to me.

Back in the kitchen I sat at the bare table with my tea and toast, forcing myself to chew and swallow but only managing one slice. The strident tones of the local news bulletin filled the kitchen and I reached out and turned the volume up, half of me eager to hear and half of me afraid.

The earnest young newsreader came on. The last time I had heard that voice I had not killed a man. Something flipped inside me and I flicked the radio off, then changed my mind again and switched it on in time for the details.

' ... early this morning. The dead man, who has not been named, was killed in a gun battle with an off- duty soldier. Police are still hunting two men who escaped on foot. A submachine-gun and a pistol have been recovered at the scene. The shooting was condemned–'

I snapped it off and the silence came back at me. Irrelevant, I told myself, trying to get the intellect back in the driver's seat. All this emotion is bullshit. He fired first. The rules are simple. I abide by them and have done all my life and if he had abided by them he wouldn't now be lying on a slab with his guts hanging out of his back. His own fault, no one else's. And certainly not mine.

For a few hours I stalked the house like an animal, doing mechanical chores to keep the animal occupied but all the time my mind was flicking through the incident again, examining all the angles, searching for excuses and justifications and going through all the 'If onlys' I could dredge up. If only I hadn't taken that road. If only I had stayed on duty a little later, or left a little sooner. If only they hadn't been going so fast.

And the girl, what of the girl? Was she alive? Was that her blood on the seats of my car? Her face kept coming back to me, blurred and indistinct with the damp hair and that pale, frightened look. Helpless. I kept telling myself that she must have done something or been involved in something, that they wouldn't do that kind of thing for a parking ticket but somehow all the excuses seemed lame and hollow and it all came down to the one last and final fact: they had tried to shoot her, an unarmed, fleeing girl. In the back. To stop her getting away. Jesus Christ, I knew plenty of people who deserved a bullet and if they wanted I would do it for them but not a girl, not a wee frightened girl.

That was a long, cold afternoon and the house felt like a prison so around three o'clock I went out for a walk in the rain and that was when I first noticed the surveillance. They weren't very good. I noticed them almost as soon as I left the house, in a car pulled up on the kerb about four doors down the avenue. Cars don't park in our avenue unless they're visiting, in which case the occupants will decant and go into the house and leave the car empty but these two chaps

37

were sitting in the car trying to look unobtrusive so I picked them up right away. I thought they were terrorists at first. You always watch, you see, you always keep one part of the brain awake so that any detail that doesn't fit in will register immediately and the subconscious can begin to act on it. I've spent my life watching for the unusual and the out of place and these people thought they could sit in a car and wait for me without being seen. Laughable, I reflected.

As I reached the corner of the avenue I heard the car starting up and the door slamming so I guessed that one of them would follow on foot while the other one leap-frogged ahead in the car. I didn't think they were terrorists because if it was the Provisionals I would never see them; it would be the bomb under the car or the sudden burst of gunfire through the windscreen but they certainly wouldn't sit in a car and let me walk away. Although, of course, I couldn't be sure. I wished the police had given me my gun back. I felt naked. I felt as though my back was a mile wide.

You get an awful urge to run when someone is following you. I was itching to take to my heels and sprint and hope to lose them that way, even though it was pointless because they knew where I lived and I had to go back sometime, but you do get these animal urges. Run. Escape. Hide. The way children hide from monsters.

I walked down into the main street, slipping into the bustling crowds of shoppers, easing my way between the old women gossiping in their head-scarves and waterproofs. The main street is wide and long and dips in the centre of the town to a cross-roads before widening out into the long market square with the old town hall sitting squat in the centre. Side roads run off the main street towards the housing estates and the countryside and on all the corners people were gathered in twos and threes, passing the time of day in idle chat. Young mothers pushed their babies in plastic-covered buggies. Old men shrugged in doorways, out of the rain. Cars whooshed slowly up and down the street, glistening in the rain. Everything normal and as it always was and always will be except that I was being followed and watched by two men I had never met.

Three men. I noticed the third one in the reflection on a shop window, straightening up slightly as I passed, noticing me too suddenly then trying to look away. Black woolly hat and expensive trainers, will they never learn, how many young men in the town could afford training shoes like that?

He followed me at a distance, keeping to the inside of the pavement. I crossed the road, using the opportunity to look directly at him and memorising his jacket, dark blue wrangler with a hooded sweatshirt underneath. In the middle of the main street I paused at the traffic island to examine the crowd on the far side because there should be a fourth one and sure enough there he was, hurrying through the shoppers too quickly and too politely to be local. Heavily built this time, tweed jacket and a flat cap and I wondered vaguely why they all wore hats. He hurried on up the street a little and suddenly paused at a shop window, feigning interest.

By then I knew they weren't terrorists. They stood out too much. The PIRA live in the community and are part of it and when they want to hide you just can't spot them, but these fellows were outsiders and looked it. Trouble was, if they weren't terrorists then who were they? Army? Police? Someone else?

'Garrett!'

Sudden flood of adrenalin but the broad red face was familiar.

'Desi. How are you?'

Desi Masters, Platoon Commander with C Company in Lurgan. Farming stock, wealthy, taste for Black Bush and a wallet to afford it.

'Never mind me, what about yourself? I hear you got one of them?'

'Good news travels fast.'

'Well, you know this place. Who was it?'

I knew that if I mentioned one of thirty or forty names Desi would know it immediately, the players, the local terrorists. We all knew them. And they all knew us.

'I didn't recognise him, Desi. I don't think he's in the book.'

'Well, he'll not be a loss, that's for sure. Well done, oul' son. You're the talk of the battalion, and you always said you couldn't shoot. Next time you're down with us you'll have to take a wee drink.'

'Desi, look, I, ah ... ' I didn't know what to tell him. I wanted to tell him about the surveillance. I wanted to ask him for help. I couldn't think of words.

'What?'

'Doesn't matter. Nothing. You working tonight?'

'No, thank goodness. Heading for Belfast, taking the wife to the pictures. She's been at me for months, nag, nag, nag. Never stops. So I'm hoping this will shut her up for a few weeks at least.'

'Sure, you love it, Desi.'

'Wait till you're caught, like the rest of us. There'll be a different tune then.'

'It'll take a hell of a girl to catch me.'

'You'll not know the day.'

'Aye.' I felt uncomfortable talking to him, knowing that four men were watching us; it was like having some kind of disease that might be passed on through contact. 'Desi, look, I have to go, I have to be in Lisburn by half five. Give us a ring some night and we'll have a few beers, all right?'

'Yeah. No problem.' He slapped me on the shoulder. 'Good work, old son.'

'Yeah. Right.'

'OK. See you about.'

I hope so, Desi. I hope so.

I watched him disappear into the crowd and wished that I had told him because at that moment I needed an ally. People were following me and I didn't know why and I had killed one of our own and I felt lonely and sick, standing there in the middle of the crowd and all alone.


I walked through the town for a long time, aimlessly wandering through the emptying streets, pausing here and there to look into shop windows and check for reflections, all the time resisting the overwhelming

41

urge to glance behind and check if they were still there. I knew they were still there. I could feel their eyes tingling on the back of my neck.

Eventually I walked into the police station at the end of town and asked at the desk for Simpson just as he came in from outside, clutching a bundle of files, his shoulders darkened with rain.

'Hello, Garrett, what are you doing back here?'

'I'm being followed.'

'What?'

'I'm being followed. I was followed here.'

He looked at me suspiciously for a moment, then pulled a handkerchief from his pocket and wiped it under his nose.

'Let's go into my office,' he said.

He waved me into the swivel chair in front of his desk. Another man at a desk across the room glanced up as we came in and Simpson jerked his head at him.

'Give us a minute, would you, Joe?'

'Sure.'

He gathered up a file on his desk and sauntered out into the corridor. Simpson waited until he was gone before perching himself on the edge of the desk, one expensive slip-on shoe dangling in the air.

'You look terrible,' he said.

'Thanks.'

'What's happened?'

'I've been followed. They were waiting for me at the house, and I've just dragged them all around town. They followed me here.'

The story welled up inside me and I was aware

how stupid I sounded, blurting the words out like a scolded kid. But I was frightened. Frightened and angry.

'Who were they?'

'Well I don't know, for Christ's sake–'

'Provies?'

'Of course not! You know who they bloody well were.'

Simpson looked at me with his immobile face like carved granite. His eyes were very steady.

'Sorry, Garrett; I know as much about this as you do.'

'Look,' I said, trying to keep my voice calm. 'Phil. All of a sudden I've been dropped into something that I don't want to know about. Not only have I been rammed, threatened, shot at, been forced into a situation where I had to kill one of our side, now I've also been put under surveillance for some obscure bloody reason. And no one has bothered to come and ask me anything, not a word, not even, Garrett, how the hell are you feeling today and would you like a sleeping pill!'

Shouting again and he let the silence ring for a few moments before replying.

'They're probably just keeping an eye on you. For your own safety.'

'Right. Yeah. All of a sudden I'm under a big threat. I'm in danger. Question is, from which side? Theirs, or ours?'

'What do you mean by that?'

'I mean, they tried to shoot an unarmed girl. For whatever reason, I don't know, they've probably got their excuses. But if they're prepared to go that far, then what would they be prepared to do to me?'

'You can't–'

'I mean, it was their mate, wasn't it? Their mate I killed. What's to stop them coming for me?'

'I think you're getting this thing a little out of proportion, Garrett.'

'Well I don't.'

'How many of them were following you?'

I rubbed my forehead and tried to calm down, forced my brain to think. 'Two in a car outside my house. Two in the centre of town. There might have been a couple of others but I'm not sure. One of the men in town was wearing a blue wrangler jacket and a black woolly hat. And expensive running shoes.'

'I see.'

'Aren't you going to write this down?'

'No point. If you're wrong, then it means nothing. And if you're right, then there's nothing I can do anyway.'

'You're going to do nothing?'

'I didn't say that.'

'That's what it sounded like to me.'

'There is nothing I can do. Officially. That's the problem. Unofficially there isn't a lot of scope either but I'm doing what I can. Until I find out something useful you're just going to have to bear with me, old son.'

Walls all round me. I felt trapped.

'You've been followed before,' he said. 'There's no need to get het up about this.'

'I always had the law on my side before. Now I don't know who's on my side. When can I get my gun back?'

'Soon. It's still down at ballistics. As soon as we get it back I'll drop it out to you.'

'I'd feel a lot safer.'

'I'm sure you would. Now look. There isn't any point in you hanging around here. Go home. Walk home and let them follow you. They won't try anything, I'm sure of that. Take it easy for a few days. If anything does happen that worries you, get in touch with me here, or leave a message and I'll call out at the house. If I hear anything, I'll give you a shout. Fair enough?'

'I haven't a great deal of choice, have I?'

'Not a great deal, Garrett, old son. Not a great deal.'

I leapt out of the car and ran towards them, my feet sliding on the wet road, watching them pushing at the car, screaming at them, who are you, who are you, reaching inside my jacket for the gun but only the empty holster flapping, where is the damn gun and they're armed, oh Jesus they've got guns, trying to stop but the momentum carrying me towards them and their faces white in the early dawn light, streaked with rain, guns, Jesus this is where I die, this is where I die, the flash of the muzzle blast flickering before the noise and the terrible thumping, hammering, jerking impact across my chest and I'm dying, dear God I'm dying, is this my blood pumping out of all these holes, where does it all come from, oh God stop that bleeding, dear God stop it, stop it, stop it, falling on to the wet road on my knees first then on to my face and breaking a tooth on the tarmac but none of it matters because I'm dying, this is the end, the noise in my head, the buzzing, growing louder, louder, everywhere, then pain in my back and the television flickering and buzzing in the corner and my mouth dry from sleep.

I lay for a long time without moving. They were outside, watching. Even as I lay there they would be somewhere close by, in a car or a room, maybe sipping coffee from a flask, always one of them awake. Taking photographs, maybe. I had an unpleasant sense of thousands of eyes outside in the garden. The room was quiet except for the television but I was afraid to turn round and look into the shadows, why didn't I leave some lights on, for heaven's sake?

One a.m. I had fallen asleep in the armchair, slouched down with my legs out, not intending to sleep but fatigue deciding otherwise and my body shutting down without permission. Stiff. Pain from the joints as I bent my legs. I rubbed my chin and it was bristly and rough.

Out of the chair and all the lights on, might as well let them see that I'm awake. I went upstairs and peered carefully out of the bedroom window down on to the deserted avenue, the yellow streetlight shining on the damp road but at least the rain had stopped and no sign of them anywhere, all the cars familiar neighbour cars, all safe. I knew they were there. Somewhere. I knew they were watching me. I knew they wouldn't give up until they were satisfied although God only knew what they wanted.

I thought about food and wandered around the kitchen absently drawing the curtains, unable to decide what to have and in the end I settled for a beer from the fridge. Watch it, said the little voice in my head, alcohol is no answer. Fuck off, I told it.

I was alone. Terribly alone. There was no one to phone, no one to talk to. I wished my parents were still alive, although they would never have understood. To them the law was the law, and that was the end of it. Black and white and none of this grey business. The goodies and the baddies and nothing else mattered, and if you didn't want to play you could go and live somewhere else. The silence of the house yawned back at me, hollow and taunting.

The beer was finished too soon and I almost went for another. I looked out of the window instead. Across the street the Johnsons' house was dark and quiet, the whole family asleep and in the morning their world would be the same as it ever was, nothing changed or altered. No one watching them. No blood on their hands. They were society, the Johnsons and their like, living quiet, happy lives, moving from day to day and weaving their lives through the brutality and terror that bubbled softly around them, ignoring the pop when occasionally a bubble burst. The society I had stepped away from in joining the UDR, moving into the edges of the other life, the silent war, taking on the fear and the sweat and the phone-calls in the night, we're coming for you you Brit bastard, and the little relief in the morning when the car starts and you're still alive. Now I was further away again, out in the wastelands, a killer without a cause.

The Commanding Officer called early. I was still dossing about in T-shirt and tracksuit bottoms, unwashed and unshaved after a sleepless night, stifling a yawn as I offered him coffee.

'This is a lovely house, Garrett. Lovely.'

'Thank you. I don't get to enjoy it too often.'

'Yes, I'm sure a few days off will do you the world of good.'

'Yes.'

He sat in one of the armchairs, politely on the edge of the cushion with his legs crossed, his off-duty twill trousers immaculate and the brown brogues gleaming. I slouched back into the settee cradling my coffee in both hands.

'I'm sorry about the mess,' I said. 'I haven't really been tidying for a while.'

'Oh, Good Lord, this is nothing compared to our place. Toys everywhere. Lego all over the living-room floor. Bloody games bleeping and chirping.'

'Yes,' I said.

He sat back in the chair and clasped his hands together in his lap, staring down at the freckles on their backs, and I could see his scalp through his thinning sandy hair. I knew he was wondering what to say next. The Colonel was a decent man. All too often in Northern Ireland he had found himself embroiled in the little whirlpools of intrigue and secrecy and it did not sit easily with him.

'How do you feel, Garrett?' he asked after a long time.

'I'm fine, Sir.'

'You look tired.'

'I didn't sleep too well last night, Sir.'

'You've seen the papers, have you?'

'No, I haven't been out.'

'I should have brought you a couple. You've made headlines everywhere. Mystery shooting. The press have- n't really got a lot to go on, I suppose our own press office is being pretty tight, and they're printing anything at the minute. You've been accused of all sorts of things.'

He attempted a thin smile but neither of us was in the mood and it faltered and died. He looked at the floor again, resumed his serious expression.

'I suppose you know the man you shot was involved in Intelligence?' he asked quietly.

'I had sort of guessed it, Sir. Have they released his name yet?'

'Not yet. I gather it will take a short time for the powers that be to make up their minds on policy ... in a case like this.'

'I see.'

He shifted in his seat and re-crossed his legs and cleared his throat.

'Unfortunate business, really.'

'Yes, Sir,' I agreed. There was a long pause. Both of us looked at the carpet.

'How do you feel about it?'

It was an odd sort of a question and it threw me a little.

'Feel about what?'

'How do you feel about the incident yesterday morning? I suppose that's not very well put, is it? I suppose I'm trying to ascertain your feelings in regard to the death.'

'Well, I'm not very happy about it, Sir; he was on our side, and I killed him. Those are the facts. On the other hand, I'm not going to shed many tears over him, considering the way he acted.'

'Yes, I believe they opened fire on you first.'

'No, Sir, they opened fire on the girl.'

'What?'

'The first shot was fired at the girl. If they had fired at me they would hardly have missed. It was thanks to the girl drawing their fire that I was able to draw my own weapon.'

'They fired on the girl?'

'Yes.'

He seemed genuinely surprised. I supposed a garbled version of the shooting had filtered back to him, and he wasn't the sort to approach the RUC to demand details.

'And then you fired at the armed man?'

'Yes.'

'I see.'

'Have you seen the statement I made to the RUC, Sir?'

'No, I haven't, actually. At the minute all my information has come through the jungle telegraph, you know how long it takes paperwork to filter through the system. I hope to see the details later today.'

'It's just that you seemed surprised when I–'

'Yes, well according to the information I was given–' He broke off suddenly, as if he had realised that he had gone too far. He shrugged and looked away. 'Rumour. Never one hundred per cent accurate, is it?' He smiled his fatherly smile, knowing and protective. He should have been commanding a battalion in Germany, where the enemy was real and wore a uniform and looked across the fence at him, rather than getting himself tangled in this barrel of lies.

'Look, Garrett,' he said, looking at his hands again. 'I want you to realise that you have the complete support of everyone in the battalion in this business. Everyone is one hundred per cent behind you, and if you need anything, you have only to lift the phone.' Warning bells were ringing in my head again. 'However, we have received certain ... instructions from HQNI, regarding yourself.' He paused again and I felt something sinking in my stomach. The boat was leaving and I was on the jetty waving it goodbye.

'We are to relinquish contact with you from now until the case comes to court. The only exceptions will be visits from the Medical Officer, if requested by either yourself or the battalion. The adjutant will visit you on a weekly basis for administrative purposes. You are to have no other communication with other officers in the battalion, nor with other ranks, for that matter. If you need to talk to us, you contact us through the adjutant.' He tugged sadly at the knot of his tie. 'I would like to add that these restrictions are being forced on me from above and that I have already used every weapon at my disposal to fight them. However, this all comes from a great distance above me, I'm afraid.'

And you've got your career to consider, you poor bastard. I felt genuinely sorry for him, sitting there, writhing and squirming; he had always tried to foster a family spirit in the battalion, always telling his subordinates that they were a team and that he would stand by them in whatever decision they took, no matter what the cost. But now all he could do was resign and even that would have no effect and he knew it. He was as trapped by the thing as I was.

'Can I ask why?'

'You can,' he replied, 'But I'm afraid I can't tell you, because I don't know. I presume that the incident is connected with some sort of high-level intelligence operation, and that they want to keep you ... under supervision ... for a while.'

I knew, in the part of my mind that reasons, that the Colonel had had no choice, that the decision had been made at a level far above his, and that with a wife and a family and a fairly promising career ahead of him he could not afford to rock any boats. Especially high-level boats. I knew all this and understood it all and yet, deep down in the back of my mind I felt hurt and betrayed. I felt the battalion would have stood with me, no matter what, yet here they were cutting the lines and setting me adrift.

I stood up and walked over to the window, still cradling the mug of coffee. The morning was dry and clear and the harsh winter sun glistened on the wet road. As I watched, a woman in a yellow waterproof pushed a pram past the gate, head down and the click of her heels reaching me faintly through the glass.

'Did you see anyone standing about outside, Sir, as you came in?' I asked him, casually. I was aware of him stiffening slightly, as if afraid to listen.

'No, I didn't. Why?'

'Because I've been under surveillance since I left the police station yesterday afternoon. Four men followed me all around town yesterday. Last night they were in a car watching the entrance to the avenue. I'm sure they'll be about today, somewhere ... ' I made a point of peering out of the window. 'I just thought you might have noticed them.'

'You think you're being targeted?'

'Not by the opposition, Sir. These people are on our side.'

'Our side.'

'Yes, I believe so.'

He watched me from the chair, his eyes calm and steady. 'You think our own people have you under surveillance.'

'Yes.'

I looked him straight in the eye and he held my

gaze for a few seconds then dropped his head and stared at the carpet again. The Colonel was one of that dying breed, a man of honour, and both of us knew that he couldn't lie to save his life.

'The thing is,' I began, 'ever since the beginning of this business I've been treated like a criminal, and I have done nothing outside the law. All right, I killed that guy, and he was one of ours; but I acted within the rules of engagement, I followed the yellow card. There was a danger to life and all I could do was shoot him. And now, I'm being watched, I'm being followed, I've been kept in interview rooms, I've been interrogated. For Christ's sake, I'm an officer, after all. Surely I'm entitled to some kind of trust?'

The Colonel was leaning forward in his seat and flexing his fingers, trying to think of something to say. Something snapped inside me, and I slammed the empty mug down on the windowsill and marched to the sideboard, snatching open the doors and jerking out the picture frame from beneath the pile of cards and photographs. I went to his chair and held it out in front of him.

'Colonel. Sir. Look at that. The Queen's Commission. Signed by Her Majesty Queen Elizabeth, appointing me to command her loyal forces. It's maybe the most precious thing I have in this house. Eight years I've had that, and I've never been able to hang it on the wall. Never been able to show it off, in case some Republican bastard looks through the window and sees it and decides to come after me. Eight years an officer. Dodging and ducking and doing what I can to help this bloody country and now all of a sudden I'm a criminal, well where's the bloody justice in that?'

I broke off, half-ashamed of my sudden outburst. I turned away. The frame was heavy and awkward, and I set it back on the sideboard. 'I just ... would like to know why they're watching me, that's all,' I explained limply. 'Just why.' I sat down heavily on the settee, feeling ridiculous. This man was on my side, and I was berating him. Fool.

The Colonel sat for a long time in silence, fiddling with his fingers, staring past them at his feet.

'Look, Garrett,' he said at last. 'I'm not supposed to tell you this, but as you say, you're an officer and a gentleman and you've been treated shabbily, so I'm going to take a chance. Needless to say, anything you hear is between the two of us only and must go no further. I ... ah ... know I can rely on you for that.

'What has happened is this. You have stumbled into the middle of a very high-level intelligence operation which was being run by the intelligence services–without, I may add, any consultation with either the RUC or ourselves–and I am led to believe that the possible results of this operation, in intelligence terms, are ... well, immense.'

He was speaking slowly, choosing his words with great care. I was staring straight ahead at the slanting rays of cold, bright sunlight flooding through the window and on to the floor, almost mesmerised by the tiny specks of dust floating and swirling in the wash of the air.

'What happened to you was highly unfortunate, by any standards, but all the more so for having happened right at the culmination of the operation. I'm assured that no permanent damage has been done–'

'Except to the fellow I killed,' I interrupted harshly.

'To the operation itself,' the Colonel continued, neatly ignoring me. 'However, the people running the operation were a little alarmed by the apparent ease with which you ... despatched ... their man. They were concerned in case they had been compromised and that you weren't who you said you were. There was a lot of hasty checking up done, I can tell you.'

'Who did they think I was?'

'They didn't say and I didn't ask and I don't think they would have told me in any case.'

I sat silent and morose, staring into the light.

'Look,' he said, patiently, 'I know how you must feel about all this. But you must understand their point of view. This business they're involved in is very ... delicate. They must safeguard themselves. Follow up every avenue, every possibility, no matter how unlikely or far-fetched. They have their own standard operating procedures, just as we have ours, and all they are doing is following those procedures.'

His eyes were sad and honest. I felt sick. As if it wasn't enough to accidentally kill someone, now I was accused of doing it deliberately.

'What gets me,' I said quietly, 'is the fact that no one seems to believe my story. No one trusts a word I say. No one listens.' I stood up and went to the window again, keeping my back to him, not trusting the quiver in my voice. Outside a milk float whirred past the gate, bottles clinking faintly in their crates.

'I suppose they've got my P-File, too, have they?' I asked without turning round.

'They have,' he replied steadily.

'I thought that was confidential?'

'It is. But they have the big guns on their side.'

'Of course.'

Along the avenue to the left, half-hidden by my neighbours' hedge, I could just make out the shape of a man's head and shoulders, immobile, leaning against a lamppost. As I watched, another head and shoulders joined the first and they seemed to exchange words before both of them moved off up the avenue, away from my house. I watched them until they disappeared from view. Even at that distance I recognised the woolly-capped man from the previous day.

'I hope you're right, Sir, I really do. I wonder if they've killed the girl yet.'

'Oh, for God's sake, Kearns, stop feeling sorry for yourself!' he snapped, and I almost jerked to attention. 'These things happen. It will blow over. You're an officer in the British army, start acting like one!'

The little switch in my head flicked over.

'Then start treating me like one!' I roared back, swinging round from the window. 'If I'm under suspicion, then arrest me! Let me stand trial! Court Martial, even; I've done nothing wrong and I'm not afraid, but do something, for God's sake!'

He sat perfectly quietly still, looking back at me, meeting my gaze and saying nothing. Which normally works in a slanging match, calming the aggressor down, but the little switch was thrown and I was out of control.

'I'll be going back to work in a few days, what then? Will these goons still be following me? Will I still be under suspicion? Whose files will I be on then? When will they forget about me? Jesus Christ, I almost prefer the Provisionals, at least they're only trying to kill you!'

He stood up suddenly, straightening his jacket, sticking his chin out over his collar.

'I'm assuming you're still under a lot of strain. That's understandable. But I can see no point in continuing this interview in your present mood. I'll call again.'

Coldness in his voice, all the quiet friendship gone. Superior to junior officer again. I suddenly realised that I might have lost a friend.

'Right,' I replied carelessly. I knew I had to say something but didn't know what, except sorry and I wasn't sure I could do that.

He let himself out and I stood at the window and watched him stalking down the path, a tall and lonely figure, completely out of his depth. I knew that he would never, could never understand the Province. He was a soldier, with a soldier's mind, equipped and trained to deal with straight lines, definitions, black and white. Right and wrong. He needed a proper war and he knew he would never get one.

They brought the car back later that morning, two uniformed policemen with a Landrover waiting at the gate to take them away again. I had to sign for it.

The front driver's seat was stained black with blood, and the dashboard was smeared with the fingerprint dust the forensic people had used. All my cassettes were gone, as were all the useless objects people normally keep in their cars; cloths for the windscreen, a few maps, the AA book. All the scrappy bits of paper. The car was like a relic, a sudden reminder of the shooting, familiar and yet so changed.

The front of the car was wrecked, the lights smashed and the bumper hanging off, and the nearside was scratched and dented from the impact with the hedge, mud-spattered right up to the windows. It was like having a wounded horse returned to you, still in pain. I felt I should put it out of its misery. The uniformed men were apologetic.

'You'd think they'd have cleaned it for you,' one of them said.

'Hard to get blood out,' I replied.

'Even so.'

'Yeah.'

He handed me a black bin-liner. 'Those are the contents of your car. I've got a list here, do you want to check them off?'

'No, I'll trust you.'

'OK.'

The policemen drove off and I sat in the front passenger's seat and looked at the bloodstains for a long time. The car felt different. Things had happened in it which would leave a bad atmosphere. I would have to sell it, I decided, once it was repaired. I wondered what the girl had done, or what it was she knew that was so important it allowed them to try to kill her, rather than let her escape. In my head I saw the gunman switching his aim to the girl and his expression as he fired, never changing, the flash of the pistol and the crack as the heavy round passed me. His face had been cool, professional. Tense, but in control. I wondered how you could shoot at a running woman and not feel something.

I sat in the house for the rest of the day trying not to think and the RUC station phoned at about four o'clock. Could I come down, they said, something about another statement, won't take long, like to get it finished with as soon as possible, etc etc. OK, I said.

I walked down because the car didn't feel right, besides which it had no headlights and I didn't want

61

to be booked by Traffic Branch on top of everything else. The watchers followed as usual, keeping well back today but still visible. In the centre of town I nipped across the main street just as the lights were changing and they had to run to keep up and when one of them came too close I turned and waved to him. He immediately stopped and stared intently into a shop window not noticing that it was a ladies' shoe shop.

The two detectives waiting for me were strangers. They took me to the same interview room and introduced themselves as Detective Sergeant Moore and Detective Constable Breslin of Special Branch. They were big men in pale-coloured suits and expensive slip-on shoes and they would have stood out anywhere as peelers. Something about them was tense, watchful, mistrusting. Battered and tough.

Moore sat down across the table from me and Breslin took a chair over against the wall, beneath the camera. I noticed that the red light was off. I began to notice a delicate hardness in the atmosphere.

'Now, Mr Kearns,' Moore began, pulling a police notebook from an inside pocket. 'What we want to do this evening is just clear up a few points from your earlier statement. It won't take long.'

'Good,' I said. He was being a lot cooler than he had to and it was irritating me. I was on his side, after all.

'Now,' he said again. 'Yesterday morning, as you were returning from your duty. You were going home from Portadown through Bleary, is that right?'

'Yes.'

'Why come that way, in particular?'

'Just for a change.'

'Seems a long way to go just for a change? When you could nip down the main road in half the time.'

'I always vary my route.'

'The route to and from the UDR centre?'

'That's right.'

'I see. Now.' I was beginning to wish he'd stop saying 'now.' 'Your personal protection weapon. Where do you normally carry it?'

'Normally in a belt holster, now and again in a shoulder holster.'

'I see. It's a thirty-eight, isn't it?'

'Yes.'

'Smith and Wesson?'

'Yes.'

'And were you carrying the weapon in a shoulder holster that night? Or in your belt?'

'In the shoulder holster.'

'I see.'

I was being deliberately short with them but the questions didn't call for long involved answers and I didn't care for their attitude. I felt somehow that they had already come to some sort of a decision about me, that this interview was merely for the sake of form.

'Now when you left your car immediately after the collision, what exactly did you have in mind?'

'I was angry. I wanted a few words with the other driver. I wanted his name and address, for one thing. For the insurance. And I wanted to tell him what I thought of his driving.'

'And where was your weapon at this point?'

'In the holster. What exactly are you getting at here?'

'I'll ask the questions, if you don't mind.'

The tone was flat and hard. So that was the way of it.

'I beg your pardon.'

'Not at all. Now, at what point exactly did you draw the weapon?'

'First chance I got.'

'Before the other man produced a gun?'

'No. Once he shifted his point of aim from me to the girl. Until then I couldn't move at all.'

'What made you think he would open fire on you?'

'Well, he had a gun pointed at me; that usually leads me to that conclusion.'

'Did he say anything to you? Like, I'm about to fire, or drop your weapon, anything of that sort?'

'No.'

'And he didn't actually declare an intent to open fire?'

'No.'

'So then you fired at him?'

'Yes.'

'Why, exactly?'

I wanted to retort with a few choice phrases but I managed to force down the anger.

'I felt my life to be endangered. The girl's life certainly was.'

'Oh?'

'Well, he fired at her, not at me.'

Over beneath the camera Breslin shifted in his chair.

'How long have you held a PPW, Mr Kearns?' he asked. Something had been niggling at me and that was it, they weren't using my rank. It had been Captain Kearns before.

'Ten years, Mr Breslin.'

'Have you ever had occasion to draw it before?'

'Yes, several times.'

'And have you ever fired it in anger?'

'Yes. Once. Only it was the IRA who were shooting at me that time, not my own bloody side.'

The two of them exchanged glances and it all seemed a little bit Starsky and Hutch, a bit ridiculous. Moore closed his notebook with a flourish and stood up. 'Well, I think that's about all we have for you.'

I stood up, too.

'I wonder would you mind waiting for a few minutes, Mr Kearns,' said Breslin. 'I think we've covered everything important, but just in case a detail pops up when we go over this. We won't keep you long.'

I sat down again. 'I'm at your disposal, gentlemen,' I said graciously.

They smiled thinly and went out and the dull, oppressive silence of the room settled around me again. I would never again denigrate the effect of detention in a small, bare room, I reflected.

Half an hour later they came back in with a third man, another stranger. Tall and thin and untidy, with a bent-over way of moving that told me immediately that he wasn't a policeman. This time they didn't bother with introductions. Breslin stood by the door and Moore took his place beneath the camera, while the newcomer sat carefully down at the table, facing me. He clasped his hands together on the formica top and clicked his knuckles. The atmosphere was hostile, I could see it on their faces and the air was dancing with it.

'Garrett Kearns,' said the newcomer, carefully, in a bland English accent.

I said nothing. We sat in silence, staring at each other. He had small, steady eyes, pale hazelnut, almost the colour of nicotine-stained fingers.

'I take it you are Garrett Kearns?'

'Yes.'

'You are thirty-three years old?'

'Yes.'

'Unmarried?'

'Yes.'

'How long have you known Alison Sharpe?'

'Who?'

'How long have you been a member of the Ulster Defence Regiment?'

'Twelve years.'

'Have you ever been a member of any other organisation?'

'No.'

'You're sure of that?'

'Well I was in the Boys Brigade for a while but I'm sure that's not what you mean.'

'Just answer the questions please. Would you consider yourself a loyal subject of the United Kingdom?'

'I would.'

'A loyalist?'

I looked at him for a few moments. His fair hair was thinning at the front, greasy, drooping over his dry forehead. He would have been about forty, forty-two. He didn't blink often. Some people are easy to dislike; no matter what they say or do you can never grow to enjoy their company, and I knew this was one of them. In appearance he reminded me of a large rat, with his small eyes and the jerky way he moved his head.

'I don't believe we've met,' I said politely, extending my hand across the table. 'How do you do?'

He stared at me from below his eyebrows.

'Would you say you're a loyalist?'

'I am a loyal subject. I hold the Queen's Commission in her land forces. Which I would imagine you don't.'

Something passed across his face as he watched me, a flicker of emotion, anger perhaps, quickly hidden.

'When did you first meet Alison Sharpe?'

'I don't know anybody called Alison Sharpe.'

'But you have met her?'

'I don't have to take this.'

'I'm afraid you do, Mr Kearns,' said Moore from under the camera.

'Who is this man, anyway?' I asked, addressing myself to Moore.

'My name is Smith,' said the newcomer.

'Oh, aye. Very original.'

'Mr Kearns,' said Smith wearily. 'If you don't

choose to be a little more co-operative we shall arrest you and hold you here until you do choose to help. Under the prevention of terrorism act you can be held for up to seven days without charge, you are aware of that, I'm sure. So I suggest, to make things easier for both of us, that you give us your co-operation and then we'll get this whole thing over with as soon as possible.'

'I came here of my own free will. And I'm getting up and walking out of that door now, unless you want to arrest me,' I announced, raising myself from the seat but before I could stand up Breslin had begun to intone in a dull, practised voice.

'Garrett Kearns, you are under arrest. It is my duty to remind you that anything you say will be taken down and could be used in evidence against you.'

A chill in my spine. I was arrested. I sat back down, slowly, disbelieving. Arrested. Thirty-three years of life, twelve years of service to Queen and country and here I was, arrested. I felt as though the floor had been taken from beneath me, as though the world had spun suddenly round and had fallen across me.

'Now let's begin from the moment your car hit the other vehicle,' Smith continued calmly. 'In your statement you said that your own car came to rest in the ditch at the side of the road, is that correct?'

'Yes,' I said in a hollow voice.

'And you were about thirty metres from the other car.'

'Yes. More or less.'

'And then you left your car.'

'Yes.'

'Your weapon was drawn at this point?'

'No.'

'It was still holstered?'

'Yes.'

'What exactly were the occupants of the car doing when you got out?'

'Ah … ' I was trying to think but my brain was reeling from the shock of the arrest and the thought processes were blurred and shaken. All I could do was thank whatever fates there were that my parents were dead and were spared all this for they would never have understood. Only bad people were arrested, criminals; the final ignominy. 'They were trying to move the car. I thought they were trying to push the car back on to the road.'

'To what purpose?'

'To drive off.'

'How many people did you see?'

'Two. One got back into the car as I approached.'

'So then you opened fire on them?'

'No.'

'Then when did you open fire on them?'

'When they fired at the girl!'

'They?'

'All right, for God's sake, he!'

'Then you yourself never actually came under fire?'

'No,' I said patiently, 'the man with the gun fired at the girl–'

'How many rounds?'

'One round.'

'Then you fired at him?'

'Correct.'

'Does the name Michael John Ledbury mean anything to you?'

'No, should it?'

'I'd imagine so. It's the name of the man you killed.'

Nasty and below the belt and I felt the stomach twist. I was a killer again, a taker of life. I swallowed quickly and tried to keep my face steady but Smith had seen the reaction and noted it. I didn't want to give the bastard anything.

'Really?' I said casually.

'You don't feel remorse? Guilt? You don't feel … perturbed in any way about killing someone on your own side?'

'Certainly not. He was a terrorist.'

'A terrorist?' His turn to register a reaction. Bastard.

'Yes.'

He smiled thinly and scratched at his nose. 'He was working for us, Mr Kearns. He was an employee of the Crown.'

'He tried to kill an unarmed girl when she was running away. I've spent half my life trying to stop people doing things like that, so in my book it makes him a terrorist. And yes, I'm glad he's dead, because if he wasn't, then I would be.'

Smith suddenly pushed his chair back and stood up, long and gaunt and tatty. He began to walk around the room and I got the impression that it was something he had practised for effect. Too many spy films, perhaps.

'Ledbury was an intelligence operative, working for ... shall we say, a Government department. He was working on a very sensitive operation. Entailing great personal danger, I might add.'

Anger.

'Oh, dear, how sad! And I suppose checking under your car every bloody morning in life doesn't count as personal danger, does it? Holding your breath every time you drive away, waiting for the fucking bang? You people make me sick. Over here for, what, two years? If that. Then back home to London with a few stories about mad paddies, well let me tell you something, Mr Smith, I've lived with it all my life so don't lecture me about danger!'

Moore coughed and tried to stifle it and it might have been a laugh.

'Nevertheless, he's dead now, isn't he?'

'Makes the world a little sweeter, if you ask me.'

He had walked around and was standing behind me. I could feel the hairs on the back of my neck prickling.

'We're all on the same side. We're all fighting the same war, just on different levels. So I don't know why you felt you had to kill him.'

'I didn't know he was one of your lot. He didn't identify himself. All I knew was that he was pointing a gun at me and making nasty noises. And let me tell you something: it could have been the Good Lord Jesus Christ himself standing there and if he did the same things I would have shot him, too.'

'Murderous sort of a bastard, aren't you?'

'I'm a live sort of a bastard. Your man isn't.'

Smith moved past me to the table and perched himself on the edge, beside me, taking a tube of Polo mints from his pocket and carefully unwrapping them. He made a point of not offering me one then nervously twisted the silver paper into a point before pushing the packet back into his pocket. All his actions, all his movements were marked by the same, nervous jerkiness, like a junkie on cold turkey, or a rat. He cracked the mint loudly between his teeth.

'Look,' he said in what he must have considered a friendly voice. 'We need certain information from you. We need to know about the Sharpe girl. We need to know who she would go to in an emergency. Who she would trust. And we need that information as soon as we can possibly get it. Otherwise we're blind.'

'I don't know anyone called Alison Sharpe.'

'You expect me to believe that, do you?'

'I don't give a crap whether you believe it or not.'

'Well you'd better start giving a crap. And soon.'

'Is that a threat?'

'Not at all. Advice, just good advice.'

He was wearing cheap, grey shoes, scuffed, with one of the laces undone. I hoped he would trip and break his neck.

'Now look,' he said, reasonably. 'You and I are both aware of the nature of the relationship you and the girl have been having. That's fine, that's not a problem, she's a very lovely girl. No worries there at all. And we don't want to delve into your private life, that's the last thing we want.' I half-expected him to say, 'Isn't it, boys?' He looked at the wall for a moment, sucking noisily on the mint. 'But we do need to know about Alison, where she would go to. It's important. A matter of national security, highest priority.'

'Look,' I said wearily, 'I don't know the girl, I've never met the girl, apart from yesterday morning because I assume that this is the girl in the other car, and I don't have any idea who she would run to. I only hope she makes it.'

Smith suddenly spun round and banged his fist down hard on the table. 'Then why did you give her your car!' he shouted.

'I didn't give her my car,' I roared back, 'she took the fucking thing!'

'You're a liar,' he hissed, and then the narrow strand of reason had snapped and I was on him, fists hammering and flailing and the chair falling backwards behind me, aware only of the hatred and soft, yielding feel of him as he tried to curl up under the assault. Squealing and shouting and I could smell tobacco smoke on his clothes and then all of a sudden big hands grabbed me and I was lifted bodily backwards and thrown face-first at the wall. Moore had his arm across my neck, pushing my face against the plaster, and I could hear Smith groaning as Breslin fussed around him. I'm not any sort of a fighter but the rage had given me a kind of strength and a kind of luck and I knew I had damaged him in some way. I felt wild, triumphant, even with my nose hard against the cold wall.

'What the hell did you do that for,' Moore hissed into my ear.

'Ah, fuck off,' I said.

I heard my chair being set up again and then I was whipped round and pushed firmly into it. Smith was sitting unhappily in the other chair holding a handkerchief to his nose, great, dark bloodstains spreading over it. I saw the hatred in his eyes.

'You little bastard,' he said quietly and very calmly. I recognised the danger in him; some men take a physical assault on their person very badly, men who have spent their lives apart from other men, away from any kind of contact, without any kind of touch. Smith was one of those and I knew I had made an enemy for life.

I sat looking at him, arrogant, gasping for breath, my heart pounding from the excitement. There were spots of blood spattered down the front of his shirt.

'Sorry about that,' I said as casually as I could. 'I must have slipped. Good of you to break my fall.'

'I'll break more than that, you bastard.'

'Why don't you press charges? Or don't you people believe in the courts?'

'Shut your mouth!'

'Aye,' I said wisely, slowly nodding my head. 'A bit too open. A bit too public.'

'That's enough, Kearns,' snapped Moore, and I decided not to push it any farther. I felt I had made my point.

'OK. No problem.'

The three of them looked awkward and out of place now that the dynamics of the interview had been disrupted. The thread had been broken and it would take them time to repair it. I sat at the table with my chest heaving and awaited developments.

'We'll suspend this interview for the time being,' said Smith through the handkerchief.

I could hear a quiver in his voice. I suppose people like Smith don't come across raw physical violence much in their kind of work; they deal in violence of the mind, of the soul. The bodily sort is alien to them and it unsettles them and they don't know how to deal with it. He pulled the handkerchief away from his face slightly and peered down into it, as a fresh track of blood began to dribble down his upper lip. He jammed the stained cloth back against his face.

'We'll be back later,' he said quietly, his voice laden with menace. 'Have a think about things. Have a good, long think.'

I tried to think. I sat in the room for almost an hour and a half, trying to force my brain to reason but the effort was enormous, like trying to push a car through mud. The part of me which should have been evaluating and appreciating and drawing deductions was dull and empty and the only thing I could find in my head was the injustice of it all. The injustice, and the sting of a middle-class conscience which could find no fault with its own conduct. I had been in trouble with the police, yes, well everybody is at some point in their lives, even if only a parking ticket or a speeding offence, and for me it had been a party which blossomed out of control and on to the street and into a charge of disorderly conduct. High spirits in the wrong place at the wrong time. The lecture from my father in the quiet of the drawing room with the curtains drawn and the clock ticking on the mantelpiece had pierced me inside; letting down the family name, the local disgrace, the shame, all the little middle-class barbs which had lain beneath my skin ever since.

So I had joined the law, worked for it and under it, served it, still slightly nervous of its massive machinery, watching it from behind and outside, a faithful mechanic ready with oil for the cogs. Now I had suddenly been pushed around in front of it, to the dangerous end, and it was unknown and frightening.

Think. They thought I knew the girl. I didn't. But why did they believe that I did? Think. Were they getting false information from somewhere? Mistaken identity? Someone who resembled me, perhaps? Similar name? Think. Evaluate. But my mind was stuck in the cloying, mute, soundproofed silence of the little room and the four blank walls held me there.

The door opened suddenly and I started and Smith came in, all speed and efficiency, the soul of a civil servant. He stood across the table from me. Moore lumbered in behind him and closed the door, positioning himself in front of it and across the small window.

'Had time to reconsider, have you?' Smith asked. I was glad to see he had a neat sticking plaster across the bridge of his nose.

'Yes, thanks,' I replied. 'I see they managed to stop the bleeding.'

'Yes. Apparently I'll live.'

'Pity.'

He glared at me. I suppose he was trying to look aggressive but it wasn't his way and he was failing sadly. He set a file carefully on the edge of the table and extracted a single sheet of paper from it which he passed to me.

'Is that your signature?' he asked.

It was a closely typed document with mistakes here and there blanked out using the 'x', scrappy looking. I had only time to glance at the signature.

'Looks like it.'

'And this? Is this your signature also?'

Another sheet of paper, similar but crumpled and worn. Looked like my signature but I couldn't be sure. I peered more closely at the text and Smith snatched the sheet away.

'You own a typewriter, do you?'

'What about it?'

'Olivetti portable, model 500?'

'I think so.'

'Where do you keep your typewriter, exactly?'

Warning bells were clanging loudly in my head.

'Why?'

'Just answer the question.'

'In the house. Upstairs.'

He smiled again. Something was wrong. My mind was racing and jerking and halting, trying to cope with the instinct screaming at it, warning it.

'This sheet of paper,' he announced smugly,

waving the first sheet, 'is a letter from yourself to Miss Alison Sharpe detailing, among other things, your love for her and your hatred of her lover, a Mr Michael Ledbury. In it you have expressed an intention of, and I quote, " ... sorting Ledbury out", and "Taking care of the English bastard". The second document is a letter from yourself expressing your desire to ...' he held the paper close to his face and peered at it, ' " ... blow that bastard Ledbury away". ' He looked down at me from the height of his long frame. 'Seems that you planned the whole thing,' he said.

The rage flared up inside me but Moore was watching me and I knew that I would not get another chance at Smith.

'I did not write those letters. Those are not my signatures.'

'Nonsense. They were written on your typewriter. We found both of the letters at the girl's house. Obviously you have not been entirely straight with us.'

'You're framing me.'

'We're discovering evidence which would imply a conspiracy to murder. A file will be produced and forwarded to the DPP. And the due processes of law will take their course. Unless, of course, you were to help us with our enquiries.'

'I told you, and you bloody well know, that I don't know this girl!'

'You must start being a little more helpful, Garrett,' Smith sneered at me. 'You could do yourself a lot of harm in a position like this.'

78

'I want to see a solicitor.'

'Sorry. Major Martin of the Army Legal Services will be coming to see you, but he tells us he's very tied up at the moment and it may be a few days before he can spare the time. Sends his apologies. Didn't seem exactly enamoured with you, old boy.'

'Then get me a civilian solicitor.'

He pursed his lips and shook his head sadly, enjoying himself.

'Can't do that, old boy, I'm afraid. The whole business touches on some very sensitive operational material and we couldn't just throw the files open to any Tom, Dick or Harry who walked in off the street.'

Bastard.

'You're setting me up!' I addressed that at Moore but his face never even flickered. 'Call yourself an Ulsterman! An RUC man! I haven't done anything, for heaven's sake!'

'You'd need to be careful what you say,' he replied gravely. 'You'll probably be charged with murder, and any statements made during your interview might be used against you.'

'I don't believe this!' I gasped. The weight of it was bearing down the anger; they were setting me up, accusing me of having a relationship with someone I didn't even know and the upshot of it could be a prison sentence and even the thought of those two words made me shudder.

'You'll be held in custody for the next few days, then you'll be officially charged with murder. And once that happens, there's nothing we can do to change it. So consider the situation carefully. I'll come back again in the morning and see what your answer is.' He slipped the papers into a thin document case.

'Look, I don't know the girl, what do I have to do to convince you? I never met her before. I was there totally by chance. By accident, that's all. What in the name of God do you want me to say?'

'You'll think of something, Mr Kearns. I'm sure you'll think of something.'

Cold. The only sound was the hum of the light behind the grille and the occasional creak of the low bed as I shifted on it, and now and again the dull thud of a door banging up in the corridor. I hugged my arms tight against my chest, partly for the warmth. All around the plain, grey-brick walls were the spidery markings of slogans and signatures in felt pen and biro, small, hesitant scratchings, little bits of personality scraped on the oppressive brick. I wondered how many criminals had lain on the little bed before me, looking up at the same, dull, bare ceiling, and where they were now. Back on the streets, perhaps, or maybe still rotting in some other cell.

And now it was me, here, on my own, waiting to be charged. The bastards. So much for democracy. So much for twelve years' service. Threatened. Shot at. Hated. Long nights with little sleep and no reward or thanks. Days spent lying in soaking fields, watching for someone who never came, cold and miserable and all for what? For this? For a coarse, grey blanket on a prison cot?

I lay there for some time and deliberately didn't look at my watch so that the time would pass a little faster. Once the shutter on the steel door opened and a pair of eyes peered in before it clanged closed again. Now and again there were footsteps outside, going past my cell. My cell. Jesus, I thought.

I was drifting off to sleep when Simpson came in.

'Garrett!' he hissed, closing the door carefully behind him. I heard the bolt shutting on the far side.

'Phil, what–'

'Look, I haven't much time.' He looked at me, then at the door, then at me again, and there was a strange look on his face which I couldn't fathom.

'Phil, they're trying to frame me–'

'I know.'

'How do you know?'

'Peter Moore told me. He's not too happy about it.'

The name threw me for a second and then I remembered the big Special Branch man at the interview.

'You know him?'

'We were at the depot together.' He paused, examining me. 'He said they had a couple of letters from you.'

'Jesus Christ, Phil, they forged the bloody things, I didn't–'

'They said the letters were written on your typewriter.'

'Well they probably broke into the house while I

was down here. I'm sure they could find someone to forge a signature!'

'OK, OK, I believe you. Peter more or less told me the same thing.'

'Why are they doing it, Phil? That's what I can't understand.'

'This fellow, Smith, is a nasty bastard. He thinks you know something about this girl, and the murder charge business is mainly to frighten you into singing. Thing is, Peter says this boy is so annoyed with you he's likely to let the prosecution go through anyway.'

'Bastard!'

'If you were prosecuted it would leave things very neat for Smith. Domestic dispute over a woman, man kills rival, no hint of Intelligence at all and that would leave them very happy. Peter only went along with it to get whatever information he could out of you, but he's involved now and can't get himself out.'

'He could turn Smith in!' I hissed at him.

'He's got a wife and three kids and he wants to be able to feed them. If he turns Smith in then he'll implicate himself.'

'He got himself there. He can take the buck when it's passed to him.'

'Anyway, that's not all. The weapons found at the scene have disappeared.'

'What?' I couldn't believe it.

'They were taken to the forensic labs, and now they say there is no record of them arriving there.'

'You're kidding!'

'I wish I was and that's the God's truth, Garrett.'

'But if I was the only one there, then who drove my car away?'

'They'll get around that one, don't you worry. You're in deep shit, Garrett. Deep shit. They're making out that you went looking for this guy, rammed his car and shot him.'

I felt my stomach twisting and heaving, real fear slamming into me.

'What about Moore? What's he going to do?'

'He's done it. He told me.'

'Brilliant. I mean, no harm to you, Phil, but I need help.'

'I know. Look, Garrett, there's only one way out of this thing.' He looked at me gravely and his eyes were very still. 'You could run.'

There was a long silence. The light bulb hummed.

'What?' I asked him.

'You could run. Get out. If you could find the girl you could clear your name.'

'You're kidding.'

'No. If you stay here you're going down. This man, Smith, is very high and he is very powerful and he hates your guts. If he can swing it, he'll send you down, and there's nothing you, me or anybody else can do about it. These people have the power.

'Now I'm giving you a chance, if you want it. I can get you out. Now. Get you away. But you have to make the decision. You have to want to do it.'

'To run?' I asked weakly, aware of the unsteadiness in my voice.

'To run, or to stay. That's the choice.'

I rubbed my chin nervously. The walls seemed to

84

be contracting around me. I knew that what Simpson was saying was true, that they had me in the palm of their hand. If I went to prison it would be years of solitary confinement, a UDR man in with IRA men; always waiting for the broken glass in the food or the rat poison in the tea. Years of it to come, relentless, unbroken days and months and years. Smith had the power and he would do it.

In life there come a few moments, here and there, when the entire future course, and sometimes the length of a man's life, depends on the one yes or no decision. Moments when he suddenly holds his destiny in his grasp and the weight appals him, when all the responsibility sits on his shoulders, and no matter how it goes there'll be no one else to blame. This was the moment and it was all up to me. Simpson watched me with his sad, battered face.

'You're right,' I said at last. 'Get me out of here.'

He swung up a big hand and slapped me on the shoulder.

'Good man.' He glanced at the door again. 'I'm not supposed to be here, obviously enough. If they find me I'll be in here with you.' He was rummaging in his jacket pocket for something. 'Here. You'll need this.' He produced a familiar old piece of polished walnut and blued steel, passing it to me butt first. I flicked open the cylinder, six rounds, their brass cases gleaming. The weight of the gun was comforting. I felt better already.

'Came back from ballistics this afternoon and I managed to get a hold of it. There's another ten rounds in there-' he passed me a small plastic bag,

'–all I could get, unfortunately. Still, better than a poke in the eye.'

'Thanks, Phil,' I said, meaning it.

'No problem. Now listen. I'll leave the cell door unlocked. In half an hour, no sooner, you leave the cell and walk out of the station. There'll be no problem, as long as you wait for half an hour. No one will stop you. Don't produce that thing–' he nodded at the gun '–or there might be a massive sense of humour failure. Just walk out nice and casually. Once you're out of the station, turn right into Sloan Street, you'll see a pale blue Escort. The keys will be wedged above the sun visor. Drive it away. It belongs to a friend, but as far as he's concerned, it'll be reported stolen about lunchtime tomorrow. I've already forced the door lock, by the way, just to keep things right.

'Drive to Belfast. When you get there, get in touch with a fellow named Mills, Joey Mills, his mates call him Bomber. UVF man, owes me a few favours. He'll help. There's an address in the glove box of the Escort and you'll find him there tonight. Don't trust him, but use him. Don't turn your back on him. All right?'

'Yeah.'

He stuck out his big hand and I took it and gripped it tightly.

'Listen,' I began, 'I appreciate what–'

'I'm not just doing it for you,' he said gravely. 'It's the principle. Too many good men are dead fighting for the law, and this bunch of whores are shitting on their memory. I won't have anyone twisting the fucking law, our side or theirs.'

He stood up. There were tears in his eyes. He punched me lightly on the shoulder, embarrassed.

'Don't get caught, all right? Or I'll be in the shit too. And hurt them, Garrett. You hurt them as much as you can.'

I nodded. He knocked twice on the door and the bolts on the far side clanged open, then he quickly turned and went out.

I listened for the sound of the bolts closing again but there was nothing, just the fading clicking of two pairs of feet on the polished corridor floor.

The thought crossed my mind that Simpson might be setting me up for something but I discounted that idea almost immediately. I knew him too well, and I knew his sister, the one who had lost her policeman husband in a gun attack on their bungalow. I knew he was honest.

My heart was racing in my chest, pounding wildly like a hammer on a bucket, fast and hollow. I checked the revolver again, and then once more before slipping it under my waistband. I felt capable again. I was moving somewhere. I was fighting back.

That half hour was the longest in my life, lying on the bed and checking my watch every two minutes and feeling the sweat breaking in my armpits and groin. I was on the run now, I told myself; there was no going back from this, no explanations, no apologies. I held the balance of my life in my hands and if I dropped it, well, it was my own bad luck. Strangely enough it was a good sensation, a feeling of power and competence. I was my own man again.

At nine forty-five it was time to go. I had to make a physical effort to restrain my breathing as I gently pulled the door open and leaned out into the corridor. Empty. The dull yellow lights reflected off the glossy walls.

I walked out of the cell and along the corridor and up the stairs, the thirty-eight tucked in my waistband and covered with my shirt and digging into me slightly but it was good to know it was there, comforting. On to the ground floor and along the main corridor, no sound from anywhere, not even the eternal clatter of typewriters. Nothing. Somewhere up ahead a door closed hurriedly. Past the CID offices. No sound at all. My footsteps echoing loudly in the dark and glossy corridor. My heart racing. Right turn into the entrance hallway and through the heavy door and beside me the enquiry desk, almost afraid to look round at it but the two policemen were carefully studying books and papers, taking care not to look up.

Through the main door and out into the cool night air, and the smell of rain in the courtyard. Everywhere brightly lit, security lights at the gate dazzling me. I walked across the yard, acutely conscious of the revolver at my back and the sangar ahead of me, my head pounding. Dodge around the vehicle boom and past the sangar and the open pedestrian gate ahead and then out and away but a voice calling to me from the sangar, oh dear God no, is this the end of it now, after such a clear run and so close. I turned slowly, hand twitching towards the gun although I knew I wouldn't use it. The small, armoured-glass window of the sangar had been slid back to reveal a face, half in shadow, young features and a dark moustache.

'Mr Kearns,' he called softly. I was ten, maybe fifteen feet from him. Act cool, I told myself. Act normal.

'Yes?'

He looked at me with young-old eyes and the bright lights glinted on the submachine-gun by the window.

'Good luck,' he said.

I swallowed hard and waved at him and then turned out into the street and the cold free air and the tears were stinging in my eyes.

They had thrown out the last of the late-night drunks and turned up all the lights and now they stood quietly behind the bar, polishing glasses and talking softly with frequent glances in my direction. They weren't just barmen. Barmen in these clubs tended to be older, experienced men who could be relied on not to dip the till. These two were there for a purpose, protection probably. They looked as though they were expecting trouble.

The room was heavy with the smell of stale beer and cigarette smoke and on all the tables lay the debris of the night's drinking: overflowing ashtrays, empty crisp packets, pools of spilled drinks. The noise and bustle of the evening seemed to reverberate in the silence. I sat alone in the corner of the empty lounge, toying with a half-full glass of flat beer, trying to look re- laxed. This was a dangerous place to be a stranger. Young men could and did vanish from this club, to reappear in the morning face down on some road- side with their hands tied and their heads blown open and I was grateful for the thick, warm comforting nudge of the revolver in my waistband when I shifted in my seat.

It was already twelve-thirty and I had been there too long, they would be looking for me now and Simpson would have told them where I was and I had to get out, run, get away, anything other than sit here and wait. Be calm. Relax. I checked my watch again, drummed my fingers nervously on the tabletop.

The two barmen had finished their chores and were now leaning against the inside of the bar, their arms folded, watching me as they chatted. I returned their stare, just as casually. Hoods. Young and thick-set and hard-looking, the sort to slice you open without a second thought. One of them had intricate Loyalist tattoos spattered all along his forearms. They had been expecting me when I asked for Mills, one going to the phone behind the bar and the other motioning me to a table, both of them ignoring a loud drunk demanding service. Very efficient and very impressive but if they were expecting me then why the delay? You're in the shit, the instinct was screaming. You're in the shit and you'd better get out.

Relax. Calm the breathing. My hands were shaking badly and I slipped them into my lap and hoped the two men would miss the nervousness. I had read the intelligence briefs on this and other clubs and I knew what went on behind the scenes, the fear and the extortion and the money that changed hands and the bloodstained chairs in the back rooms; I knew of men who had spent their last nights on earth in places like these. I had read their names and seen their last photographs, lying thick and naked on the slab with their wounds hanging open to the world, and I had imagined too much. And now here I was in the middle of it and by God I needed strength.

I decided on the emergency exit and was planning which of the two hoods I should shoot first when the door by the bar opened and a large, untidy head emerged. He looked down the lounge towards me.

'You Kearns?' he asked.

'Yes.'

'Right. This way.'

'Where's Mills?'

'Up here. He's waiting for you.'

Through the door and up the narrow stairway with threadbare patterned carpet and tatty red walls and the warm stench of body odour from the big man in front of me.

'Round to the right, the steel door.'

The door was reinforced with sheet steel riveted on to the wood and there was a peep-hole shutter which clattered back as I approached. The door swung open and I hesitated at the threshold.

'In there,' my escort directed.

One bare light bulb in the centre of the ceiling and the cigarette smoke swirling around it, a long table along one wall with three men behind and two more standing off to one side and in the centre of the room a single, upright kitchen chair. I caught the smell of body odour and cheap aftershave. One of the men standing by the wall gestured at the chair and I went across to it, my mind racing, dragging in details. The frayed carpet. The tatty settee below the curtained window. The Ulster flag stretched across the back wall.

'You're Kearns?'

'Yes.'

The man in the centre was Mills, I remembered his face from the terrorist recognition sheets: broad, unshaven, heavy, sleepy eyelids above quick and vicious eyes. The man to his right was younger, late twenties, neat and clean-cut and intelligent-looking. The third man was older, thin and cadaverous with rings below his eyes, greying hair greased back off the forehead.

'I'm Joey Mills.' He nodded to his right. 'This is Billy,' he said, 'And this is Sammy. You wanted to see me?'

'Yes.'

'Well, here I am. What do you want?'

He stared at me with his slow, nasty eyes. The room was totally silent and I felt it twanging at my nerves, fear clutching at my throat and chest. Newspaper headlines were snapping through my imagination: 'UDR man found dead on Black Mountain.' 'UDR officer murdered by Loyalist gang.' 'Body found with throat slashed.' How many men had sat in this chair before me, I wondered, and were now rotting in their graves?

'Phil Simpson sent me. He said you could help.'

'Is that right?'

I had read his file years before and there were two or three killings down to him but nothing that could be proved, hearsay most of it. Apparently he favoured a butcher's knife, when he had the opportunity; the men he shot were the lucky ones.

'I need to find someone.'

'Wouldn't be a wee girl, would it?'

I almost jolted with the nerves at that but then Simpson would have told him what I was after. I wondered just what kind of a hold Simpson had on him.

'Simpson spoke to you, then.'

'Aye.'

'Then you know I'm being framed.'

'Aye.'

Silence. The man he had introduced as Billy began to pick his teeth with a cocktail stick. Sammy fiddled constantly with a well-chewed pencil, rolling and twirling it between nicotine-stained fingers. Mills was watching me carefully, his eyes steady and calm, and all I could think about was butcher's knives.

'Simpson told you I could help, did he?'

'Yes.'

'Aye. I owe him a favour.' He sniffed loudly. Everything in the room seemed to focus on Mills and his broad, sleepy face.

'He said.'

'Did he?'

He pulled a packet of Silk Cut from the breast pocket of his shirt and rummaged in his trouser pockets to find a cheap, plastic lighter, then carefully arranged the two on the table in front of him, the lighter on top of the cigarettes, squaring them off neatly.

'By the way,' he remarked casually, 'I know you're carrying. Don't be thinking of doing anything stupid, because you'd be dead in seconds.'

There didn't seem to be much to say to that. The gun seemed suddenly very big in my waistband.

'I believe you're in the UDR?' he went on.

'That's right.'

'A captain?'

'Yes.'

'Full-timer?'

'Part-time.'

'What do you work at, then?'

'I'm a teacher. History.'

'Smart lad.'

'Not really.'

With slow deliberation he pulled a cigarette from the packet and pushed it between his lips, as though lost in thought.

'And they're trying to frame you.'

'That's right.'

'Simpson didn't say what they were framing you for.'

'Murder.'

He raised an eyebrow. 'Is that right, now? You don't look the type. I wouldn't have said you were a killer, looking at you.'

'Neither would I.'

'So who are you supposed to have killed?'

'An undercover intelligence operator. And there's no supposed about it.'

Sammy coughed violently and leaned back from the table, covering his mouth with his fist, and Mills let a flicker of surprise pass across his face. It seemed I had scored a point.

'You actually killed him, then?'

'Yes.' A long pause. One of the men by the wall shifted position and his leather jacket creaked. 'It was self-defence. He was shooting at me.'

'But they say he wasn't?'

'Yes.'

'Aye.' Mills lit the cigarette with a well-practised flourish, watching me with his dead eyes.

'So why do you need this girl?'

'She was there. She saw what happened. She can clear me.'

'What happened to her?'

'She got away, but they captured her again later on.'

'They?'

'MI5. I think.'

'So you have to find her to prove your innocence,' he said slowly, half-smiling. He stared at me for a long time and said nothing and I felt the anger beginning to rise in my chest but at least it was better than the fear.

'So how do we know you're not working for the cops?' he asked eventually, blowing a long plume of smoke into the air.

'Look, I've already had one interrogation today. Are you going to help, or not?'

'Well, that depends on what sort of help you're after. And a few other things.'

'Like what, for instance?'

'How much you're prepared to pay.'

So that was how it was to be. I felt as though a heavy weight had dropped into my stomach. To come as far as this to stop.

'I can't pay anything. All I've got left is what I took from my house tonight and that hardly fills a rucksack, so if it's money you're after you've shit out.'

'Something might be arranged.'

'Well I can't bloody well arrange it.'

He stared past me for a moment with the blue cigarette smoke drifting around his face.

'How do you propose to find this girl?' he asked casually.

'She's being held by MI5, but that's all I know. I have to get inside their organisation somehow. Or get a hold of one of them.'

'Is that all?' he sneered. 'You don't want to smuggle her into the House of Commons when you're at it, do you?' I felt the anger rising again.

'If you don't want to help, just say so. I'll find someone else.'

'Oh, don't be so bloody touchy. We'll help. But it'll be on our terms, all right?'

'What terms?'

Mills nodded to his right. 'Tell him.'

Billy clasped his hands together on the tabletop and looked intently at them for a few moments before leaning back and switching his gaze to me. He looked intelligent; quick and sharp, but cold, like a lizard. Cold, steady, lizard eyes.

'Well,' he began. 'As it happens, there's been a whole rake of people asking about this girl in the last few days. The cops, the army, MI5. Maybe even MI6.

There was even a TV crew nosing around. So what we wondered was, why all this interest in one wee girl? Now, there were only two possible scenarios; either they wanted her because she'd done something, or they wanted her because of something she might do. If she'd done something already they would just leave it to the cops and they would turn her up in due course, but they're not doing that, they're panicking. So it must be something she might do. And the only thing a wee girl like that would be able to do, is talk. So we reckon she knows something. Something very important. Something which is so important it could affect the Government itself.'

'And whatever she knows would be very useful,' Mills added. 'Especially to an organisation like ours.'

'So?'

'So we'll help you find her. On condition that you give us first refusal on whatever it is she has. All we want is the information. You can have the girl.'

I'll see you in hell first, I thought.

'What kind of help?'

'We can give you a couple of men for a while. Maybe a car. And we can give you the MI5 safehouse in Belfast.'

It was all getting like a cheap spy story and I couldn't keep a grip.

'You're joking, of course.'

Mills shook his head slowly. 'Nah,' he said. 'I'm not joking. I have their address. They're still there and they don't know we've compromised them. They think they're so fucking smart. I've had them watched for weeks and they still haven't noticed.'

'How did you find them?' I asked.

'Never you mind. All you have to worry about is getting in there and finding that wee girl. That's the deal, take it or leave it.'

The whole thing sounded ridiculous but I was in a cul-de-sac and he was showing me an exit and there was nothing else to do.

'All right,' I said.

'There's another condition,' Billy put in.

'Which is?'

'There's a TV crew in town at the minute, asking about the girl. You have to take them with you.'

'You're joking!'

'They'll pay us five thousand quid if we can find the girl for them. That means that they'll pay us for the help we give you and everyone will be happy.'

'As long as you find the girl,' Mills added.

'I can't get involved with the media, for Christ's sake! I'm on the run!'

'Look,' Mills said impatiently. 'These two are crooks. I've met their type before. They probably stand to make a fortune out of whatever the girl has and if they think you'll help find her then they'll not give you away. Besides, we'll put the fear of God into them. They won't make a peep.'

I could believe that.

'Plus you'll have the media on your doorstep when you find her,' Billy said. 'Instant publicity. And you'll need that to clear your name.'

'If the information becomes common knowledge,' I said, 'then it'll be of no use to you.'

'You don't have to reveal what she knows just to

99

clear yourself. All you have to do is produce the girl and get her to say that you killed your man in self-defence. The Intelligence lot will close round and back that up. And if these two journalists try to use any of it the MI5 people will take them out. That wouldn't be a problem to them.'

'They could take you out, too,' I said.

'I've got an organisation behind me. They'll not take me out so easily. And besides, as long as we get our five thousand quid ... '

He grinned across at me, a gold tooth glinting in the corner of his mouth. They had obviously planned the thing in some depth and that was why I had been kept downstairs in the bar for so long. I wonder what would have happened had the decision gone the other way.

'All right,' I said.

Mills looked at his cigarette for a moment then glanced up at one of the men by the wall.

'Get us an ashtray, Joe, would you?'

There was a bustle behind me and then a heavy glass ashtray was placed reverently on to the table in front of him. They treated it like an altar, I realised. No doubt it was often draped in the paraphernalia of the organisation: the flag, the gloves. Combat jackets and masks and the weapons held awkwardly for the cameras. An altar, and Mills the high-priest. He tapped the long cylinder of ash delicately on to the clean glass.

'Wise man,' he said heavily. I looked at his greasy hair and his snide, slow eyes and the great swell of his belly and at that moment I loathed him and his world, hated this little room full of the smell of sweat and cigarette smoke. I felt dirty and cheap and wanted to be away, in the night air, cold and wet and free.

'How do I contact these people?' I asked him.

'They're already on their way. I sent for them. We don't sit around on our backsides around here, you know.'

'I'm sure you don't.' I tried to keep the tone casual but his eyes hardened a little and I was sure he had caught the disgust in me.

'No,' he agreed. 'We don't.'

He was a dangerous bastard, anyway, and I was becoming his enemy and the thought frightened me because he was a killer. Those thick-fingered hands had ended other lives and would end mine without a thought. Suddenly my head filled with that burning, welling-up behind the eyes, the childish heat that comes before tears. I wanted someone with me, someone to comfort me, to put their arms around me and tell me that they were going to fix it and everything would be all right. But I was on my own and not a friend anywhere and only the fear and the loathing and the dreadful pain of betrayal. Years of obedience and service to the Crown and now come to this, hunted by its agents, forced to seek sanctuary among the scum of the gutters. For a moment I thought I would break down in front of them but then something inside me hardened, some long-forgotten part of me grew tough and scarred and bitter; at that moment some part of me died.

'So how do we get into this MI5 thing, then?'

'We'll discuss that when these journalists arrive. They'll have to agree to everything, as well.'

The bastard was enjoying his moment of power and I glanced down at my watch, afraid he might read the anger in my face. I didn't notice the time.

The man Sammy was fiddling with a packet of cigarettes and I knew he wanted to ask me something. At last he cleared his throat and spoke.

'How long are you in the UDR?' he asked. His voice was hoarse and wheezing, like that of a dying man making his last confession; with his sallow wasted face and his shaking hands, maybe that wasn't too far from the truth.

'Twelve years.'

He nodded down at the cigarette packet. He never looked at me when he was speaking, always down at the table or over at the wall.

'You ever come across a fellow called Derek Rickland? Thickset man from Castlereagh? He used to be a Sergeant in the UDR.'

Rickland. Caught stealing ammunition from the ranges. Not a great deal of ammo, only ten or twelve rounds stuffed into his pocket, but spread over a year or two that was a hell of a lot of lives. Treacherous little bastard. When the case came out in the media we got a lot of attention from the Provisionals and a culvert bomb had taken out two of my men who might be alive still if Rickland hadn't been such a bloody fool.

'Yes, I knew him.'

'Fine man.'

'A stupid, treacherous bastard,' I disagreed politely.

The atmosphere stiffened perceptibly. There was a quiet shuffling as chairs were shifted and breath drawn in.

'Some of us would look on him as a hero,' Mills said, his voice cold.

'I lost two good men through his stupidity,' I replied. 'Two men with a bit of honour about them. Decent men. I had to shovel what was left of them into plastic bags. You lot play your stupid fucking games and the decent men take the fall for you. Let me tell you something, Rickland made me sick. In my opinion they didn't put him away for long enough.'

I stopped, alarmed by the sudden edge of anger in my voice. Sammy commenced a fit of racking coughs. Billy leaned back from the table. Mills stared at me, his eyes full of threat. I thought, what the hell have I just done?

'You better watch your fucking mouth,' Mills growled. 'You're asking us for help. Don't you forget that. Without us you're finished.'

'Bollocks!'

The knock at the door saved me and we sat for a moment in the harsh yellow light with the tension settling down around us, then one of the men from the wall went across to the door and slid back the shutter.

'It's them,' he grunted, opening the door. Mills jabbed a finger at me.

'I don't like you very much, do you know that?'

The fear and the tension were twisting at my stomach and the palms of my hands were damp but I couldn't show weakness, not now.

'Yeah, well the feeling's mutual.'

'Just you watch your back when this thing's over, all right?'

I felt weak and exhausted and for a moment the room began to swim and I was afraid of toppling from the chair. Mills was not a man to have as an enemy. He would kill me without a thought, if he was sure he could get away with it, and what was worse, he would do it slowly, with knives. These were psychopaths and scum who masqueraded as an army and I hated and despised them but I needed them too and the thought made me sick.

There was someone else in the room and I looked round and it was a man and a woman, standing awkwardly near the door, noticing me in the chair and the tension in the air.

'Look,' the woman said quickly, looking nervously at me. 'If this is a bad time we can come back later–'

'No. Come in.' Mills gestured at the heavy by the door. 'Get two more chairs.'

They looked like reporters, both dressed casually in jeans and bright waterproof parkas, the man with a camera bag slung over his shoulder. He was tall and thin with a sandy beard and weak eyes. They were both looking at me, unsure.

'Who is this?' the woman asked.

'His name is Kearns.' He nodded at me. 'That's Clare and Uel.'

Chairs were produced and they sat down carefully. The man, Uel, seemed very nervous, his eyes darting round the room and his arm jerking now and again as his nerves got the better of him. Don't blame you, I thought. The woman seemed wary rather than afraid. I guessed she was around thirty. She looked as though she might once have been a model, but there were lines around her eyes and the way she held herself suggested a tough attitude and a hard mind.

'You sent for us,' she announced. 'What do you have?'

Mills rubbed his eyes roughly with his fingertips, then reached out and stubbed the half-finished cigarette into the ashtray, grinding it to and fro with more force than was necessary and I knew that in his mind it was me he was extinguishing.

'You're looking for a girl, isn't that right?'

'Yes.'

'Well, he's looking for the same girl.'

'Does he know where she is?'

'I can talk, you know,' I put in. Her eyes widened a little, curious.

'I'm sorry. Do you know where she is?'

'I know who has her.'

'Who?'

'MI5.'

'You're joking.'

'Wish I was.'

'You mean the Intelligence people have arrested her?' Uel asked hesitantly.

'Not arrested. Kidnapped, if you like. Maybe killed, I don't know.'

There was a flicker of something across her face but her voice stayed calm. Tough cookie, I thought. Her voice was polite, home-counties and privately educated.

'Why do you want to find her?'

'Kearns, here,' Mills said happily, 'is looking at a life sentence for murder if he doesn't find her. And find her alive.' He was smirking slightly, as if he had just realised how slim my chances really were. The girl nodded slowly.

'But we don't really know why you two are so keen to find her,' he went on, swivelling his gaze in her direction. 'And to pay so well for the finding.'

'That's our affair.'

'Not if we're going to help, it's not.'

'You'll be paid. All you have to do is find her.'

'Maybe we should find her, and hang on to her. Maybe auction her off. She seems to be a bit valuable at the minute, for some reason. Or would it be something she knows?'

The girl stared at him for a few moments then suddenly stood up and turned to the door.

'Forget it,' she said. 'Let's go, Uel.'

Uel began to rise obediently to his feet.

'Wait,' Mills commanded sharply. The girl stopped dead. 'Sit down.' He rubbed at his face with the two big, animal hands, aping the great statesman, waiting until she had settled again.

'All right, here's the deal.' He nodded at me. 'We'll give your man here all the help he needs to find this wee girl. He'll take you along with him. You'll pay us for the help he gets. Sound fair?'

'I said I would pay for the girl, if you could deliver her into my hands. I didn't say I was going to go chasing after her.'

'Well, that's the only way you're going to get at

her. I haven't the resources to waste looking for her, and she could be anywhere by now, or dead. He has to find her or he's in deep shit, and he's capable of it, probably. It's your only chance. Take it or leave it.'

She chewed lightly at her lower lip for a moment, then turned to me.

'What makes you so sure you can find her?' she asked.

I shrugged. 'Because I have to,' I said. She held my gaze for a moment and her eyes were very dark. 'I'll find her or die trying.' I don't think I meant it, really, but it seemed to have the desired effect.

'Mad fucker, isn't he?' Mills remarked.

'All right,' said the girl. 'How much?'

'Five thousand.'

'I can't afford that much.'

'You said you could before.'

'That was before.'

'Well, how much can you afford? I thought you worked for the BBC?'

'We work for anyone and everyone. Five thousand is too much. Two thousand.'

'Can't do it for less than three.'

'Mr Mills, I'm not buying sheep and cows and I'm not into haggling. I now have two thousand pounds to spend on this project. You can either take it or not, but it's all there is.'

Mills stared at her for a moment, his eyes hard and scheming.

'All right,' he said. 'Two thousand.'

'Half now, half when we find the girl.'

His face reddened slightly, the rising anger mottling his coarse features.

'All of it now,' he said.

'No.'

Tough cookie indeed. She held his gaze, boldly outstaring him, pushing and poking at his temper. If things went wrong here we were all dead, even if I managed to get to my gun before they had me, and I hoped she realised that.

'Look, don't fuck me about, lady. You might find you're in above your head here.'

Uel coughed nervously and looked embarrassed. His face was pale and waxy, frightened. Smart man, I thought.

'This is a business deal,' the girl explained patiently, as if to a child. 'I'm not paying you two thousand quid just for the pleasure of your company. You'll get an advance of a thousand, then a further payment when the contract is completed and we find the girl. That's the way people do business. In the real world, anyway.'

'You're pretty fucking smart, aren't you?' he hissed at her. The men at the wall were fidgeting again and the tautness had slipped back into the air.

'If you don't want to deal, just say so,' the girl said calmly. 'That way we won't waste any more of each other's time.'

He sat back in his chair and his face was shadowed and stark. He stared at her for a long time. The two men beside him looked down at their hands, and Sammy was furiously rotating the pencil between his fingers. I didn't like the way things were going and I was trying to work out exactly where the two men at the wall were standing so that I wouldn't waste the first shot when the animal face split into a wide and unpleasant grin.

'All right. Half now, half later. It's a deal.' He was still motionless and staring with the broad, empty smile hanging on his face and I knew there was more to come. 'You're a good business woman,' he continued.

'I know.'

'If you fuck me about I'll have you killed. Remember that.'

The smile was still there and the gold teeth glinted in the yellow light and the threat hung in the air like ice. The girl swallowed. Uel jerked his head nervously, all colour drained from his face.

'This is a business deal,' the girl said carefully. 'We don't want any … ah … complications.'

'Just so long as you remember that,' Mills said quietly. 'Just so long as you remember that.'


The room was small, made smaller by the neat stacks of crates and cartons of various kinds of alcohol piled around the walls and the small pool of light cast by the single weak bulb. The smell of damp mingled with the dry cardboard odours of the boxes and packages.

'You've to wait here,' our escort muttered. 'I'll come back for you later.' The key rattled in the lock as he closed the door behind him. Another cell, I reflected sadly.

The girl sat on the stacking chair in the middle of the floor and dropped her shoulderbag on to the worn carpet. Uel stood by the locked door, chewing at his lip.

'I hope you know what you're doing,' he accused her.

'Oh, for God's sake, Uel,' she snapped.

He opened his mouth as if to reply, then thought better of it and turned away. I pulled a low stack of beer crates out from the rest and settled myself on to it. The girl was fishing in her pockets for something.

'Do you smoke?' she asked, and after a moment I realised that she was addressing me.

'Oh. No. Thanks.'

'Wise man.'

She lit up and blew a long, satisfied stream of smoke towards the ceiling. It was a smooth and competent action; everything she did seemed like that.

'So where do you fit into all of this, then?' she asked. 'Is it true about this murder thing?'

'What do you think?'

'You don't strike me as a murderer.'

Uel laughed shortly. 'Not that she's ever met any, you understand.'

She ignored him and waited for me to answer.

'Well, you've met two tonight,' I told her. 'First Mills, and now me.'

'So you did kill someone.'

'I did.'

There was a little tremor in her voice as she spoke and her eyes were a little wider than normal. She was

110

locked in a room with a man who admitted killing another person, and suddenly the world had come a little closer than the end of her microphone.

'But I thought they were framing you?'

'They're accusing me of murdering him. I killed him in self-defence. There's a difference.'

'I see.'

'They're trying to put it down to a personal feud. I never met the guy before.'

'How did you kill him?'

'I shot him.'

'You shot him?'

'Do you have to repeat everything I say?'

'Sorry.'

I was trying to think, trying to work out some sort of a plan. For all I knew Mills had already phoned the police and they might be already on their way to pick me up which would be the whole thing finished. Even if he hadn't, the car Simpson had organised for me was parked a few streets away and my rucksack was in it; once they found that it was just a question of cordoning off the area and going through it house by house and this was probably the first place they'd look. And then there was Mills, who I had annoyed; he could always turn nasty and none of us would get out alive. It had happened before. The situation was very loose and I could do nothing about it and it worried me.

'So how does the girl come into it?'

'What?'

'How does the girl figure in this. Why do you want to find her so badly?'

'Because she's the only witness. They were shooting at her. That was why I shot that fellow.'

'I see. So how come you had a gun?'

'How come you ask so many questions?'

'It's my job. I'm a reporter.'

'Is that an explanation or an excuse?'

She was beginning to irritate me. I didn't want these two people with me. Things were bad enough as they were, without these two idiots getting involved.

'You haven't answered my question.'

'I'm licensed to carry a weapon. For personal protection.'

'Why?'

'I'm in the UDR.'

'You're kidding!'

'All right, I'm kidding!'

She exchanged a glance with Uel who was standing by the door, listening.

'Must be true, then,' she remarked.

'Maybe this might be worth two thousand quid after all,' Uel replied.

Now it was my turn to ask questions. 'What's true?'

She turned back to me, drawing heavily on the cigarette and blowing the smoke down her nostrils.

'We got a tip-off recently,' she began. 'Information to the effect that this girl knew something which would severely embarrass the Government. To the point of bringing it down. Not just possibly, but definitely. The source in question has never let us down before, but this one seemed a little ... what, far-fetched? However, now that we've run across you ... I mean, if they're going so far as to frame an army officer–I take it you are an officer?–then there must be some substance in it.'

'So what is the information? What does she know?'

'You tell me. Whatever it is, it's serious. Hence all the effort to put you out of the picture.'

I remembered her face in the grey morning light, the hair plastered to her forehead, the way she had fought her way from the car. The frightened eyes. Poor bitch, I thought. I hope it was all worth it.

'If there is something,' I said, 'The Government would never allow you to publish it — or broadcast it — in this country. They'd slap a "D" notice on to it.'

'That's right. No one would run it in the UK or Ireland. But the French would. Or the Germans.'

'Or the Yanks,' put in Uel.

I suddenly felt like a blind man, paddling in the deep end. This was too much to take in. Governments, international scandals. I had to concentrate on my own predicament, on clearing my name. I didn't particularly give a damn if the Government stood or fell, so long as I could go back to my own little world and leave this dark half-life behind me. But if this was all true, then my prospects were bleaker than ever. The whole security apparatus would be turned against me; MI5, MI6, SIS, SAS, RUC, Army, UDR, every man and his dog would be dug out and sent against me. Dear God. Suddenly the room seemed very small and quiet.

'What do you think of Mills?' the girl asked thoughtfully.

'He's a psychopath.'

'You think so?'

'I know it. He's got three murders to his credit already. That we know of.'

'God. Do you think he can really help?'

'I don't know. He's the only chance I have.'

'If he does help, can you find the girl?'

'If I toss a coin, will it land on its edge?'

'What?'

'Look, I'll be honest with you. The chances are that I'll be picked up again within the next twenty-four hours. At the most. If I can stay free longer, then I will but I reckon that's all I can reasonably expect, and if I haven't found the girl by then I'm screwed. I don't know what this MI5 business of Mills' is, but frankly I wouldn't place too much hope in it. He's probably been watching too much James Bond. I wouldn't imagine the security services would be so poor as to let the UVF get a handle on them. So in short, I'm not hopeful. But I can't think of any other way. This is the only straw I have, and I'm going to clutch at it.'

Her face was calm and thoughtful. It was odd that she could be so cool in a situation like this but then she probably didn't realise what sort of atrocities Mills was capable of. She looked well-cared-for, expensive, delicate, arched eyebrows and well-tanned skin.

'I see,' she said.

'I hope you're not wasting your two thousand.'

'In this line of work most things are a gamble.' She sniffed. 'Anyway, Mills seems to have a lot of confidence in you.'

'I wouldn't give much for his judgement.'

'What rank are you?'

'Captain. Part-time.'

She gave a low whistle. 'Must be serious if they're trying to frame a captain.'

'I imagine they've done worse,' I said wearily. I was thinking about Phil Simpson and the risk he had taken for me, about the girl and the risk she had taken, about the blood on the seat of my car. What did she know, what was it she had that was so important, so devastating? All the sadness at the death of the man, Ledbury, the man I had killed, was gone, and in its place was a slow, dull anger at what they were doing to me.

We sat in silence for a long while, listening to muffled voices in other rooms. Uel fidgeted a lot. Clare was definitely the dominant partner. She sat smoking and thinking, her forehead slightly furrowed, her legs crossed and one foot tapping gently in the air. She was wearing very soft leather boots, expensively made and very good quality and when she moved her toes the leather creased delicately.

'How long have you been a reporter?' I asked, not that I wanted to know but it was easier than listening to the silence.

'Seven, eight years.'

'You must have seen a bit of the world.'

'Mainly the bad bits.'

'Such as?'

'South-east Asia, Africa. Central America.'

'Sounds exciting.'

'An experience.'

'Whereabouts are you from?'

'Norfolk.'

'Never been there.'

'It's nice.'

Outside a car whooshed past in the street. Someone going home to his family, home to his life, not locked up in a stinking room in a stinking club with no friends and no hope.

'What about you,' she was asking, 'where do you come from?'

'Armagh, originally.'

'Country boy?'

'I lived in Belfast most of my life. Moved out to Lurgan about a year ago.'

'You like living here? Northern Ireland, I mean?'

'I don't think I could live anywhere else. I love this rotten little country.'

'I don't know how anybody lives here,' she said.

I smiled. 'Like you said, you only get to see the bad bits.'

They came for us about an hour later and led us back to the main room. The old man had gone. Billy was still seated behind the table and only one of the heavies stayed in the room with us. Mills was leaning against the back wall. He seemed in cheerful form. As we came in he gestured at the three empty chairs in the middle of the floor.

'Sit down,' he ordered. We filed in and took up the same seats as before.

'Right,' he began, folding his brawny arms across

the top of his protruding gut. 'We've discussed the whole thing and I've spoken to my superiors and they've given us the go-ahead. So now all we have to do is sort out the nitty-gritty.'

'Which is?' I enquired.

'The money.'

I looked at the girl and she reached into her handbag, extracting a plain white envelope which she handed to me.

'Give this to him, will you?'

He handled it carefully, as if afraid it would detonate in his grasp. I half-wished it would.

'What's this?' he asked.

'It's a bank draft for one thousand pounds, made out to your name,' Clare replied.

He leered at her, showing some of his teeth.

'You were pretty sure of yourself, weren't you?'

Clare smiled back and said nothing. I was beginning to feel uneasy. I didn't like the thought of Mills reporting back to someone, because the thing was big enough already and the more people who knew where I was, the more likely it was that someone would talk. You can't keep secrets in Belfast, not for long, and I needed more time. And if someone was pulling Mills' strings then there were other layers and other angles which I didn't know about and I didn't like that. I was beginning to feel like a fly twitching in the middle of a massive spider's web.

Mills walked around us and lifted a sheet of A4 paper from the table.

'This is the address of the MI5 safe-house in

Belfast,' he said, holding it out to me. I took it from him, squinting in the poor light. Malone Avenue, the heart of middle-class respectable Belfast.

'Are you sure?' I asked him.

'Course I'm fucking sure, you think I'm stupid or something?'

'How did you get it?'

'Contacts,' he said, tapping a thick finger along the side of his nose. 'I've got good contacts. I know everything that goes on in this town.'

'You expect me to act on that?'

'Take it or leave it. It's nothing to me.'

I didn't have a lot of choice. I passed the paper to Clare.

'Is this all?' she asked impatiently. She was a girl used to getting her own way but she didn't know people like Mills and I wished she would shut up.

'What more do you want?' Mills demanded, his voice raised slightly. 'Took us months to get that, and now we're giving it away to you. Do you know how much the Provisionals would pay for that? You're getting a fucking bargain, lady!'

'A thousand pounds for an address!' Clare retorted.

'It's enough,' I said quickly. 'It's a start and that's all we need.'

She flashed her eyes at me and looked about to say something but she seemed to think better of it and sat back in the chair. I looked at Uel and he was gripping the sides of his chair and his knuckles were white and bloodless, his eyes staring straight ahead at the wall.

118

I turned back to Mills. 'You said you could give me two men.'

'You'll have them.'

'How long for?'

'Remains to be seen.'

Helpful bastard, I thought. 'All right. What about guns?'

'Guns?'

'Can you get us guns? Anything at all?'

Mills threw his head back and laughed, a deep, braying, brutal laugh.

'You're good crack, Garrett, I'll say that for you. You're certainly good crack. Guns indeed.'

'What do you want guns for?' Clare asked. There was a flicker of something behind her eyes, concern, perhaps.

'In case I need to kill someone else,' I said, enjoying the look on her face.

'There's no way I'd give you a gun, Kearns, don't you worry about that. They're hard enough to come by these days. And anyway, I don't reckon you'll be coming back!'

He perched himself on the edge of the table and sniggered crudely and I saw the way his gut wobbled and the oil stains on the knees of his trousers and for a second I was tempted to draw my gun and kill him where he sat, blow his foul head off and to hell with the consequences. I forced down the anger. At last the smile fell from his face.

'There's two boys downstairs waiting for you,' he said. 'They've got their car outside. That's all you're getting.'

'Nothing else?' I asked. I thought he might at least have wished us luck.

'Nah,' he said.

The sun had come out at last and the bright, hard light sliced across the cold morning. A dull winter breeze blew dead leaves around the pavements. On each side of the road the big, red-brick, Victorian houses stared down through the tracery of bare, grey trees to the damp gardens, the unkempt lawns and the thick hedges. Ahead of us an old woman laboured up the footpath dragging her tartan shopping trolley behind, feeling her way with a stout wooden stick.

'Are you sure you want to come in with me?' I asked her again.

'I'm sure, for Christ's sake!'

'All right, as long as you're sure.'

Uel drummed his fingers on the rim of the steering wheel. He was the weak link and I didn't trust him at all but if the girl insisted on coming in with me then there was nothing else I could do.

'You're sure you know what you have to do, Uel?'

'Drive to the pick-up point,' he recited, 'wait there until you two arrive. If you're not there by six o'clock this evening, I go back to the hotel.'

'Yeah. Might be better if you waited a few hours before arriving at the pick-up point. Just in case you're noticed hanging around. Make it four this afternoon; I can't see us being out before then, anyway.'

'What will I do in the meantime?'

'What?'

'Between now and four o'clock? What should I do?'

'I don't know, for God's sake. Buy a book, or something.'

If he was at the right place when they needed him; if he was on time; if he didn't crash the car; if the army didn't pick him up. Too many ifs and I hated having to depend on imponderables but I couldn't think of any other way.

The car was full of tiny creaks and groans as we shifted in our seats, every sound magnified by the silence. Uel fidgeted a lot. Clare mostly sat quietly, gazing out from the back seat. I was tired, heavy in the head, my eyes numb and gritty. I had snatched a few hours' sleep in the sleeping bag Mills had provided, dozing rather than sleeping, and now the pace and the tension were beginning to catch up on me. I found myself yawning a lot.

'I didn't think you'd agree to using your own car,' I commented, more to keep myself awake than for the sake of conversation.

'It's a hire car,' Clare said from behind. 'Besides, driving a car on the open road isn't an offence over here. You had me worried when you asked Mills for guns, though. That kind of thing I do like to keep away from.'

'Don't blame you,' I replied. Images in my mind, Ledbury's body with the holes in his back, the blood smeared down the wing of their car.

'What happens if I get stopped by the police?' Uel asked.

'If that happens we're all bollocksed because you're so bloody nervous they're sure to pull you in!' I snapped at him. He shivered the way a cat would, and stared out of the side window.

'Just act cool, Uel,' Clare said soothingly. 'You're press; you heard about the bomb scare; you wondered what had happened. Ask a few questions. You'll be all right.'

'Yeah, and remember,' I said roughly, 'there'll be a lot of security activity round here once this thing starts. Two or three judges live up this road, so I'd imagine the police will be very quick. You make sure you're well away by the time anything happens. All right?'

I didn't trust Uel. There was something about him that was hidden, divided. I reckoned he was a homosexual, but there was something else he was keeping back and it worried me. I had cobbled a plan together which might or might not work but no matter how it went I was relying on him, and if he screwed up then I was finished.

The old woman disappeared over the brow of the hill. Across the avenue a young girl was coming towards us, struggling with a lively retriever. I had known a girl from round here once, I remembered, Malone Park, or was it Malone Avenue? Too long ago. All these quiet, tree-lined avenues looked the same to me, anyhow. Her father had been a doctor, I remembered that. She used to ride her pony every weekend. She had always been on at her father to buy a horsebox so she could compete in the show-jumping. A different world. I thought of Mills and his dark labyrinth of streets and alleys only five minutes' drive away, and Smith and his cronies manipulating and deceiving in their treacherous little schemes. I wondered where Smith was now. Maybe in this very house. If I ever got my hands on him he would suffer, by Christ he would. I had promised myself that.

A car appeared over the brow of the hill, moving slowly down towards us. For a moment I thought it was the police and my heart caught.

'Is that them?' Clare asked.

'I don't know.'

The two young men Mills had produced had not impressed me with their intelligence or common sense but they were all I had and I imagined they could steal a car without much difficulty. The older of the two had seemed reasonably sound and I had put him in charge, hoping he wouldn't balls the whole thing up.

It was a Vauxhall Cavalier and moving slowly, too slowly for normal traffic. Dark steel grey, the pale sky reflecting on the windscreen making it impossible to see inside. It was fifty metres from us when the headlights flashed three times.

'That's the signal,' Uel said, urgently.

'That's it,' I agreed. 'Give him one flash in return.'

The Cavalier slowed gradually and came to a halt almost level with us. A tall, thin figure jumped out and sauntered over to our car, hands in pockets and his shoulders swaying jauntily. The elder one, what was his name, John? George? Joss, that was it. Joss. He leaned down to the driver's side window, one arm on the roof, grinning insolently.

'Everything all right?' I asked.

'No problem,' he replied confidently. Typical Belfast man.

'Where's your mate?'

'Over the hill. He's waiting for me, once I dump this thing.' He nodded over at the Cavalier. 'Not a bad motor, that. Pity to waste it.'

'Vauxhall man, are you?'

'Wouldn't steal anything else.'

'Right. It's ten-fifteen now. Give us ten minutes, say, twenty-five past. Then do your stuff.'

He looked down at me and sniffed. 'No problem.'

'There better not be.'

'I wish you'd relax, mister.' He pulled a hand from his pocket and wiped it under his nose. 'Where will we meet you?'

'What do you mean?'

'After the job. Where do we meet you?'

'You don't.'

'Joey said – '

'Joey's not in charge here. I am. Once you finish here you go back to the club. I'll phone you there. All right?'

A flash of anger in his eyes because he wasn't used to people talking to him like that but he controlled it and after a moment or two shrugged his shoulders nonchalantly.

'Nothing to me,' he said. 'But Joey won't like it.'

'Like I said, Joey's not here.'

Another shrug, then he spat carefully on to the tarmac.

'You're the boss.'

He walked back to the other car, his walk a little stiffer now, nearer to the job.

'Scum,' I muttered. A nasty wee back-street gouger with a chip on his shoulder and nothing to do all day but drink and fight and steal.

'He's on your side,' Clare observed.

'So he's on my side. He's still scum.'

'You're a real humanitarian.'

'I'm just a realist. Let's go, Uel.'

I had already decided which house to use for the access to the safe-house; it was in the next avenue, backing on to the MI5 place, a big old pile of a house with untidy lawns and overgrown flowerbeds. There were plenty of shrubs and bushes in the back garden for cover and it didn't appear well-used; there had been no activity in or around it all morning. Uel pulled up outside it and we got out and walked in through the gate, trying to look casual, keeping an eye on the big bay windows with the half-drawn blinds, watching for movement: if we were seen at this stage then the whole thing was ruined. Down the side of the house as if heading for the back door, trying to look as though we owned the place, into the back garden and a strong sense of trespass, then quickly under the big, evergreen bushes which lined the lawn. The broad leaves spilled rainwater on to our backs and the air was thick with the damp, clinging smell of earth. We picked our way carefully between the bushes and the hedge, right down to the bottom of the garden, pausing now and again to watch the rear windows of the house for movement, checking round the edges of the lawn. The garden

125

had once been elegant and cared-for but now the borders were sprouting with weeds and a small ornamental pond was almost choked with dead leaves. An abandoned child's tricycle lay rusting in the overgrown lawn.

There were gaps in the hedge at the bottom of the garden and through them I could see the rear of the safe-house. It looked normal; red-brick walls, old-fashioned sash windows, curtains drawn in an upstairs room, two overflowing bins outside the back door. There were two cars parked at the side of the house, out of sight of the main avenue.

'You see the back door?' I whispered, putting my mouth almost against her ear.

'Yes.'

'That's how we go in, all right?'

'Yes.'

'When I give the word, OK?'

'OK.'

With her head so close to mine I could smell the strong, feminine scent of her, a mixture of shampoo and perfume and delicate sweat. It was the first time I had really noticed her as a woman, and an attractive woman, too, and it was an effort to empty my mind of her. The job in hand, the job in hand. Concentrate.

I picked the biggest gap and gently began to pull branches and twigs away from it, hooking them into other parts of the hedge, moving infinitely slowly in case someone was watching from the house. The garden beyond was neat and well-kept and normal, and I wondered if Mills was setting us up for something. I had always imagined safe-houses to be small, grubby, out-of-the-way places, not easily noticed, where mysterious comings and goings would not be out of place. Unremarkable and hidden. This was about as far away from the conventional image as you could get, but then, that was probably why they chose it. These people were probably very good and it would be wise to bear that in mind.

The lawn was long and flat, water lying in puddles here and there; beyond the lawn a paved terrace and beyond that the house itself. Quiet, middle-class, suburban domesticity. I hoped Mills was right about the place.

Five minutes. Seven. My legs began to ache, crouching under the damp leaves. The bastard is two minutes late, I was thinking, when I heard the screech of tyres as he braked on the corner of the avenue then accelerated up towards the house.

'Here he comes,' I whispered.

The engine was roaring, screaming away in second gear, the sound rising in volume as he approached the house, ripping through the suburban calm. I noticed a flicker of movement at one of the top windows of the house. Suddenly, the engine note changed, deeper and louder for a few seconds and then there was the massive crunch of the car against the gatepost and the sound of a door slamming and more revs as the pick-up happened, then the sound of the second car gradually disappearing. Well done, lads, I thought, well done. That should wake them up.

The back door opened. I felt the girl tense. A man emerged, dressed in jeans and a blue, zipped jacket, and walked nervously around to the side of the house, pausing to peep round every corner of the building. I noticed that he kept his right hand at his waist. I held my breath: the plan depended on their being spooked by something totally outside their experience, something they couldn't deal with. I had assumed they were watchers rather than doers, surveillance experts rather than action men. It looked as though I was right.

Ten-thirty. By now the message would have been phoned through to the *Belfast Telegraph*. I had told them to use the word 'Boatman' as a codeword. It didn't mean anything but the Intelligence people would spend a couple of hours cross-referencing it and it might keep them off our track for a bit. Allow five minutes for transmission to the police, another five, maybe ten for the nearest unit to arrive. Although as soon as the word got through to Army Headquarters they would probably contact this crowd direct.

Blue-jacket came round to the back door again, trotting this time. He was big and heavy and looked out of shape. He disappeared inside. I felt Clare brushing against me as we watched through the hedge, her face tense and excited, and again I noticed her scent through the damp smell of the undergrowth. The job, I told myself, mind on the job.

Someone was shouting inside the house, muffled yells drifting through the open door, then blue-jacket appeared again, coming out of the house and pausing briefly to shove a magazine into a pistol. Clare drew her breath sharply. I heard the familiar scrape-clunk as he snapped the slide back to put a round into the chamber but his actions were strangely clumsy, he was holding the thing awkwardly and I could see he wasn't used to it.

More shouting from inside. Someone was panicking, I thought, which was all to the good because time was moving on and the cops would arrive soon and we had to be inside by then. I hoped blue-jacket had taken the trouble to look into the back seat of the car because I had gone to some trouble over the bomb and it certainly looked the part; only an empty beerkeg from Mills' club and a lunchbox with a few wires and a lot of black tape but it would work on these men. They weren't prepared for bombs, it wasn't their scene.

A second man rushed out of the back door, knocking into one of the bins in his haste, hurriedly tucking his shirt into his waistband, and behind him appeared a third, tall and bearded and tatty-looking. Blue-jacket waved them past and they started off around the house until he shouted at them, 'Not that way, that's where the bloody bomb is!' London accent, I noticed. The two men changed direction and started to run across the lawn and my heart jerked in my chest as I thought they were coming straight towards us. I put my hand down towards my gun but they were heading for the next-door garden; it must have been some kind of prearranged escape route, for they passed within fifteen feet of us and saw nothing. I held my breath until they were safely through the hedge and and I could hear them blundering up the garden towards the house. Thank

Christ I picked this house, I thought, and not the one next door.

Blue-jacket followed them across the lawn, walking quickly but all the time scanning the area as if suspicious; he seemed cool as he passed us but his hands were tight around the big butt of the Browning pistol and I could see that his knuckles were white. A bomb is a frightening thing because it doesn't pick and choose and you can't reason with it and your first one is always the worst. He followed his colleagues into the next garden and it wasn't until the sound of his footsteps faded into silence that I let out my breath in a long, thankful sigh.

'Now?' Clare asked.

'Yeah, let's go.'

I wiped my palms on my jeans. My armpits were damp and sticky. My bladder was bursting. Jesus, what a way to live.

'Follow me and keep low in case they're still watching from somewhere. We'll go around by the hedges then across to the patio from that yellow bush there. Got that?'

A quick nod. She was nervous, too.

'OK, then. Let's go.'

I ran carefully across the garden feeling acutely visible and vulnerable. At any second I expected to hear the rip of automatic fire or the crack of a pistol because I didn't really expect them to leave the house unguarded. My heart pounded in my throat. It seemed to take hours but all of a sudden I was inside the house with my back hard against the kitchen wall and the girl slamming in against me.

130

'All right, we're in.'

I reached behind my back and drew the revolver from my waistband. Clare's eyes widened when she saw it.

'Where did you get that?'

'Shut up. Stay here.'

'All right. No need to snap.'

I checked every room and opened every wardrobe and cupboard and the place was empty, thank God. The bedrooms smelt of feet and stale sweat. One of the beds was still warm, the sheets pulled and wrinkled. The downstairs dining room had been turned into an office-cum-operations room, with a desk and some filing cabinets and a large-scale street plan across one wall. A cork pin-board was covered with mug shots and collages of wanted terrorists. Back in the kitchen the girl was standing nervously by the door, her hands thrust deep into her pockets.

'Anything?' she asked.

'They've all gone,' I told her. 'I didn't really think it would work.'

'I feel like a burglar.'

'Better than a murderer.'

'Mm,' she replied.

She took the upstairs and I took the downstairs and we went through the house carefully and methodically. I didn't have any real idea of what I was looking for but I hoped there would be something to give us a lead, to give us a direction. Something, anything to hang on to.

The office seemed the best bet and I started there, pulling out the bottom drawer of the filing cabinet. I went through the files carefully, pulling them out one by one and flicking through the contents before replacing them in the correct order. I didn't want to leave any obvious sign that we'd been there. All the time I was working out the timings in my head, guessing and estimating, hoping. We would have around four hours, at most, before the army discovered the bomb was a hoax; two hours at the very least and that should be ample time to search a house.

The police arrived a few moments after I started, the sirens wailing at the far end of the avenue. The girl clattered down the stairs.

'What's that?' she called out.

'What does it sound like?'

'The police!'

'Correct answer. They'll have to evacuate the area.'

'Oh.' She stood uncertainly in the doorway. 'What if they come here?'

'They won't come here. The bomb is here, remember?'

'Won't they want to check that it is a bomb?'

I shook my head, my attention on the files in the drawers. 'Not their job. Anyway, they'll take the word of the Intelligence crowd. I hope.'

She stood on and I looked up at her.

'There's nothing to worry about. Go back upstairs and carry on searching. And stay away from the windows, all right?' I thought about smiling to reassure her but I just didn't have it in me.

'What'll happen if they catch us here?' she asked.

'Oh, you'll more than likely get away with a suspended sentence. First offence and all that.'

'What about you?'

'Life, probably. If they don't kill me first.'

I didn't like the direction the conversation was going and I was glad when she turned on her heel without a word and hurried back up the stairs. I was constantly aware of the situation I was in, it was always at the back of my mind, the sure and certain knowledge that once I was caught my life would be finished, one way or another. It was hanging around my neck like a millstone. I just didn't like to think about it too often.

After an hour or so we took a breather and sat in the hallway on the floor with our backs to the wall, facing each other. Neither of us had found anything of value. The files in the office were just personal dossiers on most of the local players, probably used for briefings and so forth, and most of it pretty mundane information about their homes and their cars and what pets they kept. None of it was of any use to me. Upstairs Clare had found a pair of good-quality binoculars under one of the beds and I told her to keep them as a souvenir. Now we sat on the cold parquet floor and looked at each other. There didn't seem to be a great deal to say.

'Do you really think we'll find anything?' she asked, after a long while.

'I hope we do.'

'But you're not optimistic.'

'We'll give it our best shot. Let's hope we're lucky.'

'It would help if we knew what to look for.'

'You'll know it when you find it.'

She was looking hard at me, her head slightly to one side, her expression quizzical.

'You're very calm for a man on the run,' she said.

'It's all a front. I'm shitting myself, really.'

She smiled at that but I wasn't kidding.

'You must have been a good officer.'

'I am a good officer,' I reminded her. 'They haven't fired me yet, and I don't intend to resign. But thanks for the compliment.'

'No, I mean it. That was a good plan you came up with. And you're pretty cool under stress.'

'You're not so bad yourself.'

'I've been frightened before.'

'There's no fear like Irish fear.'

She smiled thinly. 'South American fear would beat it hands down,' she said, running her fingers through her hair. 'So would Cambodian fear. So would Angolan fear. There are worse places than Ireland, believe me.'

At that moment they did the controlled bang on the car and one of the windows came in and Clare screamed as she threw herself on to the floor. I grabbed her as quickly as I could and slapped my hand over her mouth, praying that no one had heard her.

'You stupid bitch, keep quiet, would you!' I hissed at her. Her eyes were full of tears and she was trying to nod so I slowly took my hand away. The hall seemed very quiet. There was broken glass on the floor. I was lying almost on top of her.

'I'm sorry,' she said quietly. 'It was so sudden ... '

'It's all right.'

She was shaking. Her face was pale. A tear had streaked out of her eye and down her cheek and I wiped it gently away and suddenly I was aware of her again, as a woman, soft and feminine and just for a few seconds wanting only to be hugged. She felt small in my arms and the soft smell of her hair and the perfume from her sweater filled my head and just for a moment something jumped between us, linking, joining, half-understood. Her shell had dropped and she was alone and frightened and she clung to my chest with a strength that surprised me. I wondered what it was that frightened her so much.

We lay like that for perhaps thirty seconds and then she began to return to the shell, slowly pulling away from me, pushing against me with small, hesitant thrusts. I rolled off to one side and let her raise herself to her feet, brushing imaginary dust from her thighs.

'I wasn't expecting it,' she announced shakily in her hard, business voice. I watched as she hoisted on the persona again, the career girl, the woman on the move, a century away from the frightened child I had come so close to.

'It's OK.'

'It was the shock.' She stared down at me, all challenge and aggression, one hand on her hip, and I realised that I had seen through a door she preferred not to open.

'Yes,' I agreed. 'The shock.'

'Was that ... was that the bomb exploding, do you think?'

I looked at her for a second. 'It's not a real bomb, Clare.'

Blushing. Embarrassed. She looked away. 'Of course not. I forgot.'

Shortly after the first explosion I found the gun, slipped under the seat cushion on one of the cheap settees. Smith and Wesson nine millimetre with a large capacity magazine, a real handful and very welcome. I rubbed my hands together like a child with a new toy before slipping out the magazine and clearing the pistol. Twelve rounds, clicking together in my palm, bright and shiny and new. Twelve more chances. Terrific.

I reloaded the gun and shoved it into my waistband. I had to trust Clare and Uel to an extent but until this thing was settled I was on my own and I was damn sure they wouldn't go down to save me. The oldest military principle, always have a reserve. This would be my reserve.

All credit to her, it was Clare who found it, upstairs, in the pocket of a jacket hanging in a wardrobe. A notebook, small size, with a plastic cover and a pencil thrust through the spine and all the used pages torn out except for one, the one we'd been looking for. She brought it down to me.

'What about this?' she asked hopefully.

'Let's have a look.'

Someone had taken notes at a briefing of some kind; there were various rough headings and titles scribbled in pencil, some underlined. One was underlined more heavily than the rest. 'Sharpe, Now at scrapyard. PZ i/c, move in three days.'

I felt a quick surge of excitement because that was obviously the girl and at least we had found a beginning.

'Well, that's the girl all right,' I said. 'I wonder what "scrapyard" is.'

'Code?'

'Obviously, but how do we break it?'

There were doodles across the top and bottom of the page, triangles intersecting and a darker, furred mess which might have been a word. I stared at it for a second until suddenly I saw the letters and the word leaped out at me.

'Drumkeary! Look, this doodle. He wrote Drumkeary, then doodled all over it. Must have been bored out of his skull.'

'So?'

'What if there is a scrapyard at Drumkeary?'

'You mean a real scrapyard?'

'Yes. Why should they use codenames at an internal briefing? Anyway, a scrapyard would be bloody good cover for a covert headquarters. Strange-looking people coming and going at all hours of the day and night. Disreputable men hanging around. Piles of scrap arranged to prevent surveillance.'

'You're clutching at straws,' she said.

'Well that's all I have to work with at the moment.'

'Still. You could be right.' She brushed her fingers through her hair. She looked tired. 'I'll go back up then and carry on, shall I?'

'Yes. I'll finish off down here.'

She clattered up the stairs again and I went back into the kitchen and began to rummage through the cupboards, trying to concentrate on the search but with my mind always wandering back to the girl. I wondered how she could take all this so calmly, being on the wrong side of the law, on the run, associating with a fugitive. She was pleasant and calm and helpful but there was something about her that was always held back and hidden and it made me wary. Sometimes, when I accidentally caught her eye, there was a hardness, a cruelty about her that was almost unnerving. I supposed it was her job. That sort of job would harden you, over the years; too many war-zones, too many bodies, only natural that some of it would rub off.

I started sliding open the kitchen drawers and search- ing through the contents, only half-aware of what I was doing. I kept thinking about Clare. It was Clare now, I noticed, and not 'The Girl'. She had clung to me. Held tightly on to me. Frightened.

The kitchen smelt of unwashed dishes. There were three empty milk bottles by the sink. It was devoid of the usual feminine trappings of a kitchen: no bright tea-towels, no pleasant little notice boards, no pretty cups and saucers or colourful containers, nothing but cheap, functional kitchen equipment and a couple of plain white dish-cloths.

She was too much in my mind and I told myself to ignore her, forget about it. Save yourself first, and there would be time for the rest later. She was nothing, she didn't care about me, all she wanted was her story, the end product, and everything else was of no importance. It suddenly struck me that no matter how this thing ended, Clare would still have her story to sell. Clever girl, I thought. Clever, clever girl.

Half an hour later the army did the second controlled explosion, smaller this time and no damage to the house although the windows all rattled in their frames. Clare came down the stairs and leaned against the kitchen door.

'Shouldn't we be going soon?' she asked.

I shook my head.

'Once they're satisfied with the car they'll search the surrounding area for booby-traps and come-ons. If we leave now they'll pick us up during the sweep.'

'If we stay here they're sure to find us.'

'They won't be back today. By the time the ATO is finished it'll be getting on for three or half-three. That only leaves about an hour of daylight, and I can't see them coming in here in the dark. They'll be suspicious, they'll want to check everything for themselves before they move back. And they won't want the army in here before them, I can guarantee that. So I think they'll wait until tomorrow morning, by which time you and I will be long gone. I hope.'

'You've got it all worked out, haven't you?'

'I hope so,' I replied, closing the last cupboard door. 'Well, that's it. I don't think we'll find anything else.'

'All we have to do is find this place Drumkeary.'

'Drumkeary. Was that a cellnet phone in your car?'

'Yes, but–'

'We could ring Uel and tell him to find out where it is before he picks us up.'

She smiled and shook her head. 'Wouldn't work. Uel would panic. We'd probably never see him again. He's very good at doing one thing at a time, but you must be careful never to confuse him.'

'He's a dickhead, that's what you're saying.'

'He's good at his job. Maybe the best in the business. He knows his stuff backwards. He's just not the action man type, that's all.'

'Yeah,' I replied. 'I had sort of gathered that.'

'Oh, he's all right once you get to know him. Once you know his limitations. Besides, they'll have a tap on this phone, won't they?'

And of course that was when it struck me that the only thing I hadn't checked was the phone and that all the security people I'd ever met recorded their phone-calls as a matter of course, so I raced back into the office and flicked the button on the answerphone to rewind. Clare watched me from the doorway.

'Surely they wouldn't use an answerphone?' she asked. 'Wouldn't they have this place manned around the clock, or something?'

'This isn't an answerphone. It's a special recorder, tapes both sides of a conversation. Scrambles it as well, I think. I've seen them at Army Headquarters.'

The tape clicked back to the start and I stabbed at the play button. Through the smoked-plastic window I could see the two tape rollers begin to revolve. The machine beeped twice.

'But–' Clare began.

'Quiet!'

The phone rang twice and a hoarse voice said 'Yes?' and then there was a thin educated English voice and the sound of it twisted something in my stomach. Smith. The bastard.

'Kearns is out,' he said. The whining tone of his voice was flat and a little distorted by the hiss from the machine but I recognised him instantly.

'How did that happen?'

'Inside job. About four hours ago.'

'Got anyone for it?'

'Not yet.' Thank God, I thought. 'I want you to concentrate on Kearns now. Drop everything else. He gets priority.'

'What about the Maguire thing?'

'Drop it. It can wait.'

'We're very close–'

'I said drop it. This is more important. Kearns is more important. We can pick up on the other business any time. Besides, it shouldn't take long to pick him up.'

Silence for a moment. The tape hissed.

'You're the boss. Any news of our new man?'

'Yes, he's arrived. I've sent him to Drumkeary for the time being. They're a bit short-handed down there.'

'We're a bit short-handed down here, too.'

'You'll manage. Conference tomorrow, two o'clock. I'll pick you up, all right?'

'All right. Look, this business about Kearns. Do you want him picked up, or–'

'Pick him up if you can. But I wouldn't make it an imperative.'

'But you don't want him disposed of?'

A long pause.

'Look, I'll leave it to you. If you can do it cleanly, then do it. But make sure he isn't found.'

'Fair enough. Just so long as I know the score, that's all.'

'Just make damn sure everything is clean, all right? No more screw-ups. See you tomorrow, all right?'

'All right.'

Click-click-buzz. The tape hissed on. I sat for a full minute on the edge of the desk, stomach churning and my head empty, frightened because I had just heard my own death warrant being signed and it was a chilling feeling.

'My God,' Clare breathed.

'That was Smith.'

'You know him?'

'He interviewed me. I reckon he's behind this whole business.'

'MI5?'

'God knows.'

'What did he mean, dispose of you? Did he mean kill you?'

'Probably.'

'Dear God,' she said again. She was staring at me, her expression suddenly quizzical. 'Aren't you scared?' she asked.

'Scared?' I replied. 'You'll never know how much.'

We sat in the front room for a long time, on the floor, watching as the grey light began to fade with the evening. I was angry and I was afraid. All I could think of was Smith and his whining little voice. I think I was making him into a symbol, turning him into some kind of receptacle for my rage. He was a person. You can hate a person. You can't hate a system. The girl sat quietly against the wall, saying little.

'What actually happened to you?' she asked after a moment. 'I mean, when you shot that chap.'

'Well, I happened on a kidnap. They were kidnapping this girl, Alison Sharpe, and she tried to get away, and they fired at her, and I then fired at them. They missed, and I didn't, and there you have it.'

'What happened to the girl?'

'She stole my car, the wee bitch. There's gratitude for you.'

'Did she give you anything?'

'What like?'

'I don't know ... anything at all?'

'Why?'

'Just curious.'

She retreated into her shell again for a while and I looked at her and wondered. There was something about her which said, watch out, be careful. The sort of girl you could find attractive, very attractive, but the sort you could never trust.

'How did you find out about the girl, anyway?' I asked.

'Contacts. Every good journalist has contacts.'

'So what is it she has that's so important?'

'That, I don't know. Information, probably. Maybe papers, maybe a tape. I don't know.'

'And you're going through all this business on the strength of that?'

'It's a good source.'

'Need to be,' I said.

She was hiding something and I didn't like it but then it was that sort of a game and I would just have to live with it. In any case, I hadn't mentioned the Smith and Wesson pistol which was digging into the small of my back. I pushed my head back against the wall and waited.

At last we heard the scrape of metal on metal from the direction of the front gate and I thought that it must be the ATO, satisfied at last that the bomb was a hoax, coming out to check the wreckage in person. I was sitting under the bay window and I moved my head slightly to peer out between a chink in the net curtains. I could see the front drive where it swung round to disappear behind the great shrubs at the front of the house. I was just thinking how well-hidden and secluded the house was when the ATO appeared in the drive, dressed in the massive green armoured suit, looking for all the world like a lost spaceman. I shrank down below the level of the windowsill just as he swivelled his head round to look towards the house.

'What's he doing?' Clare hissed at me.

'Just having a wee nosey,' I hissed back.

I waited for the distant crunch of the heavy boots on the gravel before lifting my head to the window again.

'All right,' I said. 'Let's go.'

The air was cold and damp and the evening gloom was already settling round the garden as we sprinted across the lawn towards the safety of our hedge. The shrubs and bushes loomed around in the dim light, dark and menacing. I helped Clare through the hedge and we crouched in the near-darkness beneath the damp foliage.

'Now we wait until they lift the cordon,' I told her.

'How will we know when that happens?'

'Good question.'

In the event it wasn't long before the traffic began to circulate along the avenue and we could see the headlights flickering through the hedges so I led her out on to the road and right towards Malone, walking as casually as I could. I felt naked walking so openly along the footpath, after a day in hiding.

'Link arms,' I said quietly.

'What?'

'Link arms! Do it!'

The polished visor of his cap was shining in the gloom and that was what had given him away. Not that he was trying to hide. He was standing at the junction with Malone Road, thumbs hooked into the straps of his body armour, his dark green and black uniform almost merging with the shadows. He was middle-aged and looked bored and that was bad because the old fellows always trusted their instinct and their instinct was rarely wrong. I had worked with them often enough to know that. Clare jumped slightly when she noticed him and I squeezed her arm, partly to reassure her and partly to try to control her. If she panicked now we were both finished. As we approached he stepped out into the pavement to meet us.

'Hello,' I said. 'Is the bomb scare over?'

'Aye. They've just cleared it. Only a hoax.'

'Bastards, aren't they?'

'They are indeed, Sir.'

This was the point, this was where he would either ask me who I was and where I was going, or step back and let us pass. If he asked any questions I had no story to tell, and the hesitation would be fatal. Think of a name, I thought, at least think of a name. Harvey, Peter Harvey. I forced the name through my mind.

'Where are you headed to, Sir?' he asked.

'Just out for a walk, to see what was happening.'

'I see.'

Sweat was breaking on my forehead and I hoped he wouldn't see the sheen. If they took us now, just

when things were starting to roll ... My stomach was
turning over and over.

'What's the name, Sir?'

'Harvey, Peter Harvey.'

Pause. Make your mind up, damn you.

'Right you are, Sir. Have a nice evening.'

'Yes,' I said. 'Right. Thank you.'

It was raining by the time we arrived at the pick-up point; I had chosen a car-park three miles from the safe-house but it was a long walk in the dark and the thin drizzle soaked us. Uel was agitated, standing by the car, not sure what to do.

'What kept you?' he demanded.

'It took a bit longer than we thought,' I told him.

'I was worried sick!'

'Relax, Uel, ' Clare said. 'It's all right.' She threw herself into the back seat and began to drag off her wet jacket.

'I've been here for nearly four hours! I thought you weren't coming!'

'Well, we're here now, aren't we,' she replied wearily.

'Thank God.' He looked ruefully at me from the driver's seat. 'Anything could have happened to you.'

'Look,' I said, as calmly as I could. 'Either you shut the fuck up, or I'm going to break your leg. Which do you prefer?'

'All right, all right, no need to get all macho with me.'

He turned and stared petulantly out of the windscreen.

'Uel, you ever heard of a place called Drumkeary?' Clare enquired.

He hesitated slightly. 'Of course not,' he said. 'Why?'

'Only asking.'

We left the car-park and slid out on to the main road, heading south out of Belfast, the wipers scraping the drizzle from the windscreen. I had to find Drumkeary, but first I had to find food and shelter, somewhere to rest. I was tired and hungry and the two pistols in my waistband were digging into me and my eyes were dry and sore, my brain wanting to close down for sleep but the animal pushing and poking at it, keeping it going. I hadn't really slept for more than thirty-six hours and the organism was complaining. Of course I could go on, I could push myself and maybe get another twenty-four hours but after that I would be useless and it looked as though this business might go on for a while. Better to get proper, organised rest if possible, keep the animal on its feet and functioning.

'Where are we going to?' Uel asked me.

'I don't know yet. Towards the motorway.'

'You'll have to give me directions.'

'Oh, for Christ's sake!'

'Next on the left, Uel,' Clare said calmly from the back seat.

I flicked on the radio, hoping to catch the news.

Twangy country and western music, Dolly Parton whining about her blues. Honey, you should try my life.

'Do we have to listen to that?' Uel asked, but a quick glance at my face answered his question.

'Have you got a map in the car?' I asked Clare.

'Should have. Just a road map.'

'Might be worth having a look at, for Drumkeary.'

'Good idea. It's in the glove compartment, I think.'

A big, comprehensive road map, plenty of detail, and I folded it to the area of Donegal and London-derry, holding it close to my face to read in the meagre light of the dashboard instruments. Some-thing told me that Drumkeary was in the South, maybe someone had mentioned it in passing or I had read it somewhere; certainly I knew most of the small towns in Northern Ireland by name, and Drumkeary wasn't one of them. And I thought it would make sense to have a safe-house across the border. There would be fewer questions asked, especially in the border counties. Make an allusion to the 'RA', act suspiciously, and as long as you didn't annoy the Gardai no one would bother you.

Clare brushed her damp hair in the back seat, giving occasional directions to Uel who drove in an irritatingly harsh manner, clashing the gears and braking roughly, taking corners too hard. The radio news came on and I turned the volume up; I made the fourth item, after a new investment for West Belfast, a shooting in Fermanagh and the bomb scare in Malone Avenue.

' ... The search is continuing for the part-time UDR

150

man who disappeared from his Lurgan home late last night. The man, who is in his early thirties, was last seen near the RUC station in Lurgan in the early evening. He is believed to be suffering from a rare mental illness and may have lost his memory ... '

'Bastards!' I reached out and snapped the radio off. The sudden quiet was accusing. 'Bloody bastards!' I spat again. Clever of them, though. Very, very clever. Spread a rumour about mental illness and then even if I did find the girl and get some evidence, no one would ever take it seriously. Bastards.

Clare sat quietly in the back. Uel drove on. After a moment he glanced across and caught my eyes and looked quickly back at the road. Suddenly I realised what they were thinking.

'Oh, come off it,' I protested. 'You know it isn't true!'

'I wasn't thinking that,' Clare said.

'You bloody well were.'

'You don't seem mentally ill to me. Honest.'

'Well, thank goodness for that.'

'But it's good thinking on their part. If you ever try to go public they can use it against you. The "big lie".'

There was nothing I could say and I turned and stared out of the side window for a while. I could feel the odds stacking up against me like a massive pile of heavy crates teetering awkwardly and about to fall. I was alone against the world. Suddenly it all seemed too unfair and too much to bear, and at that moment I might have packed the whole thing in, had there been a way. Given myself up, relied on honesty and justice. Taken whatever happened. But the thing had run on too far and there was no easy way out now; either I finished it or it finished me and that was about the size of it.

The window was cool and juddering against my forehead as the familiar nightscape slipped by outside, all the lights, orange and yellow and white, scattered up the dark bulk of the hills, bright clusters of houses and glittering strings for roads. How many times had I driven this same motorway, looking at those same lights, submerged in my routine and hardly noticing their scattered beauty? Now everything had changed, subtly and definitely. The lights were different, the hills were different, the long, rushing barriers along the motorway were different. They seemed somehow altered or renewed, as though I was seeing them for the first time, a stranger in my own land. I had stepped outside the world and couldn't get back in. I felt like crying.

'I hate to bring it up,' Clare said, 'But where are we going?'

'We're going to stay with a friend of mine,' I replied, with more confidence than I felt. 'Uel, take the next exit and find a phone-box.'

I wedged the door of the phone-box open with my foot to let out some of the stench of stale urine. Across the road the wind ruffled the bushes under the yellow streetlight. I dialled the number. Of course he might not be in, or he might not want to help, or he might not even believe my story but he was the only one I could think of who was close enough to trust but not so close as to fall under suspicion and–

'Hello?'

'Desi?'

'Who is this?'

'It's Garrett.'

Long pause.

'Jesus, Garrett, you're in some trouble, mate.'

'I know. Desi, I need your help.'

'What kind of help?'

'Somewhere to stay. One night.'

'You want to stay here?'

'Yes.'

Another pause. The wind cut in through the broken panes of glass. Rain began to spatter into the puddles on the footpath.

'That fellow you shot.'

'Yes. What about him?'

'They say you shot him over some girl.'

I had known he would have to ask me that because he was a blunt and honest, straightforward man, and that was the way he liked to do things; ask the question and judge the answer. I knew that if he believed me he would back me to the hilt. But if he thought I was lying he'd report me himself.

'I never saw him before, Desi, that's the God's honest truth. And he fired at me first.'

Silence. If he didn't want to help I could always head for the border, try to get into the South and find Drumkeary and maybe get some rest because that was most important, rest, sleep, a wee bit of peace for a while–

'When can you get here?'

'Forty minutes.'

'I'll be here.'

'Desi, there's three of us.'

'Three?'

'I don't want to say too much now. A fellow and a girl. I need them.'

The phone went quiet and I thought I heard a chuckle.

'How do you do it, boy? You're always picking up these women.'

'A man needs a hobby.'

'Yeah. All right. I'll see you later on, then.'

'Good man.' Thank you thank you thank you.

Uel and Clare changed places and Clare drove us out on to the motorway again, using the car easily, confident and relaxed.

'So where are we going?' she asked, glancing sideways at me.

'Follow the signs for Armagh. Once we get there I'll give you directions. We're going to stay with a friend of mine.'

'A friend?'

'Yes.'

'Can you trust him?'

'Yes.'

She looked at me again, then shrugged her shoulders.

'You're the boss,' she said.

'You don't believe in trust?'

'I wouldn't like to rely on it.'

'You must live in a very sad world.'

'I never trust anyone. I make a point of it. That's why I'm successful.'

'I have no reason not to trust him,' I said. A bridge drifted up to meet us and flicked overhead and away.

'It's not so important for me,' she went on. 'They won't be able to hang anything on me. You're the one who should be worrying.'

'I'm too tired to worry.'

She flicked on the windscreen wipers but the drizzle was too thin and they began to screech across the glass. She flicked them off again. The night-time whipped past us.

'So what made you join the UDR?' she asked, after a while.

'God knows.' I was tired and my eyes were sore and my head was numb with fatigue and all she wanted were stupid answers to stupid questions.

'No, really, I'd like to know. I've never met anyone from the UDR before.'

'We're no different to anyone else.'

'But it must be a strain, living under that threat all the time.'

'You get used to it. You can get used to anything.'

'This man we're going to see, he's one of your UDR mates, is he?'

'Yes.'

'Are you sure you want to involve him in this?'

Well, fuck you for asking that, I thought.

'I need his help. We need a base. And I can trust him.'

We sat in silence for a while. I closed my eyes and tried to doze but there was too much going on in my brain, and I ended up staring out of the window again. Lorries passed us, big artics in the outside

156

lane, the beams of their headlights sweeping through the inside of our car. Uel was sitting quietly in the back seat. He said nothing but I knew he wasn't sleeping. There was something about him which made me uneasy, nothing in particular, just a general sense of unpleasantness which gnawed away at the subconscious. I wondered how well Clare knew him.

'Where did you two meet?' I asked.

'Paris, five years ago,' she said. 'I had just got back from South Africa and Uel was in between jobs. We got drunk together.' She smiled over her shoulder at him. 'We've been together ever since. We make a great team.'

'You just cover wars, then?'

'Mostly. That's where the money is.'

'And you work for the BBC?'

'Freelance.'

'So what brought you to Belfast?'

'Work. The promise of work.'

'Did you come specially to find this girl?'

She looked across at me.

'No,' she said after a moment. 'Not especially.'

'Tell me,' I asked her. 'If this thing the girl has turns out to be important, how much do you stand to make?'

'You mean money?'

'Yes.'

'Depends what it is she has. From what I've heard, it could be another Watergate. Which might make us a fortune, eventually.'

'You've no idea what sort of information it is?'

'Nope.'

'But you're willing to risk a couple of thousand quid on it?'

'Yep.'

You might be risking more than that, I thought. For a time I tried to imagine what sort of information would be so important as to be worth so much trouble but I was too tired and my mind was muzzy so eventually I just watched the lights go by in a kind of daze. I had enough to worry about for the time being. We were driving through the countryside now, peppered here and there with little clusters of lights, farmhouses and villages. People in their own lives, comfortable around their television sets with their families and their friends. Whole existences whirling round and never glimpsing the world I was moving in now, the world of deception and fear and death.

'What will you do if we don't find the girl?' she asked eventually.

'I'd rather not think about that for the time being, thanks.'

'All right.'

Desi had stoked up the fire in his back room and he took us straight down there, the curtains pulled and the muted sound of the television coming from somewhere deep in the house. The house was big and old and smelt of the country, the musty odour of old boots, the smell of drying waterproofs, the flour fragrance of fresh-baked bread. I introduced Uel and Clare and we sat down in the warm and comfortable armchairs.

'Wife's away at her mother's,' Desi explained.

'Probably better off up there, really.' He sat on the edge of one of the armchairs beside the hearth, toying with the antique bayonet he used as a poker, his attitude friendly yet still reserved and guarded.

'Desi, I'd better explain what this is all about. Then you can decide whether or not you want to get involved.'

He nodded slowly. 'Sounds fair,' he said.

I explained what had happened, leaving nothing out. I explained what we planned to do, and I told him what we needed from him, if he decided to help us.

'Just a place to sleep tonight and some food and you'll not hear from us again until this thing is finished with, one way or the other.'

He nodded slowly as I talked. He had a slow way of moving which came from his country upbringing and which some people confused with stupidity, usually to their cost. Most were later surprised to discover the speed and grasp of his mind.

'What are you going to do when you find this girl?' he asked.

'If I can get her to a police station we should be all right. Failing that, I suppose I'd try to get her out of the country.'

'After she talks to us, that is,' Clare put in.

'Yes. After that.'

Desi sniffed loudly and ran a thick finger backwards and forwards under his nose.

'You've been straight with me, Garrett,' he said, 'So I'll be straight with you. You're in a bad situation, old son. Half the country is looking for you. They're digging out anyone who can walk and talk at the same time to do VCPs and man radios. We had a full-scale brief on you from the Intelligence cell last night, biographical notes, photographs, the lot. They say you're looking for this girl to kill her.'

His voice was slow and casual but the last three words hung in the air and he raised an eyebrow and looked me in the eye. I returned his gaze as steadily as I could, letting him search and find his own answer.

'You don't believe that, though,' I told him, my voice taut.

'No,' he said at last, leaning back and straightening his long legs. 'I don't believe that. You're not a killer, Garrett, not by nature. It wouldn't sit easily with you.'

'It doesn't, Desi.'

'Aye,' he said, sucking in his breath. He looked down into the fire for a moment, then leaned forward and shoved the bayonet into it, pushing around among the glowing coals. 'I must admit, I had heard that there was another side to this whole business. You know what the jungle drums are like. People are saying that you were framed and they aren't too happy about it. These are bad people you're up against, Garrett. Vicious. You'll need to watch yourself.'

'I know. Will you help us?'

He looked across at me for a long time and I was beginning to worry again but then his face split into a grin and he set the poker down on the hearth.

160

'Aye,' he said cheerfully. 'Of course I'll help.'

'Thank God for that,' I said. 'Now what about some food?'

Dawn. Cold, cold air and the sun dull and red and the clouds above the horizon glowing in oranges and yellows and golds, a bright wash of colour seeping into the ink-blue morning sky. From where we stood I could see over the bare hedges and the soft rolling fields towards the twin spires of Armagh cathedral five or six miles distant. The air smelt of daybreak. Behind us, twin trails of dark green in the silvery dew marked our tracks through the damp grass, stretching away across the sloping field.

Desi hung his forearms on the top rail of the heavy steel gate and stared thoughtfully out across his land, his breath clouding around his face. I remembered other mornings like this, emerging from our sleeping bags like shivering green larvae, faces caked and grimed with camouflage cream and dirt, cleaning weapons and cooking breakfast on the tiny hexamine stoves. Long weekends on the border, soaked to the skin, freezing in the damp hedges. Good times.

'How well do you know those two, Garrett?' Desi asked at last.

'About as well as you do.'

'Do you trust them?'

'No.'

'Neither do I. There's something crooked about them.'

'Yeah, I know what you mean. The girl would sell her mother for a story. But they might be useful. Instant media access, that sort of thing.'

'That's true.' He spat over the fence into the long grass beyond. 'She's a good-looking girl, that one. I'm surprised you haven't made a move on her yet.' He grinned at me.

'I've a few other things to sort out first, Desi, actually.'

'Well, there's time yet. About time you got yourself settled down and married.'

'Piss away off, Desi, would you.'

He put his head back and laughed, that deep, barking farmer's laugh of his, then we stood leaning on the fence for a long while, staring out across the countryside, savouring the fresh calm of the morning. I felt a weight begin to lift from my shoulders. All of the deceit and treachery and violence seemed somehow distant here, as if belonging to another world, or another century.

'So what's your next move?' he asked me.

'Find this Drumkeary, I suppose. Find the girl, if she's there. Get her back across the border. Somehow.'

'Tall order.'

'Tell me about it.'

'You got a gun?'

'Yes.'

He nodded slowly, watching the sunrise. A pair of crows whirled into a nearby tree, cawing harshly.

'You might have to use it.'

'I know that.' I looked across at him and he seemed to be waiting for something else. 'Look, Desi. If I don't get this girl out and get her to testify then my life's finished. I'll be marked as a murderer for the rest of my days, or a lunatic. Now, if anyone tries to stop me then I'll go straight through them and if I kill someone, well, that's just too bad. I didn't ask for this. I'm not doing this through choice. I have no choice. Besides, I've nothing more to lose, have I? If they take me in I'll be going down for murder and I might as well be hanged for a sheep as for a loaf.'

I listened to my words and could hardly believe I was saying them. Kill. Murder. Hanged. Jesus, what had happened to me?

'Fair one,' Desi said quietly.

'I'm a bit bitter, to be perfectly honest.'

'Understandable.'

'Twelve years I've given them, twelve bloody years, and they do this on me.'

'Typical,' he said flatly.

'Bloody typical,' I agreed.

I felt tears behind my eyes and I wanted to let it all go but Desi was still staring evenly out across the fields and the air was still and quiet and somehow I found a kind of strength beginning to seep into me, the way the damp from the grass soaks into your

164

boots. I felt it moving through me, slowly easing into every part of my body, something wild and strong and as old as the ground we stood on.

'Bitterness isn't a good thing, Garrett,' Desi said. 'You're better off without it. It's heavy baggage. But of course, you know that, anyway.'

'Yeah,' I said, my voice choked. 'I know that.'

There was no sound but the occasional cawing of the crows and the distant hum of the traffic in the town. The air was cold and clean and I felt purified, washed, as though all the filth and grime had been rinsed from me.

'You're a lucky sod, living out here,' I said.

'It's like anywhere else, really. There's the good, and there's the bad. Bloody hard work.'

'I can imagine. Rewarding, though.'

'Aye, it's rewarding, right enough.'

'What about those threats you were getting? Did you ever find out who it was?'

'No. Haven't had any phone calls for a while now, but I had my death notice in the paper the other night. Didn't worry me, really, but the wife was upset. Those bastards don't half know how to turn the screw. They're still watching. Out there, some-where.' He pointed out towards the horizon. 'See that big grey house on the hill out there, about a mile away? And the bungalow to the left of it with the red roof? The boy that lives in that bungalow is the main dicker for this part of the country. Fellow called Matchett; his grandfather used to work for my father down at the quarry, strangely enough. He's a bitter wee bastard. I've caught him following me three or four times now, in this old half-wrecked Lada he's got. I'd lay money he's the one doing the threats.'

'PIRA?'

'Yeah, probably. Peelers know all about him, but there's nothing they can do about it. They dug a load of arms and ammunition out of his yard three years ago but he cried coercion and the court let him walk.'

'Sick world, isn't it?'

'Aye.'

'Listen, Desi–'

'Don't say it, you'll only embarrass me!'

'But I really–'

'Now!' he commanded, holding up one finger. 'You'd do the same for me, if things were different. So no more of that rubbish, all right?'

'All right.'

He grinned at me, slapped me hugely on the back, then turned and began to walk slowly back down the field towards the farmyard. I watched him for a moment, the big, square, honest back swaying as he walked, his hands thrust deep into his trouser pockets, sauntering along as calm as you like. I wished I had his peace of mind. And his strength. I pushed away from the gate and followed him.

'So you're heading for Drumkeary?' he asked when I caught up.

'Yes.'

'When?'

'Soon as I find out where the hell it is.'

'You mean you don't know?'

'Haven't the faintest idea.'

'Ah, for God's sake, I used to be in Drumkeary

every summer for the fishing. It's just outside Sligo. Well, seven or eight miles out, I think. Wee arsehole of a place. I thought you knew where it was.'

I could have kissed him. It was about time my luck changed.

'Can you draw me a map?'

'I'll give you an Ordnance Survey map and mark it for you, what about that?'

'Desi, you're a bloody marvel!'

'Ah, everybody has to be good at something.'

'Don't remember a scrapyard around there, do you?'

'There's a big car dismantler's yard outside the village itself. Why?'

'I think that could be their safe-house.'

Desi sucked at his teeth and nodded slowly. 'Could be, right enough. It was a hell of a size of a yard for that size of a town, as I remember. Mind you, I haven't been down there for a while, you know. Must be nearly seven years.'

'They could have had the place for longer than that.'

'They could. They could indeed.'

I was moving now and on the right track and the girl would be there, I was sure the girl would be there.

'When do you want to leave?'

'As soon as I can.'

'Your best time would be late afternoon. Just before dark. If you can get to the border by nightfall you should make it all right. The Guards don't like to come out at night too much. Too many bloody terrorists about.'

The big danger would be from VCPs on the way to the border; if they flagged us down at all we were in trouble because for all my puffing and blowing I knew there was no way I was going to shoot at policemen or soldiers.

'What can we expect at the road-checks, Desi? What are they looking for?'

'They're looking for you, one man on his own. They've got a reasonable description of you, and the mug shot from your ID card. Photocopied.'

I pulled my wallet from my pocket. The ID card was four or five years old and I had been sporting a bushy moustache then which was now long gone and that would probably help a little.

'Look,' I said. 'Imagine I presented that to you at a checkpoint. You'd never recognise me.'

'No, you're right there. Having said that, if I saw that character standing on a street corner,' he nodded at the ID card, 'I'd arrest him right away. Give him a good kicking, too; bound to be a terrorist.'

'Very funny.'

'You'll need to shave before you go anywhere, because you do look a bit suspicious. And I'll lend you a shirt and tie. You'd best look as neat as possible.' He looked down at the toes of his wellingtons.

As we drew closer to the farmyard I could hear a dog barking cheerlessly somewhere in the distance. In the hedges the trees were grey and bare and their tracery of branches seemed brittle in the crisp clear air.

'I suppose you've no idea what you're going to do once you get there?' he asked eventually.

'No. I'll have to play it by ear.'

'If you need somewhere safe to hide the girl you can bring her here, you know that, don't you?'

'Thanks, Desi.'

'Don't worry about it. You can do the same for me someday.' He thrust his hands deep into his jacket pockets and looked up into the sky, as if searching there for inspiration. 'When these bastards set you up,' he said heavily, 'they set us all up. They didn't realise that.' He glanced round at me and grinned. 'But something tells me they're about to find out.'

Clare was standing by the kitchen sink as we came in through the back door. She brushed her hair nervously away from her face.

'I woke up and couldn't find you,' she said. 'I didn't know where you were.'

'We went for a walk. Talked over a few things.'

'What sort of things?'

'A policeman wouldn't ask you that,' Desi said easily, hauling off his wellingtons.

'Where's Uel?' I asked.

'Upstairs, in bed. I think he's still asleep.'

'It's a beautiful morning,' I said. 'Gives you a whole new outlook on life.'

'It's freezing!'

'Oh, that's right,' Desi said suddenly, 'I forgot to light the fire. The wife's not even away a day yet and I'm already going to pieces.'

Clare went upstairs and woke Uel, and then we sat around the old table in the kitchen and had tea and thick slabs of hot toast smeared with marmalade. I had already decided that it was time to lay everything on the table so that everyone knew exactly where they stood and exactly what they were getting into. The whole thing had been rolling along under its own momentum and it was about time we took some sort of control; if there was any sort of confrontation with these Intelligence people then there would be shooting and probably deaths, and the last thing I wanted was someone screwing up because they hadn't realised the risk involved.

Clare was in a strange mood and kept fidgeting and fiddling with her hair; I put it down to the strange surroundings and the odd situation but it seemed out of character for her. Uel said nothing but his eyes took everything in and now and again I noticed Desi watching him carefully.

'Drumkeary is across the border, near Sligo,' I told them. 'Desi knows the area quite well. So I think it's best that we're clear on exactly what we might be getting into here. Firstly, once we get down to this scrap- yard, I intend to do whatever is necessary to get this girl away, including the use of weapons. If I have to shoot at anyone I will, and I'll not be shooting to injure. So you'd better be perfectly happy about that. Secondly, there is a great risk of arrest, because by now every security agency in the North will be after me, and probably the Gardai and the Irish Army as well. And we've got a long way to go, apparently. Thirdly, these people don't hesitate about using their weapons. So there's a chance that one or all of us might get killed.' I paused to let that last word sink in. 'If you're both happy with that, then fine. If not, then we'd better come to some other arrangement.'

'We're in,' Clare said firmly. Uel opened his mouth as if to speak, then thought better of it and sat back in his seat.

'You're sure of that?' I asked.

'Listen, we were in Nicaragua last month. That makes this place look like a picnic, believe me.'

I shrugged. 'Well, it's your choice. You're a big girl. What about you, Uel?'

'Ah ... yes,' he said, glancing over at the girl. 'Yes. I'm ... happy about it.'

I was beginning to wonder if he ever made any decisions himself.

'Where are we going to take the girl, assuming we get her out?' Clare asked.

'Where do you suggest?'

'Well I don't know, I'm not the local expert. I just think we should have it arranged before we go down there, that's all.'

'We'll get her across the border again, then take her to whichever police station is nearest.'

'Are you sure that's wise?'

'What do you mean?'

'The police were going to stitch you up; I'd have thought it would be wise to steer clear of them now, that's all.'

'It wasn't the police,' I pointed out. 'It was MI5. And that was only me, on my own. There'll be the two of us this time, and they won't be able to explain that away so easily.'

'And what about our story?'

172

'What about it?'

'This girl is valuable. You're suggesting that I just walk her back into the clutches of the government. I'm after a story here, you know. I'm going to need her.'

'All you need is to find out whatever it is she knows,' I said. 'That's your story.'

'You obviously don't know very much about the media, do you? I can't just go on the air with a half-baked claim and nothing to back me up! I need her, talking to a camera, telling it herself!'

'Well, you'll have to make do with what you get, won't you!'

'I think we're getting a wee bit out of control here,' Desi said quietly. 'Let's calm down now and discuss this like adults, shall we? Garrett, she does have a point.'

'What point?'

'You can't just walk into a police station and expect them to believe everything you say, even if you do have this girl. The peelers will lock you up, the Intelligence crowd will arrive and the two of you will just quietly disappear. Simple as that.'

'They wouldn't–'

'They've already kidnapped her, remember? Why shouldn't they do it again, and you with her? All right, the local cops will be honest enough, but don't forget it won't be some face from the Intelligence services telling them to hand you over, it'll be their own Chief Superintendent on the phone and giving orders and they won't argue about it. These people are the Government, don't forget. I imagine they could fix that sort of thing quite easily.'

'Well, if they're acting for the Government then there's something rotten in the state of Denmark.'

I sat back in my chair and folded my arms and glared out of the window. Of course Desi was right but this was my plan he was tearing apart and it was the only one I had.

'Well, what do you suggest we do with her, then?' I asked testily.

'Get her out of the country,' Clare suggested. 'At least that will buy us time. We sell the story, she proves your innocence, and you return a free man.'

'And how do you propose getting her out of the country? Take her to the airport and put her on a flight to Paris, or something?'

'Dublin airport, why not?'

'Because the British and Irish security services are close enough to co-operate on this thing,' Desi said.

'They'll be looking for him,' Clare said, jerking her thumb in my direction. 'Not for two girls and a man with a beard.'

'If you think you're taking her away without me you've got another bloody think coming—'

'Garrett!' Desi said sharply. 'Calm yourself, for Christ's sake.' He rubbed at his mouth for a moment. 'Now look, it seems to me that the one advantage you have is numbers. At the moment they're looking for one man on his own. If you get the girl away, then they'll be looking for a couple. But not for a group of four people. If you can get her away and get to an airport fast, you might have a good chance of getting out together.'

'There's an airport at Galway, isn't there?' Uel remarked.

'There you go,' said Clare.

'So who is going to pay for the tickets?' I demanded. 'I mean, I hate to keep this conversation down to the nitty-gritty, but you don't get airline tickets for nothing, you know.'

'Money isn't a problem,' Clare said coolly.

I fought back a wild urge to slap her about the face. Cow. She looked at me with her steady, hard eyes and I remembered the little girl I had held on to in the safe-house and I thought, you aren't fooling me. You aren't fooling me at all.

' ... Downtown radio news at twelve o'clock, Gavin Micheals reporting. The search continues for the man who escaped from Lurgan RUC station late on Monday evening. The man, who is in his early thirties, is believed to have been helping police with their enquiries into the shooting in Balinderry on Sunday night when one man was killed. The RUC have admitted that the man, who is believed to be suffering from a rare mental illness, is a part-time member of the UDR and may be armed. There has been criticism of security at the RUC station from local politicians ... '

We hung around and waited. The morning dragged by. Uel brought a massive camera bag in from the car and started to lay out an array of lenses and filters on the kitchen table, handling each one carefully and tenderly, polishing them with a soft cloth before laying them down on the worn, wooden tabletop.

Clare lay slouched in an armchair with her leg hung over the arm, scribbling quietly in a notebook. She had pulled her hair straight back from her face and tied it in a ponytail with a length of green ribbon, and with her dark eyes and tanned skin it made her look a little Spanish. The big, old carriage clock ticked heavily on the mantelpiece. Outside, the weather was changing for the worse; at around eleven the rain began to spatter on the windows and the sky darkened with dark, drifting clouds. I felt sorry for Desi out with the cattle.

'There is something about guns, isn't there?' Clare said quietly over my shoulder. I hadn't heard her come up behind me.

'Like what?' I asked. I had broken the revolver down and was cleaning the cylinder, pushing a short wire brush through each of the chambers in turn, carefully scraping out the carbon. She picked up the body of the gun and turned it carefully in her hands.

'I don't know exactly ... danger. Lethality. It's actually quite a pretty thing and yet it's designed to kill people. Is this your own gun?'

'Yes.' I almost told her about the Smith and Wesson from the safe-house, now stowed safely away in my rucksack, but some instinct held me back. She stood quietly watching as I used some of Desi's gun oil, rubbing it gently on to the polished steel.

'What does it feel like, living with a gun all the time?'

'You get used to it.'

'You never feel like James Bond? Never show it off to the girls?'

'There's only one person who should know you carry a gun and that's the man you're about to kill. James Bond never had that problem. He could flash it around to his heart's content. The bloody thing never fell out of his holster in the middle of a supermarket, for instance.'

'Oh.' She stood for a moment longer. 'It's strange. Everything here seems so normal, yet here you are sitting at the kitchen table, cleaning a gun. It doesn't seem to fit in.'

I reached up and gently took the body of the gun out of her hands. She pulled up a chair and sat down beside me.

'I grew up on a farm like this,' she said. 'In Norfolk. Almost exactly the same. Right down to the smelly wellies.'

'I used to live on a farm, too. Outside the city. Smaller than this, though.'

'When was that?'

'Until I was thirteen. Then my parents moved to Belfast.'

'Don't you ever think of moving out to the country again?'

'Too bloody dangerous.'

'Dangerous?'

I fitted the cylinder back on to the gun and screwed it up tight, then snapped it open and closed a few times.

'You know what the country is like; everybody knows everybody else's business, everybody gossips. If you're a policeman or a UDR man out here, everyone knows it. They know where you live, what car you drive, where you work, everything. It's just the way things are around here. But of course, it means that the opposition know it all, too. Because they're not just the opposition, they're also your neighbours.'

'It seems quiet enough.'

'Compared to Nicaragua, it probably is. Desi's father used to own this farm. He was a Major in the UDR. The Provisionals put a bomb under the seat of his tractor. Blew him to pieces.'

'Here? On this farm?'

'Out at the back of the yard. Desi was twenty-one. He was first on the scene.'

'My God. How long ago was that?'

'Well, Desi's, what, thirty-six now? Fifteen years ago.'

'And he's run the farm ever since?'

'Yeah.'

'I don't think I could live here after seeing something like that. Seeing the same spot every day.'

'That's what they want,' I told her. 'They want him to sell up, to get out. To leave. But you can see what the big lad's like; they'll have to kill him before they get his farm. This is his father's land. It's precious. He'll live here, or he'll die here. Stubborn big fool.'

I squinted along the short barrel and pulled the trigger a few times, listening to the smooth, oiled click of the action. 'Thing is, the man who planted the bomb was arrested and convicted. He lived about a mile away from here. I think he got about twenty years, altogether, but with the remission and so forth

179

he got out three years ago. And now he's back in his old house and Desi sees him in town and driving round, happy as you like. That's what it's like out here. At least in the city you can hide.'

I set the gun down on the table and leaned back in the chair, waiting for her to speak. She seemed to want to talk but her features were still hard and composed and her voice still had the trace of an edge to it. Wary. Still the career woman. She was sitting with her legs crossed and her foot dangling idly, her wrists crossed casually in her lap, leaning forward and staring sadly into space. Desi was quite right, I thought; in the grey, rainy light from the window she did look beautiful. Beautiful and hard. I found myself wondering what she had been like as a girl, as a teenager, before her job had hardened her. I wondered if she had ever been loved.

Desi came back and we had a lunch of bread and cheese and pickle and cans of beer from the fridge. No one said very much. Even Desi seemed preoccupied with his thoughts. Afterwards he went back out to the fields and Uel went upstairs to sleep and Clare and I were alone in the sitting room. There was an armchair by the window and I settled myself into it, slouching down and staring out at the grass and the trees and the distant, rolling fields. After a while the sun came out and a shaft of warm light fell around me and I felt like sleeping again.

'This must be a hellish experience for you,' Clare said, gently. I opened one eye and squinted at her. She was perched on the white-painted window-sill, one foot cocked up on the arm of my chair.

180

'You don't know the half of it,' I said.

'It'll be all right. It'll work out.'

'Woman's intuition?'

'Something like that. Good always wins.'

'Not in the real world, I'm afraid.'

She was quiet for a while, staring out at the countryside. In the background the clock ticked. I closed my eyes again and wondered what she was after.

'Are you angry?' she asked eventually.

'What do you think?'

'I'd be angry, in your place.'

'Let me tell you, angry isn't the word for it.'

'What will you do when you find them?'

'I'll get the girl away.'

'Is that all?'

'I'll be doing bloody well to get that far.'

'That doesn't answer my question.'

'I know.' I opened my eyes again and she was watching me intently, her face serious. 'Put it this way,' I said. 'If a few of them get killed I'll not shed too many tears.'

She nodded. 'That's understandable,' she said. She was sitting very close to me and I was all of a sudden aware of her body, her legs, the denim of her jeans brushing lightly against my trousers. 'Just make sure you get me this story, all right?'

'Oh, I imagine you'll get a story, in the end. No matter how it goes.'

She was good at altering moods, subtly changing the atmosphere by the tone of her voice or the way she was standing. It was as though she were slipping on different masks; the business mask, for Mills and his lot; the professional mask, for Uel. And now, for me, the caring mask.

'Are you married?' she asked.

'No.'

She let it hang in the air and I thought I should say something.

'Are you?'

'Was once.'

'But not any more?'

'No. I was young then. Too young. I was married when I was eighteen, you know.'

'That is young.'

'He was a very handsome, very dashing Italian polo player. And he was a super lover. I think that was what attracted me to him in the first place.'

I had a sudden image of Clare lying naked on a warm, wrinkled bed with her tanned skin and her delicate feet and felt, despite myself, a sudden, roasting surge of blood to the groin.

'What happened to him?'

'I, ah … well, he died, actually.'

'I'm sorry.'

'It was a long time ago,' she said. She was trying to act tough but her eyes were full.

'How did he die?'

'A brain tumour. No one knew until after he was dead. No one even suspected anything was wrong. I never suspected. I just woke up one morning and there he was beside me and I couldn't wake him … '
Her voice trailed off and a single tear slid down her cheek. I felt suddenly embarrassed.

'Oh, look,' she said. 'I'm sorry. You've got your

own problems, the last thing you need at the moment is to hear about mine.'

She was lifting herself off the window-sill and the tears were beginning to flow now and I wasn't sure what to do. I stood up, anyway. She seemed very small beside me and I put my arm round her shoulder and she let herself melt into me.

'I'm sorry,' she said.

'It's all right,' I said softly, wondering what I should do next. She buried her face in my chest and I patted her gently on the shoulder. I could smell her hair. The image of her on the bed shot back into my mind again and I felt guilty about it and tried to lose it but she was making small, jerking motions, like a small animal caught in a net and then suddenly I knew that if I wanted to kiss her I could and she wouldn't resist and her face was moving up towards me now. This isn't right, I thought, this isn't right, but then her eyes were closed and her lips were thin and dry and her tongue was a tiny bud between them and then we were kissing and I could taste a hint of nicotine in her mouth. The sun came out again and warmed us both and we stood for a while and kissed and I was thinking all the time that it wasn't right but I couldn't think why. Eventually she pulled away and looked sideways out of the window.

'I'm sorry,' she said.

'It's all right.'

'No, it isn't. I shouldn't be doing this. It's not right.'

'I could be dead tomorrow.'

'We could all be dead tomorrow,' she said.

183

She sat for a while on her own, smoking, and I stayed by the window and felt my thoughts jerking and jumping around in my head. I was confused now, and the confidence and direction I had become used to was all screwed up and twisted. Now all I could think of was Clare and how her lips had tasted. All I wanted was to go and hold her and kiss her again. After a long while I went over and crouched down beside her.

'Are you all right?' I asked.

'Yes. I'm fine.' She put her hand out and let it rest lightly on my forearm.

'Don't worry,' I said awkwardly. I was trying to think of a way to get her out of the chair and into my arms again.

'Don't worry about what?'

'Oh ... anything. No point worrying. Never helps.'

She giggled a little. It was the first time I had heard her laugh.

'Thanks for saying that,' she said. She pulled on her cigarette. 'You're a nice guy.'

'One of my many talents.'

'Except when you use daft lines like that.'

We both laughed and I moved over to another armchair and sat down, facing her. There were slight red rims to her eyes. She stubbed out the cigarette and stared coolly across at me and I suddenly wanted to take her to bed, more than anything else, let me die tomorrow but let me take her to bed.

'What about this girl, then?' she asked after a while.

'What girl?'

'This Alison Sharpe.'

'What do you want to know?'

'How long have you known her for?'

'I don't know her at all. I only met her once, remember?'

'Sure you're not keeping anything secret?' she asked, jokingly.

'Positive!'

'What's she like, anyway?'

'Well, she's about your height. Long hair. Dark brown, I think, but it was wet when I saw her. Slim. Good looking.'

'I'm surprised she didn't try to pass anything to you,' Clare said. 'I mean, if she had anything, that would have been the ideal opportunity to get it away, wouldn't it?'

'She didn't give me anything. I've told you that before.'

'Oh, yes. Sorry.'

'That's all right.'

I thought the best thing would be to just ask her directly and I was thinking of the best line to use when the back door opened and there was a sound of wellingtons flopping on the floor and Desi was back and it was too late. Bugger, I thought. Bugger, bugger, bugger.

Shortly after that I went out into the yard for a bit of peace, to try and get my mind in order. The thing with Clare had unsettled me. It was like being reminded that there was much more to life than just living, and surviving was now just as important as winning.

I picked my way carefully through the slurry of mud and manure down to the gate at the back where Desi's father had been murdered. The two concrete pillars on either side of the entrance had never been repaired and still bore the scars of the explosion, great scrapes and gouges all down one side. I knew that Desi often came to sit on the wall. He would take an unpleasant delight in telling polite visitors the precise details of the killing, all burned on his young mind for fifteen years, and probably still as clear as the day it happened. I also knew that each year, on the eleventh of November, a single poppy was placed on the wall by the gate.

From the gate the track led down the side of the field and across to the lane beyond the hedge. The ground was churned and muddy, puddles of water in the hoofprints and fresh green cowpats here and there. I could hear the cattle lowing somewhere nearby. The air was cold and still, and it seemed that nature was all around me, folding in all around, holding on to me, cold and fresh and smelling of the mud and the cowshit and somehow mine, as though it belonged to me and I belonged to it. Suddenly I felt an understanding of mortality, as though some curtain had been lifted. Death was not the occasional unwelcome visitor by the fireside I had been used to, the grim reaper, the stealer of souls; death was near me now, it travelled with me, was in me, had always been in me. I was born and I would die, the only truths in life. Everyone had their time and their place. For Desi's father it was by this gatepost, on his land. For me it might be only hours away. After this twilight I might never see another dawn, and tomorrow's sun might find me sprawled in some ditch with the dew collecting on my eyelids and a bullet hole in the head. Strangely, the thought gave me no fear: no matter what happened to me the world would turn on and the sun would rise and in the spring the leaves would return to these bare and frozen trees.

I shrugged my jacket up around my shoulders, pulled the collar in close to my neck. This was too morbid. There should be no thought of death. I remembered the girl and her lips and the tiny bud of her tongue, the way her small frame had quivered and shook. I found myself imagining Desi's father in his last few moments on this earth, mounting the tractor, fumbling with the ignition key; was it a cold day like this? Then at last the tractor kicking into life and blue smoke from the exhaust and the big machine lurching down the yard towards the gate to the last and final jolt before the blinding flash and the percussive thump and the disintegration of man and machine. I imagined the shreds remaining. Desi running down the yard. Finding. We aren't made of much, in the final analysis, blood and meat and hair. I pushed my hands deep into my pockets and turned to walk back up the muddy yard.

Desi came off the phone and into the kitchen and jerked his head at the door, motioning me to follow. I set down my mug of coffee and followed him, wondering what had happened. He was standing in the back porch, waiting for me.

'What's wrong?' I asked, alarmed by his expression.

'That was the wife on the phone,' he said. 'She was trying to ring me this morning. She always does when she's up at her mother's, to make sure I'm out of bed. Sort of early morning alarm call.'

'So?'

'So this morning she couldn't get through. The line was engaged.'

I ran it through my head and tried to see what that meant but couldn't.

'I don't follow.'

'When she phoned here, you and I were away up the field, remember? So someone else was on the phone!'

'Who?'

'Well, who do you think? Who was here when we were there? The point is, one of them was using the phone!'

'It wouldn't have been someone ringing in?'

'Who would phone me at that time of the morning? Apart from the wife?'

I was suddenly angry because we were all in this together and all our lives were on the line and she was mucking about and it was just too bloody dangerous. Not to mention all this smooching earlier in the afternoon which I hadn't been able to put out of my head, all done on top of a lie. Bitch, I thought.


I called them both into the kitchen and we all sat around the table and Clare looked a little concerned, her eyes moving from my face to Desi's and back again.

'What's happened?' she asked.

'Here's the situation, Clare,' I said. 'You can come clean with us now, or I put you in that car and drop you in Armagh town and to hell with your bloody story.'

'What are you talking about?'

'That's the choice. You choose.'

'But I haven't a clue what you're talking about!'

'Who were you phoning this morning?'

Her face flickered briefly but her expression held and I thought, you're good, Clare, you're very good. Uel shifted uneasily in his seat.

'I wasn't phoning anyone!'

'Bollocks!'

'What makes you think I was?'

'Must have been you, then, Uel. Who were you talking to? What was so important that you had to hide it from Desi and I? Well?'

'I don't know anything about that.'

'So it was the bloody fairies, then, was it?'

'This is ridiculous,' Clare said. She made to get up but I grabbed her by the wrist and pulled her down again, hard.

'You get up when I tell you and not before, all right?'

'Fuck you!'

I'd never hit a girl before, and certainly not one I'd been kissing less than an hour previously but the fast slap across the face came swiftly and easily and the shock of it widened her eyes for a moment.

'Now you listen to me,' I said. 'You ought to know by now how dangerous this thing is. I'm playing with my life here and it may not seem like much to you but it's the only one I've got and I want to hang on to it. But I'm not going to hang on to it if you insist on playing your stupid little games and keeping your stupid little secrets! Now, you tell me who you were phoning and why, and we'll take things from there, all right?'

'You're being very stupid about this,' she said, but her voice was faltering. I reached around behind me and pulled out the revolver and pointed it straight at Uel's chest. His face drained of all colour and a tiny muscle in his eyelid started to twitch.

'I don't need you that much,' I said to her. 'And I've already killed one man so I might as well be hanged for a sheep as a loaf. And after today, shooting the pair of you might be a pleasure!'

'Clare! For Christ's sake!' Uel bleated. I pulled back the hammer and the ominous double-click filled the quiet kitchen.

'All right!' Clare said quickly. 'All right! I'll tell you! Put the gun down, and I'll tell you.'

I eased down the hammer and rested the gun on the table but still left my hand on it. 'Go on,' I said.

'I was phoning my editor. We're not really freelance, we're working on this for an American TV company. They gave us the tip in the first place. I've had to keep in touch, that's all. They're pulling the strings on this one.'

'You were phoning America?' Desi said, appalled.

'No, they have an office in Dublin.'

'What's the phone number?'

She gave it and Desi scribbled it down.

'We'll check that out later,' I said.

'Go ahead. It's genuine.'

'It better be. What else?'

'That's all–'

'No, it fucking well isn't!' I shouted suddenly, slamming the gun down hard on the table. Even Desi jumped. 'You're not coming clean with me, Clare. My life is hanging on this business and possibly yours as well and the only way to get through it is by working together and that means no secrets! Now you tell me the rest or I'll not be responsible for what I do!'

'All right!' she cried out, worried for the first time. 'OK. Look. I know what the girl has. She has a tape.'

'What sort of tape?'

'A tape of a meeting between a Government minister and the Army Council of the IRA. Apparently they tape all these things as a matter of course.'

'How did the girl get this tape?'

'I don't know. I just know that she did.'

'What were they meeting about?'

'I don't know!'

'What else?'

'There isn't anything else,' she said, almost shouting.

'There'd better not be!'

If it was true then I could understand all the effort to retrieve the thing before it was made public; it might never stand up in court but it would put the Government and the IRA in the same room and that would cause damage, severe damage. A minister of Her Majesty's Government, meeting with a bunch of terrorists. While we, the cannon fodder, stuck our heads above the parapet day and daily, for nothing. I felt sick in my stomach. It was as though the whole carpet of my life had been swept from beneath me. I had somehow imagined that the whole business was just some dreadful mistake, something Smith had engineered off his own bat, that once the authorities knew the truth then everything would be put right. Now it seemed that the authorities were in on it, too.

'I'm sorry,' Clare said. 'We just ... didn't know how far to trust you. And about this afternoon, too ... Sorry.'

'Look,' I said wearily. 'You don't seem to realise what we're up against here. If this thing about the tape is true, then they'll be happy enough to kill us and leave the bodies in some god-forsaken bog somewhere. Your life could end, Clare. And you, Uel. You could die. Finish. End. This isn't some TV film, this is reality, and you only die once and then that's it, all over. For ever.'

'I'm sorry. I said I'm sorry.'

'Well, that's all very well, but where does it leave us now?'

'What do you mean?'

'Do I take you along, or not?'

'Everything is the same. All we did was keep a secret from you. I'm sure you're keeping secrets from us.'

'Clare. We have to trust each other. Is this all, everything? There's nothing more?'

'There's nothing more,' she said. I remembered the thin lips and the tiny tongue and the smell of her small, quivering body. I remembered how my mind had whirled.

'All right,' I said. 'Let's leave it at that.'


We loaded up the car and by four o'clock we were ready to leave. I quietly checked that the Smith and Wesson automatic from the safe-house was still in my rucksack, which went into the boot. Desi took me to one side and went over his sketch map of the village again for me.

'You're sure you've got all that?' he asked for the third time.

'Yes, for heaven's sake. I'm sure. The church. O'Brien's bar. The railway bridge. The scrapyard. I'll be able to find my way about blindfold, for God's sake.'

'And you're sure you don't want me to come?'

'I'm sure. But thanks for the offer.'

We grinned at each other. He was a good friend and I would have been glad of him but he had done enough already and he had a wife and home to live for. He deserved a quiet old age.

'Don't trust those two, Garrett,' he said conversationally. 'They're rotten. I can smell it from them.'

'They're just stupid, Desi. They'll be all right. And besides, I will need the media on my side.'

'Still, don't turn your back on them. By the way, would you have really shot them?'

I grinned at him. 'Not in your good kitchen, Desi,' I said.

'Very funny. I didn't think so. But you were very

convincing. You even had me worried, for a moment or two. But watch them, all right? Keep your eye on them.'

'OK, OK. I'll watch them.'

'And you're happy enough about the route?'

'Yes. And I've packed my thermal underwear.'

'That's the thanks I get for being concerned, is it?'

'You're getting like an old woman, Desi.'

'Aye, maybe you're right. Maybe I should retire.'

'Give my love to the wee woman.'

'You can come back and give it to her yourself.'

'Aye.'

He walked around to the front of the house to where Clare and Uel sat waiting in the car. Our feet crunched on the gravel. I lowered myself into the driver's seat and pulled on the seatbelt and he leaned down to look in at us.

'Well, good luck, the lot of you,' he said.

'Thanks very much for everything, Desi,' I said, thinking that it sounded very lame.

'No problem. Remember what I told you, Garrett.'

'I will.' I slammed the door shut. He stood back. I started the car and it spluttered into life and I remembered Desi's father and hesitated for a moment and then thought, to hell with it and let out the clutch.

As we slid down the long drive to the road, Desi stood at the front door with his hand raised in a kind of salute until we were out of sight. As I turned the car out on to the main road I wondered if I'd ever see his face again.

The traffic was sparse around Armagh and we quickly made the motorway, turning west for Enniskillen and Belleek and eventually the road to Sligo. Clare and Uel said little. Clare sat in the front seat, staring out of the side window, her small hand toying with the seatbelt. She was still annoyed at being found out, I reckoned. Tough. I flicked on the radio and turned to RTE for a change but the reception was weak and after a while I turned it off again.

After we left the motorway the roads cleared slightly and we made good time through Clogher and it was just outside Fivemiletown that we hit the VCP, red torches circling slowly in the gathering dusk and the few cars ahead slowing down to a halt. Dark figures stood around near the shadowed bulk of the Landrovers parked across the road, familiar silhouettes with their helmets and their visors and the SA80s strapped across their chests. I was aware of Clare tensing up beside me as she realised what was going on.

'What is it?'

'UDR checkpoint,' I told her. 'Let me do the talking, all right? Just act relaxed. Pretend you're tired, or something.'

Only two cars ahead of us and my heart was hammering because now I was a criminal and the VCP was not the familiar and friendly sign of security it had always been before. I couldn't just produce my ID card and drive on through. I could feel the butt of the revolver tucked in my waistband. It felt huge. They couldn't fail to notice it. We looked suspicious. They had my photograph. Strange sensation, knowing that the armed men in combat gear were looking for you, waiting for you, wanting to catch you. I noticed the sentries lying in the grassy verge at the side of the road, facing back the way we had come, half in the ditch. Almost invisible unless you knew where to look and that was where I would have put them, too. Maybe a little further down. Poor bastards, it was cold out there and I knew how they felt.

One car ahead of us and my window wound down and the headlights off, cold air coming in but ignore it and try to fix a pleasant smile; I knew what they would be looking for, the signs of guilt. I had looked for them myself often enough, at a thousand other checkpoints on a thousand other nights. Staring in through the window and wondering if this was the one, if this man was a killer or that man was a killer, and sometimes knowing.

'What are you going to do?' Clare hissed. She was so tense I could feel it myself, her hands tight on the edge of her seat cushion.

196

'I don't know. I don't know.'

Rolling up to the check now and the NCO waving me forward, holding up his gloved hand as I drew level, leaning in to look at us. His face was camouflaged with green and brown cream.

'Hello. Got your driving licence on you, please?'

'Ah, yes, somewhere,' I said. I fiddled in my inside pocket, patted my jacket, reached into my trouser pockets. 'God, I've forgotten it. Have you anything, darling?' I asked, turning to Clare. She proffered her driving licence and I passed it out to the corporal.

'Where are you heading, Sir?' he asked, the tone flat and bored.

'Enniskillen. Weekend on the lakes.'

'You could have picked a better time of the year for it.'

'Well, it's peaceful now, isn't it. Fewer tourists.'

'Yeah.'

He straightened up and spoke into his radio. My eyes were level with his belt buckle. My heart was racing. He bent down again, looking at me.

'What's the name, Sir, please?'

'Ah ... Thompson. Philip Thompson.' I got it out fast but not fast enough and he would have caught the hesitation. I should have had a name ready on the end of my tongue. You don't hesitate over your own name. I've blown it, I thought, I've blown it. I looked out at the camouflaged figures standing around and began to think about shooting it out but there wasn't any point, the thing was set up so that they could take us out in seconds. And it wasn't their fault, anyhow, they were only doing their job, and doing it well.

A uniformed RUC man had appeared and the corporal was talking quietly to him, still holding Clare's driving licence.

'Drive on,' she hissed at me.

'Shut up, would you!'

'If you don't go now, we're done for!'

'Shut up!'

Maybe it would be worth trying as a last resort, but I would be playing with all our lives and it was poor odds. I pushed the clutch down and then changed my mind and released it again without putting the car into gear.

'Hurry up, for God's sake! Do it!'

The policeman strode over to us and bent down to look in. Young face with strong eyes and a dark moustache, pale from the cold. He stared at me for a second then passed the driving licence back to Clare. He looked back at me.

'I'm afraid I've got some bad news for you, Mr Kearns,' he said.

It took a moment for the enormity of what he had said to sink in but then it hit me and I thought, so that's it, all finished. All this way for nothing. I felt my stomach plummeting.

'There are VCPs further on down this road,' he was saying. 'Two of them. If you take the next on your right and swing round outside Fivemiletown you'll miss them, then keep on that road and it'll bring you into Enniskillen.'

I couldn't believe what I was hearing. I opened my mouth and closed it again, like a fish. The peeler smiled, then gave me a massive wink, then stood up and motioned to one of the soldiers who stopped the oncoming traffic to let me out.

'On you go, then,' he said. 'Don't want to hang about all night, do we?' I needed no second bidding. With the tears stinging my eyes I pushed the lever into first and eased out and around the Landrover. Oh, you people, I thought. You hard, proud, loyal people. Pride welled up in my chest until I thought it would burst.

'What happened?' Uel was asking. 'I thought we were done for?'

'Desi mentioned that the word had spread,' I tried to explain. 'They knew it was me. They know what's going on. They know I'm innocent!'

'I don't understand,' Clare said.

I looked across at her and her face was furrowed and pale and I realised that she could never understand, not really. Even if I could ever explain it properly. It was something you had to know, deep inside, something which had grown in you with every day of your life, something which spread among the people and linked them and made them strong. I shook my head a little, and I think tears of relief were streaming down my face.

'I'll tell you someday,' I said.

I rolled down into the longer grass at the bottom of the embankment and bumped into the girl and we both lay still as the train thundered by above us, the ground shaking and rumbling and the lights from the carriages flicking past on the grass. I lay with my arm across her back until the noise had faded well into the distance. All the lucky people with their simple, innocent business, I reflected, going home to their families and their beds; lucky, lucky people. The silence returned, the only sound the gentle buffeting of the sea breeze on our ears and the soft hiss of the waves.

'OK, let's go.'

I raised myself up again, my jeans damp at the knee from crawling around in the wet grass, hands chilled and wishing I had brought a pair of gloves because of the cold and the persistent stinging of the nettles. At the top of the embankment I paused and looked down the line towards the distant lights of the town, where the dark bulk of the train was merging into the general darkness. The steel rail was still quivering slightly, like something not quite dead.

'Come on.'

Clare pulled herself up beside me and we lay across the track, breathing heavily. She had pulled her woolly hat down over her ears and her face shone slightly, even through the camouflage cream I had smeared on her.

'Where is it?' she hissed.

'There.'

We were about a hundred and fifty metres from the house itself but the fence at the edge of the scrapyard was just visible in the shadows at the bottom of the embankment. It was an old, neglected thing, concrete posts and chickenwire with weeds growing up through it but sturdy enough and hard to get over. The house itself was a big, old, Edwardian affair with blocky modern extensions at the back and prefabricated outhouses spread around. Lights glowed in three of the curtained windows, two downstairs and one on the first floor, and a powerful lamp illuminated the yard at the back. The strong, white light reflected on the edges of the car hulks piled around on three sides of the yard, shining on chrome and glinting on the old-fashioned shapes so that the scrapyard took on a peculiar kind of beauty, like the surface of some alien, fantasy world.

I focused the binoculars on each window in turn but there were no gaps in the curtains and nothing to be seen. There were two cars parked in the open yard but some of the outhouses had large double doors and might have been garages, and there was space enough to hide a small fleet of vehicles. I passed the binoculars to Clare.

'See if you can spot anything.'

I felt dreadfully exposed on the top of the embankment but it was safe enough because they would only see to the limit of the powerful lamp at the rear of the house; beyond that all would be pitch blackness. The only danger was another train, and that would be unlikely so soon after the first.

'What are we going to do?' she asked after a while.

'I have a cunning plan,' I smiled at her. I felt better now that we were getting close to something, now that I had an objective in front of me. They were down there and they didn't know I was here and the thought tickled me immensely. I hoped that Smith was down there, too. Bastard. I felt the old warrior blood begin to pump.

'I should hope so, after all this time. I'm soaked to the skin.'

'Your skin's waterproof. Stop complaining.'

I didn't trust her at all now but I needed someone to work with and she was all there was. Back on the beach she had produced a dark blue waterproof suit and I had made her listen to the rustle it made as she walked and she had discarded it. Which had saved me the trouble of discarding it for her. I put my face close to hers and whispered.

'The way I see it, we have to get her out of the house somehow, before we get her away from them. There's no way we can get into the house and bring her out ourselves, they'll have to bring her out for us. And once they do that, we can snatch her.'

'How?'

I tapped the side of my nose and grinned. 'Never you mind. This is what I want you to do, all right? It's important. Go back to the car, wait there with Uel. In an hour's time, go into the village to the phone-box by the bar. Phone the Gardai, you'll find the number in the box. Report a burglary at the house; tell them the intruder is still in the yard somewhere. And try to sound frightened, all right?'

'Yes, but–'

'Never mind but, off you go. I'll see you later.'

I made to crawl over the side of the embankment and she put her hand gently on my arm. Her touch was very light. Her face was smooth in the dim, reflected light.

'Garrett,' she began. She opened and closed her mouth, then shook her head a little. 'I'm sorry, about this afternoon. And this morning. But what happened this afternoon ... well, it was good, you know?'

Looking back on it I think she was probably trying to be honest but at that point in time I was still hurting from the business of the phone call and I didn't trust her an inch.

'Nice of you to say so,' I said. A look of sadness slipped over her face for a second, but then she looked away. When she looked back the hard-bitten professional was back. I smiled thinly at her, then crawled on over the railway line and pushed myself down the wet, grassy slope to the fence.

I had no wire-cutters which was unfortunate but the fence was old and rusted here and there and I thought there would have to be a gap so I worked round until I found it, near the back of the yard, a section of the chicken-wire bent and distorted at the bottom by dogs or children scrabbling beneath. All the strands had been carefully cut through at some point in time, but the gap had been repaired with thin fuse wire, just enough to hold it in place. I pulled gently at it until there was a big enough gap to step easily through. I would be bringing her back this way and I wanted to be sure of an easy exit.

The yard smelt of old grease and congealed oil. The muddy ground was strewn with tiny pieces of glass which sparkled here and there as light hit them, shards from forgotten windscreens. Small fragments of metal rattled as I put my weight on them. Jagged edges pulled at my sodden jeans. The car hulks were piled on top of each other in heaps of two or three and I picked my way carefully through them, holding my breath at each step as I felt for the ground in front of me. The breeze whispered through the tin graveyard. I listened all the time for noise from the house and thought about Smith and his cronies and how it would be for them soon.

It took half an hour to get through the scrap to the front of the house, near to the road, then I moved back again along the same route and this time it took ten minutes and it still wasn't very fast but it would have to do. I marked the spaces and lanes between the decaying hulks with hub-caps set upright against the rusty metal, positioned so that even in a hurry I would be able to find the same route out again. Finally I was satisfied and an hour after I left Clare I was settling into a fire position in the low, scrubby hedge in the front of the house, right in the middle with the dry twigs scratching at my neck and the musty hedge smell filling my nostrils. The road was only feet away. I pulled the revolver from my waistband and checked the cylinder yet again, six rounds, their bases gleaming dully in the dim light. From where I squatted I could see a lighted downstairs window and the small courtesy light over the front door. The house looked tatty and uncared for, the small lawn overgrown and raggy. I watched the shadows for movement. I felt comfortable and relaxed and confident, completely and utterly confident. No worries. This was where those bastards would get a taste of their own medicine; let's see if they enjoyed it.

The plan would stand or fall on my assumption that they would take the girl out of the back door and across the yard towards the back of the place, probably to a prearranged escape route across the open ground beside the embankment. That was probably the reason for the lightly repaired gap in the fence; one good tug would have had it open, and away they would go. The thing was that if they went some other way then it was all screwed up but what the hell, I was too close to worry. Once the thing started I would play it as it came and roll with the punches and suddenly there were headlights and I crouched down quickly as the police car bounced through the gate and swerved down the short driveway, bumping to a halt on the lawn. Two Gardai jumped out, neat in their blue uniforms, their insignia and numbers glittering on their tunics. I watched as they went to the door and rang the bell.

There was a twitch at the curtain before the door was opened and a tall man stood in the doorway, slightly to one side to avoid being silhouetted against the light which I thought was very professional. I could hear their voices on the breeze but the words were indistinct, although I could make out the pleasant Tipperary accent of one of the policemen. I would have to be careful not to hit them when the shooting started. They spoke for some time and then the voices rose a little in pitch as the policemen began to ease themselves politely away from the door. Terribly sorry, must have been a crank call, sorry to have bothered you at this late hour. Goodnight. They went back to their car, relaxed now, waving at the tall man who remained standing just inside the door- way. They sat for a moment in the car and I saw their arms move as they strapped on their seatbelts and then the car started up and the reversing lights came on. Here we go, I thought. I settled myself into a comfortable crouch and ignored the cold and damp and the scratching branches and concentrated on the revolver in my hands and the foresight and the rearsight.

Their car began to crunch slowly up the drive. It was important that the firing should be seen to be coming from the area of the house and I didn't think the two policemen would be too skilled in locating hostile fire so I pushed the revolver right to the edge of the hedge where the muzzle flash would be instantly obvious. The car slowed at the gate then eased off into the road and right into my sight picture. I aimed at the front wing above the wheel arch and fired three rounds, then switched to the rear door and emptied the cylinder. The noise was deafening, bursting open the night after the endless quiet, the muzzle-flash half blinding me. I pulled the gun back in and pushed myself out of the hedge, crouching and running for the cover of the scrapyard as all the lights in the house flicked off and the police driver revved hard to get out of the danger zone. Waste metal crunched and clattered beneath my feet. Voices shouted, panicky, inside the house.

I had already chosen my spot, behind the house, not far from the main yard, the hulk of a van with the rear door hanging off and the window out so I had a reasonable view of the back of the house. I raced to it, dodging and weaving down the silent ranks of the hulks, head down and trying to avoid the jagged metal edges, arriving just as the back door of the house open- ed and a man appeared. I pressed down against the van, just my eyes showing through the shattered window, breathing hard. My heart was hammering in my chest.

Two men emerged from the house, big fellows with overcoats on, squinting into the darkness. One went to an estate car by one of the sheds and pulled a sports bag from the back seat. They were only twenty metres away. The enemy. I opened the cylinder of the gun and stabbed out the empty cases, fumbling a speedloader into the chambers and silently cursing my shaking hands. My ears were still ringing from the noise of the shooting. They were so close to me I was terrified in case they heard me gasping for breath.

The gun was loaded again and I felt a little better but the two men were very close and one was fiddling with something under his coat which was bound to be a weapon; I know they say you never think of the danger at times like that but you do, it's always there at the back of your mind, the damage they could do to your frail, earthly flesh if things went their way instead of yours. The man with the bag went back into the house and I thought for a moment about taking out the fellow left in the yard, an easy shot at that range but a little too much like murder and I lowered the gun again and then they brought out the girl and it all began to move very fast.

She looked very small and frail between the two heavies, each with a firm grip on one of her arms, her wrists bound in front of her, her head up, watching. She was asking them what was happening and they were ignoring her, guiding her quickly across the floodlit yard towards my hiding place. This is it, I thought urgently, this is it, Jesus; wipe the hands on the trousers in case the grip on the gun should slip, control the breathing. Be ready. Two men with the girl and one behind fiddling with his coat, maybe he was armed and I would have to watch him, ten metres away, this was it and I was wild within my soul.

'Stand still! Don't move or I'll kill you!'

I screamed it at the top of my voice, standing square in front of them, well lit up by the floodlight and the big bore of the gun gaping at them, wishing they would move so that I could shoot. They stood immobile. The girl's face was white. We stood for a few seconds like that, frozen in the shock of contact.

'Let her go!' I roared.

The man at the back was moving his hand very slowly beneath his coat and I snapped the gun down and fired carelessly towards his feet and the sound was immense and the bullet kicked up a splash of wet earth beside him.

'You, stand still!' The revolver back to the other two men. 'Now let go of her!'

The two men looked at each other, then back at me. 'It's Kearns,' one of them said.

'Look,' the other one said nervously. 'What do you want?'

'I want the girl.'

'We're Government. British Government.'

'I know.'

'I have to tell you–'

'Tell me all you want, I'll be glad to listen. The Gardai will be here in a few minutes, in force. I'm sure they'll be interested to listen, too.'

'I'm prepared to wait for the police,' he said, but his voice was shaky.

'Sure. You're prepared to wait for the police. You're armed to the teeth and you've got a young girl tied up and you're happy to wait for the police. I believe you. Now let go of the girl before I blow your fucking brains out!'

The thing was dragging on too long, it was nearly a minute since I had first confronted them and by now I had hoped to be well on my way but it was turning into a stalemate and I was getting angrier. The longer we stood like that the more their confidence would grow and I knew I had to act and act fast. So I snapped the gun down again and shot the chap who had spoken very quickly in the leg. He let go of the girl and collapsed, grabbing at the hole in his thigh, his face contorted into a scream but no noise coming out. The deafening report rang in my ears. The girl tugged herself away from the other man and I thought, good girl, let's go but then something in her eyes warned me but not in time, not in time to move or escape and I felt the sudden force of the thud on the back of my head and the last thing I remembered was a dark, mud-coloured blur as I dropped straight towards the ground and the shadows rushed up to meet me.

There was the smell of bacon and eggs, bacon and eggs and some other smell that I knew but couldn't remember, turf, that was it, the dry, earth-smell of burning turf and then I moved my head and the pain flashed round inside my skull. Bright, screaming pain. Jesus Christ.

I was lying on a bed, with a coarse grey blanket under my cheek and saliva had dribbled from my mouth and darkened the cloth and my head hurt to move and somewhere they were frying bacon and eggs. I could hear it, too, sizzling in another room. For a long moment I lay there, glad to be still and to let the pain ease, but then the business came back to me and I remembered the scrapyard and the shooting and the girl. They had knocked me out. A blow to the rear of the skull, hope it wasn't fractured. Bloody sore, anyhow.

'Are you awake?'

Someone else in the room. Jesus, God, everything

seemed to hurt, my arms, my legs, nausea in my stomach. I lay still again.

'Who's that?'

'My name's Alison.'

'Not Alison Sharpe, by any chance?'

'Yes. How did you know?'

'Oooooohhhhhhh, what a balls-up,' I moaned, and if I hadn't had all the pain I might have laughed. I moved my eyes around until I could see her, sitting on a bed across the room, her hair hanging lank across her face. She looked as though she had been crying, eyes red-rimmed and her cheeks shiny.

'Where are we?' I groaned.

'I don't know. It's a farmhouse of some kind. We arrived last night.'

'Oh.'

My hands were bound in front of me, plasticuffs, pulled tight and biting into my skin. I moved my wrists and the sudden pain sliced up my forearm.

'They're very tight,' she said.

'Tell me about it.'

'You were in the car. The other night.'

'That's me.'

'Who are you?'

'What do you mean, who am I?'

'You had a gun. Are you the police?'

'Just an innocent bystander.' She looked worried at that so I tried to smile at her. 'I'm army. UDR.'

She nodded, understanding.

'I'm afraid I've got you into a lot of trouble.'

'I got myself into this, thanks very much.'

'I had a look at your head when you were asleep.

There's a little blood, but I couldn't feel any fracture. I imagine you'll have a headache for a while, though.'

'Ha!'

Stupid bitch, I thought ungratefully. I was angry at the pain and the way I couldn't move without hurting and I swung myself suddenly upright, swinging my legs over the edge of the bed, blinding pain in my head and almost sick in the stomach but upright at last and a little more dignified.

'Are you all right?' she asked, kneeling beside me. I was swaying a little. I noticed the purple weals beneath her own plasticuffs. Her tired eyes. Her pain. I felt ashamed.

'I'm fine. Don't think I could run a marathon at this moment in time, though. What happened at the scrapyard?'

'They sneaked up behind you, and one of them hit you with the butt of a rifle. I thought they'd killed you. They took your gun. Then they dragged you away.'

'And then?'

'We got into a car and drove to a beach. It wasn't far from the big house. There was a car there, and they put us both into it and drove us here. That was about four hours ago.'

'And I've been out cold ever since?'

'Yes.'

A bedroom, small, low ceiling and a window, very dirty, letting in a smear of rainy, grey daylight. Two beds. Army blankets. An old chest of drawers, at one time painted white and now battered and chipped.

213

Bare floorboards. The girl was looking up at me, her eyes concerned.

'Are you sure you're all right?' she was asking. My head was floating.

'Perfectly,' I replied, then the walls spun round and the darkness came again.

Her face was close to mine, I could smell her breath, soft and slightly sour. Her eyes were large and dark.

'Are you back?'

'What?'

'You were unconscious again.'

'For how long?'

'Five minutes. You should lie still. That knock on the head could have been serious.'

I moved my head again which was a mistake and the bright pain flashed through me again.

'Jesus!'

'Lie still!'

She had tucked the blanket in around me and was still kneeling on the floor, by the bed, one arm across my chest holding the blanket over me. I focused my eyes on her face, neat and small, elegant even with her red-rimmed eyes and her pale skin, big eyes and upper lip protruding slightly but very attractive. I remembered her in the grey, rainy half-dawn, crouching in the ditch with the rain in her hair. Felt like a million years ago.

'Well,' I said, 'I've really fucked things up now, haven't I?'

'Why did you come?' she asked simply.

'To get you out.'

'But why? Where's the police?'

'After me, probably.'

'I don't understand.'

'Neither do I, Alison, neither do I.' I waited for a moment. 'They're framing me for murder.'

'Whose murder?'

'The fellow I shot the other morning, when you got away.'

'He's dead, then?'

'Yes.'

'They wouldn't tell me anything.'

'They're bastards.'

'Yes.'

So that was it, finished. The run was over, the dice had fallen and I had lost. I felt empty inside, numb and insensible, nothing but the dull weight of defeat and the sadness at the end I faced. I thought they would have to kill me and now it could only be a matter of time, but strangely the thought gave me no fear. Sadness at the way it would be, but no fear. Very odd.

'You said they had a car at a beach?'

'Yes.'

'Did you see anyone else there? A man and a woman?'

'No. There was a man there, with the car. But no woman. Why?'

'Nothing.'

'How's your head?'

'Bloody sore.'

So Clare and Uel were still free which was something to hang on to but not much; Clare was a tough lady but she wouldn't get near this lot, besides which, her natural reaction would be to use the media, the press, the world she knew, and even if she could work something it would take too long. At that point I was measuring the rest of my life in hours, not days.

I was looking up at the cracked plaster of the ceiling and I switched my gaze to the girl. She was the crux, the centre of the thing. It had started with her and would probably end with her and for someone so important she didn't look like much, tired and damp and frightened.

'Let this be a lesson to you,' I said to her. 'Don't go stealing people's cars, all right?'

'All right,' she said seriously. I almost laughed.

'What about this bloody tape, then?'

'What tape?'

'I know about the tape, Alison. What exactly is on it?'

'I can't tell you.'

'Why not?'

'Because ... I don't know what they'd do with you if they thought you knew.'

'I don't know what they're going to do with either of us, for that matter. So don't let that worry you.'

She gnawed at her lower lip for a moment.

'I can't,' she said.

'For Christ's sake, Alison. Whatever is on this

217

tape, it has screwed up my whole life and now they're probably going to kill me over the head of it, and I think that does give me the right to know what the hell it's all about!'

I was almost shouting and I regretted instantly when her lower lip began to quiver a little.

'Do you think they'll do that?' she asked in a very small voice.

'No, no they won't,' I reassured her, trying to sound convincing. 'No, they won't kill anybody. Don't worry.'

We sat for quite a while in silence, staring at each other. She was very pale; the talk of death had got right inside her. It's a subject the mind ignores, unless some unpleasant sod sets it right out in front of you and makes you look at it. I thought they would kill her too, eventually, but I didn't want to tell her that. Eventually she made as if to speak, then changed her mind, then opened her mouth again.

'It's a tape of a conference,' she said. 'A meeting.'

'Go on.'

'It arrived on my desk by mistake. I should never have received it. I don't know–'

'What do you do for a living, Alison?'

'I'm a confidential secretary with the Northern Ireland Office. I've got one of the highest security clearances you can get. One of my jobs is to transcribe the tapes of these important meetings, you know, write down what was said, and so on. They tape everything, now. Or everything that's important. But I never should have got this tape. It wasn't properly classified, it should have been marked "EYES ONLY" instead of only "SECRET". If they had classified it properly I would never have listened to it.'

'The meeting, Alison? Who was at it?'

She listed their names, the Government ministers first and they were big names, people I had only ever seen on television. I felt my backbone shiver, and I wondered if I really wanted to hear this. Then she went through the other names, the terrorists, and I recognised some of them, too. Provisional IRA, most of them. One from the INLA. I had chased them for years, come close to them sometimes. There was one in particular who I recognised because he was the PIRA boss in Lurgan and I knew his face from the intelligence photographs they gave us and I knew his voice because he phoned me at home one morning and told me that he was going to kill me that day. Bastard. I felt hollow inside at the memory of it.

'What did they talk about?'

'They were striking a deal. Our side wanted some of the hard-liners in the IRA and INLA taken out of circulation. Their side wanted the authorities to turn a blind eye to their racketeering. The deal was that if they assassinated the hard-liners in their organis-ations, then the Government would ignore their crim-inal activities, providing, of course, that the money they made didn't exceed certain limits. They even discussed how much the IRA could make in a year. An "Income Limit", they called it. Our side reckoned that with the political hard-liners out of the way the armed struggle would collapse under its own weight, and they decided the best way to achieve that would be to have their own sides kill them.'

'Anything else?'

'Isn't that enough?'

I looked at the floorboards for a very long time, trying to understand what she was saying but the intellect refusing to accept it, the way it is when you hear of the death of a loved one. Reality becomes too unreal and the data will not work and the brain jerks to a halt, focusing on the one thing only. I focused on an old nail in one of the floorboards, the top of it worn smooth and silvery from years of feet. I knew it was true. I could see the logic behind it but it was a cold and inanimate and uncaring logic which took no account of the people who had lived and died fighting these same people our leaders were now talking to. It was unthinkable and unbearable but somehow I knew it was true. A big old bell had knelled inside me and I knew it was true. Bastards. So this was what we were dying for.

'And you've got this tape?'

'Yes.'

'And that's what they want?'

'Yes.'

Obviously Clare had been tipped off. Certainly it was worth two thousand pounds. If it ever got out it would destroy more than the Government, and would make her a fortune and a half. Smart girl.

'I take it you've hidden this tape?'

'Yes.'

'Good.' She was delicately twisting a corner of the blanket in her fingers, her head down and the heaviness of tears about her, and I thought that this thing was a hell of a weight for a young girl to carry with her. I gently put my arms around her and hugged her a little, half of my mind still on what she had said.

'Are you all right?' I asked her. She nodded quickly.

'Sure?'

'Yes. I'm just glad you believe me. I didn't think anyone would.'

'I believe you,' I told her, then whatever was holding her together broke and the tears came and she twisted the blanket into her face as the small shoulders jerked and quivered, and I pulled her tight against me and held her and let her cry.


Rain began to spatter on the dirty window.

'Feeling better?'

'Yes, thanks.'

'Good.'

'I'm sorry about the crying.'

'Don't be silly. You're very brave.'

'Not really.'

'Yes, really. I don't think I would have had the guts to do what you did.'

'You came here to get me.'

'I didn't have any choice.'

'A coward wouldn't have done it.'

We lay in silence for a long while.

'I'm frightened,' she said, at last.

'Don't worry.'

'What do you think they're going to do?'

'I don't know.'

'I was never frightened before, not really. I was

always angry. But now you've come and I'm terrified. I don't want to die.' Her voice was very small.

'You're not going to die.'

'They said they would kill me.'

'They're trying to frighten you, that's all. Be brave. You've been very brave so far. There's a lot of men who wouldn't have been so brave.'

'I'll try.'

Silence again.

'I'm going to let them have the tape,' she said after a long while. 'There's no point both of us suffering for the damned thing any longer.'

'No!' I said.

'But we're not going to get out of here otherwise, are we? They'll hold us here for as long as they like and eventually they'll find out where it is. They've got drugs they can use. They'll find it anyway.'

'You can't just give it to them.'

'Why not?'

'Because … '

'If I give them the tape they said they'd let me go. I'm sure they'd let you go, too. They'd fix it all up again. The tape is all they want.'

'You're not going to give it to them, Alison. You can't give it to them. You can't let them win. Listen. When the Provisionals kill a soldier or a policeman the only thing that family has to hang on to is the thought that their loved one died for something. That his death had some sort of meaning. That he was defending something worthwhile. They hang on to that thought and sometimes that's the only thing that keeps them sane. Now these people are going behind everyone's back and undermining it all. It's as if they were pulling the carpet from underneath every one of us and saying, now you can sleep on the floorboards. We can't let them do that.'

'But what else can we do?'

'We can wait. And watch. They'll make a slip sometime, they're bound to. We just have to be ready for it, that's all. And once we get that opening, by Christ, I'll make these bastards pay. So keep ... fluid, all right? Always be ready to move, because when it happens, we won't have much time. And forget all this stuff about handing the tape over to them, all right? Are you with me?'

'Yes,' she said, in her small voice, 'I suppose so.'

Smith. All morning there had been the soft chatter of a television set from another room, the muted sound of children's programmes, until around noon there was a thin, whining voice raised in anger and the quiet chatter ceased. I recognised his voice instantly and was happy to hear the tension in it.

He came in shortly after that, stooping slightly at the low door, sandy hair lank and greasy and his face expressionless as he looked at me, then at the girl, then back at me again.

'We meet again,' he said casually. I stared back at him and said nothing. 'You're a fool, Kearns,' he went on. He was trying to hide it but the anger was plain in his face, his little eyes burning as he stared at me. Again I said nothing. Then he stepped quickly across the room to where I sat on the bed and slapped me roughly across the face. The blow knocked my head sideways and I wasn't ready for it and I felt skin rip inside my mouth, the warm, metal taste of the blood seeping round my teeth. I didn't make a sound. Inside I thought, I'm going to kill you, you bastard.

I saw the girl start up and I shook my head quickly at her and watched as she subsided back on to the rough blankets, her face boiling with rage. Smith kept his eyes on me. There were two heavies crowding round the door behind him and he nodded at the girl and stepped aside, letting them move in past him. They grabbed her roughly by the arms and hauled her upright.

'Get your hands off me, you scum!' she hissed through clenched teeth. Her eyes were wild and flashing and if her hands had been free I knew she would have blinded them. They bundled her quickly out of the room, and I heard her swearing at them in the hallway, listened to her voice until a door slammed and the noise faded to a murmur.

Smith stood looking sadly down at me, shaking his head slowly, then he sat down on Alison's bed and leaned forward towards me, clasping his hands in front of him like a friendly uncle settling down for a man-to-man chat. Another heavy lurched in and leaned against the door jamb. I dabbed my fingers at the trickle of blood from the corner of my mouth.

'What are you going to do to her?' I asked him.

'So you can speak, after all,' he said lightly. I stared at him without replying. He held my gaze. 'Miss Sharpe has stolen some Government property. It's our job to get it back.'

'At all costs.'

He shrugged. 'Ours is a dirty business, Mr Kearns.'

'So I've noticed.'

'You might be interested to know that you caused only minor injuries to the man you shot last night.'

'Flesh wound, was it?'

'That's right. He'll be a little tender for a few weeks, but there's no lasting damage, I'm told.'

'Pity. I'll do better next time.'

'You seem to be making a habit of shooting at your own side.'

'You're not on my side.'

He gasped out a brief laugh.

'You're a pathetic figure, Kearns, you really are. You've caused a lot of trouble, sticking your nose in where it wasn't wanted. You've killed one man, tried to murder another, escaped from legal custody. You've really screwed it up for yourself, haven't you?'

'Not half so much as you've screwed things up for yourself,' I told him. His expression never changed but I saw it in his eyes, the flicker of anger, almost but not quite caught in time. He was a man trained and practised in deception but there was something on his mind and he was showing it. 'What will happen to you when all this gets out, eh? How many years do you think you'll get? And it will get out, don't you worry about that. Some day, maybe not this year or next year, but it'll get out and they'll need a scapegoat. And you're the obvious choice, aren't you?'

Of course I was only pulling straws out of the air in the hope of grasping the right one and of course he was very good and showed no emotion but there

226

was still the faintest flicker in his eyes and a blood vessel was pumping minutely in his temple and I knew I was on the right track. Whatever was going on, things were out of control and he was out on a limb. Maybe the business was Government-inspired or maybe it was something his people had set up themselves without any sort of clearance but he was on his own and he knew it.

'You're ridiculous, Kearns, you really are.'

He stood up and looked at me and for a second I thought he would hit me again. I knew he would have liked to. But if he hit me again I would go for him, handcuffs and all, and even in the seconds before his bodyguard pulled me off him I would still do him damage. I think he realised that.

'What are you going to do with the girl?' I asked him.

'That depends entirely on her. If she gives us the tape, she can walk free today.'

'What if she doesn't?'

'That really isn't an option. She will give us the tape, it's just a question of sooner or later.'

'And then you'll let her go?'

'She'll be of no danger then.'

I wanted to ask what his plans were for me but I wouldn't give him the pleasure.

'I wouldn't worry too much about the girl, if I was you,' he said thinly, smiling with his mouth only. 'Your own predicament should give you cause enough for concern. You've stepped on a lot of people's toes, Kearns, and some of them would be quite happy to see you quietly disappear. It wouldn't be all that difficult to arrange.'

He shook his head a few times and made a show of looking unhappy, then grinned again. 'I'll never understand you people, you know. I've been stuck in this pathetic little province for five years now, and I'm still convinced that all you Paddy bastards are thick.' He grinned again, then stuck his hands deep into his coat pockets and ducked out through the door.

I lay back on the bed and listened to the key rattling in the lock and wriggled my fingers to ease the pain in my hands. The plasticuffs had worn the skin away in places and blood was beginning to smear across my wrists. My head still ached from the thump I had received. Something was worrying me. Some detail was niggling away in the back of my mind and I couldn't put my finger on it so I emptied my mind completely and let it come through and then it was obvious; he hadn't once asked how I had found the scrapyard, or how I had got there. The man was a professional intelligence operative, information was his game, and yet he had never bothered to ask the how or why. Which could only mean that he already knew. Which meant that he had picked up Clare and Uel, too. Or maybe he had got to Mills in some way. But he knew. He knew.

Thinking was annoying me and I needed activity to take my mind off things, so I stood up and began to go carefully over the room, looking for anything that might function as a weapon. It was in my mind that I would either escape or at least kill a few of them before they killed me. I was sure they would kill me. Without even running through the reasoning process, I was sure of it, and yet the thought caused me no fear at all. Sadness, yes. Regret. And a mad urge to damage as many of them as I could before the time came. And I wanted to die well, above all, I wanted that. No snivelling or crying when it came, not in front of these bastards. I suppose when you have lived with the possibility of death for a long time it becomes a little easier to accept when it finally comes around; when you've spent all of those long, warm, sheet-sticking nights staring at the ceiling and wondering when your turn would come it somehow seems more natural when you find out that it's close.

The chest of drawers was empty except for some twenty-year-old sheets of the Irish Times spread out in the bottom of each drawer. The curtain rail above the window was made of ancient, yellowed plastic. The beds were old, steel-sprung affairs held together with large bolts and some of the cross-members would have made good clubs but the bolts were tight and with my hands cuffed I couldn't get leverage on them. There was a tatty old lampshade on the end of a short, braided flex hanging from the ceiling but it wasn't long enough for a garrotte. Besides which, I didn't think I had it in me to cold-bloodedly strangle a man to death. I sat down on the bed again, pissed-off and angry and a bit light-headed still.

After a while I pulled the chest of drawers away from the wall and looked behind it. The back consisted of vertical tongue and groove, greyed and bent with age, and at some time in the past a long, thick length of timber had been nailed diagonally across it, perhaps for strength or to stop it wobbling but it was just what I needed, if I could get it off. I tugged at the top end of it and the wood creaked and a nail appeared, still half-buried in the wood of the cabinet. I pulled again. I tried hooking the plasticuffs over the wood and heaving on them but the pain was too much and I had to sit down and rub my fingers to get the blood moving again. The pain in my head had settled down to a dull, repetitive ache, squeezing at my skull. It was obviously going to take a while to get the thing off and they could come back into the room at any time but I still had to try, because I needed a direction and because I didn't want to think about the girl.

After ten minutes of working it backwards and forwards the last nail came out and it pulled free, four and a half feet of solid timber and four long rusty nails at each end and I was happy again. Armed. I swung it happily around the room. Using the steel frame of the bed I pushed out the nails at one end to make a comfortable grip, waved it about a little more and then set it on the mattress and covered it carefully with the blanket. The perspective had changed now and certain people were going to get one hell of a shock.


The key rattled in the lock and I started out of the semi-stupor and rubbed at my eyes, wincing at the pain from my wrists. Action. Get ready. Prepare. I sucked air into my lungs, flexed and tensed all my muscles. The length of wood was covered only by the

230

edge of the blanket and I had practised drawing it out and swinging it; the problem had been space, but as long as I kept the swing horizontal I could manage it, just. So long as they didn't come too far into the room, in which case I would have to improvise. Pain in my head and still hungry, ravenous, but it makes you wilder and I could feel the rage bursting up through me, pushing it, forcing it into every muscle and bone, the bastards, they wouldn't take me alive again, stinking arrogant bastards. Then the door swung open and they pushed the girl in.

She stumbled as she entered and sprawled on to the dusty, grey floorboards and I noticed that her eyes were red from crying which fuelled the madness and at the same moment I stepped upwards and outwards, pulling the club from the bed, swinging it around as I fixed my gaze on the man who had half-entered the room, tall and dark-haired with a neat moustache and looking like every squaddie I had ever known but there was no going back now. He saw me and had just enough time to register fear and I saw the reaction flashing through his eyes but it was too late because I swung the club down and straight into his face, the nails gouging into flesh and blood spurting outwards, a terrible roar from him as he clawed at the wound and moved his head downwards to protect his eyes. I stepped back and swung again, upwards this time, into the face again and missing with the nails but some bone breaking with the force of it. The girl was scream-ing. Just time for a third blow as he sank to the floor and this one laid him out cold, snapping the club off near the handle and leaving my hands twanging. The screaming stopped abruptly as he collapsed and I smashed my foot hard into his face, just to make sure, before reaching into his armpit for the warm butt of the pistol. Deep inside me something was sick at the damage I had caused to another human being but I was too far gone to pay too much attention. They were here by choice and I wasn't and there was an end to it. I grabbed the girl by the arm and pulled her to her feet, stepping over the crumpled body on the floor.

'Come on, hurry up! Time to move!'

'Is he dead?' Her face was white and frightened.

'Never mind him. Come on!'

Twelve seconds since the screaming had started and I had the pistol in both my hands, hard to pull the slide back to cock it with the plasticuffs on but I managed it and was ready for them. A hallway of some sort, peeling wallpaper and the smell of damp and daylight at the far end and suddenly a figure, silhouetted against the light, lurching towards me but halting in surprise, turning his head to shout.

'It's Kearns, he's–'

His voice was cut off by the sound of my two shots, both of them hitting him square in the face and he fell, wriggling, on to the floor. I ran past him, ears ringing, nostrils full of the sharp, dry smell of the cordite, blue gunsmoke swirling in the shadows. The door he had emerged from was the danger area and I kept the pistol pointed at it, aware of the girl behind me, wildness bursting inside me, fast and lethal and mad with a soaring, violent joy. People say that violence is a horrible thing but when you're winning there's no high like it. Invincible. Stand aside, boys, or I'll kick your ass. There was another man standing at the door as if about to poke his head around for a look and I fell across the threshold and saw his face and the pistol in his hands and shot him from the floor, upwards. Blood spattered the wall behind him. He spun back into the room. Cordite stink. Daylight from larger windows, more shapes moving in the background and only half-seen, screaming from the injured man and someone scrabbling to get through a doorway and I fired at him but missed, the bullet knocking a cloud of plaster from the wall beside him as he disappeared. Fuck you, I thought. Deaf from the noise, checking that the girl was with me, through the kitchen and bumping my thigh on the kitchen table, bloody sore, ignore it. I was almost at the back door when a door across the room was opened and I swung round, pushing the girl down with my clasped hands as I drew the pistol towards the new outline of light and the figure standing in front of it and I focused on the target and it was Clare, face white and eyes wide. What in the name of God, I thought.

'Clare, come on! We're getting out!'

I looked around at Alison and she was pulling herself up and towards the door and when I looked back Clare hadn't moved but I noticed what it was she had in her hand, a revolver, stainless steel and snubby and at that moment something collapsed inside me and all pity was gone. For a fraction of a second I stared into her eyes. She was one of them. All that way and one of them all the time. They thought I knew where the tape was and they wanted me to take them to it. For that fraction of a second my mind tried to encompass such treachery, to take in such massive deceit. All the talk, all the questions. That afternoon in the farmhouse in the sunny window. Nothing.

She was beginning to move her mouth and I think she wanted to say something, perhaps what she had always needed to say but her hand was moving too and I thought, too late you treacherous bitch, jerking the pistol up and firing one round which hit her in the face and went through and burst open the back of her head. I stood for a second and watched as her small, strong body crumpled on to the floor, the revolver clattering down beside her, but there was no time for reflection and I turned back to the door. Alison was already through and I rushed out after her, into the daylight and damp, clean air. A small yard, unkempt and empty. I began to run, pushing Alison ahead of me, half-aware of whitewashed walls and old tiles and corrugated iron sheets rusting against a shed, splashing through puddles and al-most sliding on the muddy ground.

'Look out!' she screamed at me and I slid down and hit the ground turning, the bullet pinging past my head, another snapping at the mud beside me. The girl was rolling over against the flaking white-washed wall of a shed.

'Where are they?' I roared.

'The window!' she screamed back. I noticed a movement and it was just like the firing range, line up the foresight and squeeze and I banged off three rounds at them, hearing glass break and a ricochet whining off into the sky and someone inside shouting in pain. Catch that in your teeth, you bastards.

Up again and dragging at the girl to get her moving before they started shooting again and round the corner of the shed, hard against the wall to catch my breath, my heart hammering in my chest.

'What do we do?' she gasped.

'Car,' I heaved. There were trees in a row all around the yard and the house and two cars were parked beneath them, a tatty old escort and the shiny new Volkswagen estate in which we had travelled from Belfast. Clare's car. I sprinted to the estate and wrenched open the door and the keys were dangling from the steering column, thank you Lord once again and keep doing your stuff. I bundled the girl into the passenger seat. There was shouting coming from the house, but they wouldn't follow too closely because they were not brave men; having said that we were talking seconds rather than minutes. I wondered how many of them there were; I had taken out five of them, including Clare. Clare. How could she have done that?

I twisted savagely at the ignition and the engine coughed and whirred then caught and I revved it hard and slammed it into first and ploughed off across the wet grass, bumping round in a circle and on to a track of sorts which seemed to lead somewhere. I was looking all around, trying to get my bearings, but all I could see were grey, misty trees. One of the side windows shattered as a bullet snapped through the car and the girl screamed but we were hauling around the back of the outhouses, the wheels sliding on the wet ground, too much torque and I eased off a little and the tyres found a purchase and we began to accelerate down the track. The engine was screaming and we needed second gear but my hands were still cuffed and I was hanging on to the wheel.

'Alison,' I shouted, 'Second gear!'

I pushed in the clutch and she understood and leaned forward to pull the gear lever back into second. The car wobbled on the uneven ground. I could hear shooting behind us but no noise from impact so they were just doing it to feel better.

'Keep your head down!' I told her. She crouched lower in the seat. It was difficult to hold the wheel with the cuffs and we would have to get rid of them soon but not until we had cleared the danger zone which was the farmhouse and the immediate area. I braked hard as we slid into a T-junction with a public road and wrenched the wheel round to the left, the car bouncing on to the tarmac and juddering on to the verge on the far side, gaining traction suddenly and boosting us on to the road again. I pushed my foot down hard, the engine screaming in protest.

'Third!' I yelled. She moved the lever again. 'Tell me if they're following!'

'I can't see anyone!'

'Keep an eye out!'

I drove hard for about five minutes, keeping the revs up into the red most of the time and maintaining fifty miles per hour which was fast on these roads, all bends and high hedges. There was hardly any traffic which was lucky because we used both sides regardless, narrowly missing a Ford van which swerved almost into the ditch as we ripped past on the verge. The girl watched behind for signs of pursuit. I tried to establish where exactly we were from the roadsigns, which were in English and Irish so that put us across the border but I didn't recognise any of the placenames. My breathing was coming in short gasps and my heart was still racing. In the back of my mind I was aware that I had killed or injured five people but worst of all was Clare, what she had done to me and what I had done to her. I kept seeing her face as the bullet hit her, small red rose blossoming suddenly on her cheek and the shock in her eyes before she fell. I knew there were nightmares ahead. She would have killed me, I knew that. But it didn't make it any better.

We needed a place to stop and lose the cuffs and get our breath back and I found a lane which seemed abandoned and overgrown and reversed back into it. I stopped when we were out of sight of the road and switched off the engine and the sudden silence was heavy and thick, only our breathing and the clicking from the engine as it cooled. My hands were shaking violently. I let my forehead drop on to the cool rim of the steering wheel, letting my breath out in a long and grateful sigh.

'Well, we're out, anyway,' I said, and I tried to smile at her but it felt like a grimace. The girl was white-faced and her hands were shaking even more than mine. Now and again her head would jerk slightly with the nerves and she stared straight out of the windscreen, her eyes damp and shining.

237

'I've never seen anything like that,' she whispered. 'All those people.'

'Alison, it had to be done. Their choice, not ours.'

'I know, but even so.'

'It's a shock, right enough, when you see it for the first time.' I remembered the first time I had seen the results of a violent death, a young soldier killed in a booby-trap bomb. His body sprawled in red fragments across the seat of his car, and the way I had retched for hours afterwards.

'Are we murderers?' she asked, in her small voice.

'They would have killed us. We're survivors. That's all.'

There was a lot to do and little time to do it in and I eased myself out of the car and into the cool, damp air, picking the pistol off the floor and sliding out the magazine to check the load, only five rounds left. Five rounds, and half the Secret Service after us. Dear God. The girl got out on her side and stood by the hedge, her arms held tight by her sides and the soft breeze tugging lightly at her hair. She was shivering.

'Alison, check the boot, would you? See if you can find anything useful. Maybe something to get these damned cuffs off.'

She nodded and moved around to the back of the car. She was holding up well, considering, but the stress was beginning to show; before long she would withdraw into herself and when that happened she would be nothing more than luggage.

I leaned back against the side of the car and bowed my head, rubbing my eyes with the backs of my bound hands. I was cold and numb inside, empty, as if someone had reached into my heart and scooped out my soul. My mind was full of Clare, standing in that doorway, the urgent look of apology in her eyes and the little silver gun moving slowly upwards. I tried to remember the exact moment when I decided to kill her but all I could drag from my memory was the look on her face and my hands moving automatically, the animal registering danger and dealing with it as the intellect tried to keep up. I hadn't killed her, my body had. I just hadn't been quick enough.

I had never trusted her, not really, but I had wanted her, wanted her badly. It was one thing to kill someone you didn't know and who was shooting at you, but it was a different thing to shoot someone you had once desired. To destroy that body. I remembered the feel of her small body in my arms. Destroyed now, food for maggots. It was a peculiar kind of virginity I had lost and I felt dirty, like a schoolboy with a whore. But she had betrayed me. All that time, all that way; the questions about the girl, about the tape. She thought I knew where the bloody thing was. They needed to follow me to see where I went, and what better way than with me? The enormity of it staggered me. I couldn't envisage such massive deceit.

'Look at this!' the girl called, and I raised myself reluctantly.

'What is it?'

'There's a rucksack!'

My rucksack, the one I had hurriedly filled after walking out of the RUC station, obviously forgotten and untouched and I wriggled my arms deep into the sack and there it was, cold and hard between my fingers, the pistol from the safe-house. They had never checked the bag.

'Well done, Clare,' I said beneath my breath.

'Where did that come from?' Alison said, wide-eyed, as I checked the magazine and loaded it again.

'Long story.' I felt better now. Luck had swung back to our side again. 'Look in the side pocket of the bag. You should find a survival knife.'

The knife had a serrated back and it was oiled and sharp but it took nearly ten minutes of heavy sawing before both of us were free, released at last from the dull throbbing ache of the hard-edged plastic. I rubbed the tender flesh on my wrists, looking around at the quiet countryside, painfully aware that we were wasting time.

'We have to get moving,' I said. 'Are you all right?'

'Yes. Just glad to get those things off.'

'I know what you mean.' I picked up the remains of the plasticuffs and threw them over the hedge. 'Probably choke some poor cow,' I remarked.

'So what do we do now?'

'Get that tape.'

'And then?'

'We'll cross that bridge when we come to it. You hungry?'

'Starving.'

'There should be some biscuits and spread in the rucksack. See if you can find them.' She reached for the rucksack and began rummaging. 'By the way,' I went on. 'Where is the tape?'

She froze, her hands inside the bag, staring down

into the boot of the car, afraid to look at me. I knew what she was thinking.

'Alison, I've just killed or injured half a dozen of them. You saw that yourself. I'm not working for them.'

She hesitated.

'You knew one of them,' she said after a moment. 'In the house. You called her name.'

'Clare?'

'Yes.'

'She was a plant.' Soft lips, small frame, the light warmth of the sun through the window. Bitch. 'They planted her and another fellow with me, right at the beginning. Told me they were journalists. She's dead now.'

'You killed her?'

'I had no choice.' But the little voice inside saying, you did, you did have a choice. You killed her because she betrayed you. 'She had a gun.'

She nodded. 'Still. It's hard to trust, isn't it?'

'Yeah, it is.'

'The tape is hidden in a derelict farmhouse.'

'Where?'

'In the chimney breast.'

'No, I mean, where is the farmhouse?'

'In the North.'

'I'm not going to get any closer than that, am I?'

She shook her head. 'I'll give you directions,' she said. 'I just ... don't want to trust anyone, at this stage. You know?'

'Not much of a way to do business,' I grinned at her.

'It isn't a business.' She pulled out a plastic bag

full of army issue biscuits and held it up, grimacing. 'Do you seriously expect me to eat these?'

We picked up the first of them just outside Castle-blayney as we drove past a filling station. He pulled out just a little too quickly, turning to drive after us, and I picked up his urgency in the rear view mirror. Not very professional, I thought. Or perhaps very nervous. These people weren't used to violence and I had probably shaken them up a good deal when we escaped; professional soldiers would have shot the both of us before we had left the yard.

'We've picked up a tag,' I said.

'A what?'

'We're being followed. Don't look round like that, he'll know we're on to him. Use your mirror.'

She twisted her head so that she could see him in the wing mirror on her side. 'The red Sierra, is that him?'

'That's him.'

He would drop away soon because we were on a straight road with only three or four junctions along it before the border and they would have those covered; no matter which turn we took there would be a car sitting quietly by the road and man speaking unobtrusively into a radio mike. Vehicle-borne surveillance in a rural area is a funny thing, you work it on junctions. Although the maps were covered with tangles of small country roads, they only ever lead to a few main junctions and if you know the general direction your target is going then all you have to do

242

is cover those junctions and wait for them to arrive. He could drop away now and his mates would sit waiting for us, right up to the border where the game would change because they would have the police and the army pick us up. Here in the Republic we were all strangers, playing our little games of hide and seek in someone else's garden.

'What do you think they'll do?'

'They'll follow us as far as the border, make sure they know where we cross and then have the army waiting for us at the far side.'

'Can they do that?'

'I imagine so.'

The map was still stuffed into the glovebox and Alison had smoothed it out and spread it over her lap. Now she was tracing our route with her finger so as not to miss any junctions. She was very cool now that something was happening at last.

'What does PH stand for?' she asked.

'Public house. We just passed it.'

'Ah.' She moved her finger on a little.

'We need a side road that takes us away from the border and towards a town, back into Castleblayney, even. Is there anything coming up?'

'Mmmmm ... yes, I think so. Next on the left. It's quite a bit on, though.'

The thing was, we could play hide and seek along these quiet little roads for years and nothing would ever happen, because they couldn't afford an incident on foreign soil. They would watch and wait because that was what they were good at and they would do it very well. Then the minute we crossed the border into home they would have the police and army waiting for us, and it would suit them down to the ground if we went down fighting. But we had to get to the tape, which was over the border, so we had to get across unnoticed and unannounced.

'Left here. Here!'

'All right, I see it.'

A narrow road with high hedges and a lot of sharp bends, twisting suddenly into more bad bends, up steep gradients and down into more bends. Water glistened on the damp uneven tarmac. Above the hedgerows the sky was an even silver-grey.

'How far to the next junction?'

'I don't know ... not far ... there's a crossroads.'

They would be waiting at the crossroads to see which road we took, then they'd radio ahead to a car waiting at the next crossroads and no matter which way we turned we would always find them there, waiting. Our only chance was to lose them and run for it, heading away from the border and then arcing back on it, perhaps, making for the most complicated road system on the map. They couldn't have all that many cars. Our only advantage was that they would be expecting us to turn north and head for the border and if we could surprise them we might gain a few seconds and leap a controlled junction before they got to it. Speed might give us the edge. Speed, and a lot of luck.

'Which way at this next crossroads?'

'Going where?'

'The border.'

'Ah ... turn right.'

'OK. We're going to go left. Don't be surprised. As soon as we turn, I'll be accelerating quickly, and I'll be making a few sudden turns. Try to follow them on the map because we'll need to know where we are.'

'Roger.'

I looked across at her but she had her head down to the map. She was lasting well, considering. Still reasonably bright and alert, even after all she had been through.

Suddenly we were at the crossroads and there was a shop with an old-fashioned petrol pump outside it and a few signs for tobacco, and across the road a yellow Peugeot parked against the hedge, facing north. I pushed down hard on the brake pedal and wrenched the wheel round hard to the left, feeling the car juddering as she came round, Alison bracing herself against the dashboard. On to the wrong side of the road and down into second to accelerate away, a glimpse of flurried activity in the Peugeot as we passed it.

'Caught them, the bastards!'

Now speed was the thing because we had to make the next crossroads before they got a car to it and if we managed that then we had a chance of losing them.

The road dropped for about half a mile, swung right and then began to rise and I saw another road coming up on the right and I swung into it, slightly too fast and grazing the hedge with the dry branches scratching at the car. We were up around fifty, the car almost airborne over some of the bumps and potholes, the steering wheel tugging and pulling as the wheels fought for purchase. Another right turn, down beside a big farmhouse. That made two turns they didn't know we'd made, and that put us ahead. The rain began to drift on to the windscreen and I flicked on the wipers.

'I think we come to a T-junction soon,' Alison said, trying to hold her finger on to the map.

'How soon?'

'Not too far, I–'

Then we were on to it, slamming on the brakes as hard as I could but still sliding out across the main road, a Ford van blaring his horn at us as he recovered control of his vehicle.

'Whoops!' I muttered. I pulled the car back on to the tarmac and headed left, slipping up through the gears more sedately now as there was more traffic about and I didn't want an accident, not with two pistols in the car.

'You'll have to give me a rough idea of where the tape is,' I told her, 'So that I can work out the best route.'

She looked across at me for a moment as if working something out in her head.

'When we get across the border, head for Castlewellan. That general direction.'

'Fair enough. I was worried in case you'd hidden it somewhere miles away, like Portrush.'

'Where's Portrush?'

'You really don't know?'

'I've only been in Northern Ireland for six months. You can't visit everywhere.'

'Listen,' I said after a moment. 'I've been

wondering. What on earth made you take the tape in the first place? I mean, I could understand a local girl getting annoyed and stealing the thing. But you're English. This isn't your problem.'

She was staring out of the side window, away from me, her small hand held delicately to her chin. She sat like that for some time.

'It's a long story,' she said.

'Tell me. I'm interested.'

I slowed down for another right turn on to a narrow road with a lot of trees along it. Still no sign of them and things were looking up.

'I was very worried about coming to Northern Ireland, at first,' Alison said.

'That's understandable.'

'It was a promotion, though, so I thought, what the heck, couldn't be that bad. But I felt like a stranger, at first. I didn't know anyone, I was living in a poky flat in Belfast which cost too much. I was sitting in every night. Really miserable time. But there was a chap who worked in the office beside mine, Bob, his name was. He was very good to me, right from the start. He was always asking me how I was, did I need anything, you know, he was just genuinely nice. He was in his late forties, I think. A nice, decent man.

'Anyway, I got to talking about the flat and how I wasn't really happy in it and he said that he had a bungalow in the country which had once belonged to his mother and it was vacant and why didn't I use it? Well, I went with him to have a look at the place, and it was really nice, and there were nice people living next

247

door, and someone produced a bottle of whiskey and we all got drunk and it was nice, you know. I was happy for the first time in ages. So I moved in.'

'They took you from that house on the night we … first bumped into each other, didn't they?'

'That's right.' She was silent for a bit. 'They dragged me out of the front door by my hair,' she said at last.

'Go on with the story.'

'Yes. Well. Basically, Bob was very nice. I met his wife and kids and we all became very friendly and everything was lovely. They were beautiful kids. Thirteen and nine, both with blond hair. And his wife was really great, took me with her to aerobics classes, and so on. I really liked her.'

She looked out of the window and was silent again and I knew she was hurting. I kept my eyes on the road, moving as fast as I could between the thick, high hedges. The window wipers began to squeak and scrape across the windscreen and I snapped them off.

'Anyhow, there was a shooting in Belfast a few weeks ago, outside Donegal Pass. Maybe you heard of it. They were shooting at the police station.'

I remembered hearing the news coming through on the Ops Room radio that night, sipping at my coffee as I noted down the details in the logbook. The Provisionals had set up a shoot to 'blood' a new recruit, getting him to open up at the police station but the boy had been nervous and the rounds had gone everywhere, a full magazine from an Armalite all over a busy street. One woman had died instantly and another died in hospital and there had been several other casualties. Three bullets had struck the police station. Three out of thirty, and the police had picked up the wee lad a few hours later. A good night's work for the Provisionals.

'Bob and his wife had been in town for a meal and were just walking back to their car when the shooting started. They heard the first few shots, and then his wife was hit in the head by a stray bullet. Killed her. Just like that. Apparently she was dead before she even fell.'

There was a wrenching sob in her voice but she held it back bravely. I wondered how many similar stories I had heard over the years, all of them brutal and all of them intensely sad. And all the same.

'I went to the funeral, of course, and did what I could for him, but he wasn't the same man. He was broken. He couldn't understand why ... that was all he kept asking, why did they do it? What could I tell him? What could I say to him? I couldn't even begin to understand. And those poor little boys, crying their eyes out.'

Welcome to Ireland, I thought.

'The IRA issued a statement on the day of the funeral saying they were sorry and I think that was the hardest part for me. They destroyed a whole family and they were sorry. Anyhow, two days later this tape landed on my desk and I couldn't believe that our Government, our leaders, could possibly talk to the men who had done this ... thing! How could they? For all they knew, they might have been talking to the men who had killed her! So something snapped inside me. I took a copy of the tape and stashed it away.'

If what she had told me was true, then they had been talking to the man who had ordered it. I glanced across at her and saw that she was near to tears. I thought it must have been hard for her, not born and brought up with the cruelty and hypocrisy of the place, not having it in her blood to turn away and erase the mind. Expecting civilised values in a land without honour.

'So how did they find out?' I asked her.

'I phoned a newspaper, to see if they would print it. That night they took me from the house.'

'You did the right thing,' I told her, after a while. 'I'd have done exactly the same thing in your place. Just plain awkwardness and bad temper. I suppose that makes you an honorary Ulster woman.' I smiled across at her and she smiled back and she seemed a little brighter, as though some part of her had been cleansed by the telling of it. She blinked and wiped her eyes with the back of her hands.

'I'm sure you've been through worse than that,' she said.

'There's nothing worse than what happens to you and yours.'

'That's very wise.'

'Thank you. Now get back to that map and tell me where in God's name we are.'

She bent over the map again and began to peer intently at it and then I caught them in the mirror, a long way behind but still there, keeping pace with us and I thought, oh, shit.

'They're still with us,' I said. She twisted round to look.

'They're miles away,' she said.

'It's a straight road. They have a map. When we turn off they'll know where we're headed.'

I should have realised it was all far too easy, after all this was their profession and they were the experts and they would have been on to us all the time. We had to try again, that was all, and again and again until we lost them. Or until the fuel gave out. Suddenly I was aware of the tiredness, the thick rubbing numbness behind my eyes; too little sleep and too little food and my head still light from the concussion and I was tired of the whole thing. The intellect was telling me to chuck it in, to pull in at the side of the road and go to sleep and to hell with it, get some rest and let the body recover but deep down the animal was snarling and growling and I wanted to hurt these people badly.

'To hell with this,' I said, then I braked hard and turned right, heading south off the main road, accelerating again to make the break. 'Try to follow this as best you can, Alison. And hang on tight.'

They would only be trailing us like that if their net was broken and there was no one to head us off, and so this would be the only chance to slip them using speed. If we could go faster than they could then we might lose them. I pushed the accelerator hard down to the floor and felt the car pick up quickly, a good powerful engine in there, thank God. There was no plan now, no strategy or scheme to confuse or deceive them, just plain bad temper and anger and fear, all pushing together and all blind. I hated to admit it to the girl but I thought we were finished; they were good at surveillance and there was no way we could lose them because they were professional and practised and capable. The only thing that might throw them was madness, total lunacy, doing the unthinkable and acting on instinct. These were men who had lived by their minds rather than their guts, and that would perhaps be their only flaw; they would never be able to cope with raw instinct because you couldn't quantify it, you couldn't practise it, you couldn't allow for it in the manual: 'Chapter four: human nature: classifications and recognition aids'. All you could do was move with it when it happened. Or in my case, use it.

The road dipped then swung up by the side of a low, scraggy hill, where the fields and the hedges gave way to burnt brown heather and grass. On each side of the road the countryside rolled off into the distance, spotted here and there with white bungalows and houses. Just as we crested the hill a shaft of sunlight slid out of the low grey cloud and lit up a part of the hillside in glowing greens and yellows and I fought down a sudden urge to stop the car and stare at it.

'It's beautiful,' Alison said quietly.

'Yes.'

'Such a beautiful, sad, rainy country.'

Then the hedge hid the fields from view and we were once again on a cold, wet country road, tired and scared and going too fast for safety. The moment of beauty was gone but it had sparked the wildness in me and I felt a tiny glow, deep inside, like the flimsiest connection to the raw beauty of those hills. It was a good feeling.

I missed two right turns and then took the third, bouncing over the pot-holed tarmac, sliding into the hedge and a stone clunking heavily against the underside of the car. I was driving as fast as I could, now and again losing the car a little on the tight bends, feeling the drift to the outside as I slipped down the gears with the engine screaming in protest but we were moving south-east most of the time and away from their net.

'Where are we?' I asked.

'I'm not sure.' She was turning the map round in her hands. 'Near Dundalk, maybe. I don't know.'

'OK.'

A sudden blind bend and a tractor and trailer on the far side, too close to the centre of the road and for a second we were sliding helplessly towards it as I wrenched and pulled at the steering wheel and time stretched out again, long seconds lasting for hours as we drifted and the impact came slowly closer, the driver's face shocked and white beneath the tatty flat cap then suddenly there was purchase and the wheels caught. The gearbox screamed in second as we pulled away from the tractor but the trailer caught the rear corner of the car, crunch of bodywork and glass almost lost in the roar of the engine.

'Jesus Christ,' I said. 'That was close!' My heart was flapping wildly in my chest. The girl was hanging on to the handle above the door, her knuckles tense and white, legs jerking towards imaginary brake pedals.

'My God,' she said quietly.

Left on to a main road and following the sign for Newry, to hell with them, I was going across the border and there was an end to it.

'Keep an eye out behind, would you,' I told her. 'Watch for any strange cars. Let me know if you see any.'

'What does a strange car look like?'

'You'll know it when you see it.'

The main road was not good because there would be a check at the border and we looked too suspicious, with the damage to the car and the tiredness obvious and my untidy growth of beard, they would be sure to pull us in because I would in their shoes. So we would have to use the unapproved roads which brought their own difficulties; snap VCPs in the border areas and a lot of covert activity and I didn't want to run into any of that. Better odds, though. I turned left off the main road and accelerated down a long straight with hedges on one side and a forest on the other, into sudden gloom as the trees cut away the meagre sunlight. The girl shivered.

'You all right?'

'Just cold.'

And then I saw them, quite a distance away, a yellow Peugeot parked by the side of the road and facing us and the road too narrow to turn in.

'Shit!'

'What is it?'

'The yellow car. Up there.'

'You think it's them?'

'It's them, all right. Keep an eye out for somewhere we can turn, a gateway, or something.'

I slowed down a little, watching them all the time, waiting for the sudden movement and then there it was, they were moving, pulling out across the narrow road and blocking us. They were trying to hold us, trap us there until another car came up behind us and put the cork in the bottle. He was facing us, right in the centre of the road, moving slowly towards us. The grey clouds reflected across his windscreen.

This was it, then, I said to myself, looking across at the girl and maybe it was the fear in her eyes or the way she was gripping the edge of her seat but something inside me gave way and the old, raging wildness slipped back in.

'Well,' I said to her quietly. 'Shall we take him?'

She looked at me with a curious expression on her pale face and I thought that she hadn't understood the phrase but she understood the tone all right; this was it, finale, we could risk it all and see where we ended up and if we went out we would go out in style. Maybe the world would never get to hear about it, but we'd make sure these bastards remembered us. She swallowed heavily. She nodded.

'Yes,' she said.

'Good girl. Hang on tight.'

I braked hard and slammed the lever into reverse, foot hard down and yawing off down the road at speed, my arm across the back of her seat and the raw smell of her still feminine and fragrant in my face, glancing round to see what he was doing and yes, taking the bait, nervously following to see what I was up to, accelerating towards us gradually and I judged his speed and distance then banged on the brakes again. Hard into first and the revs up in the red before letting the clutch out again and the car taking off like a rocket, speeding up the road towards him as he came towards us, second gear for more speed, a hundred metres left and this was a calculated risk, using the animal and the instinct and they wouldn't expect it, certain death for all of us if we hit and I was banking on their will to live. Thirty-five, forty miles an hour, fifty metres left and I could see their faces through the windscreen, closer, well everybody has to die sometime, what was that from Shakespeare? We owe God a death? Looked like He was about to collect, very close now and only seconds away and the girl with her eyes tight closed and very beautiful and my head full of the impact to come and the sweetness of the life I was leaving, then the Peugeot swerved into the hedge and bounced up past us, wrenching on the wheel to give him room and the blur of colour as he went past the window and the crunch as he came down on to the road again, spinning and bumping but now concentrating on my own car, the steering wheel alive and standing on the brakes as we smashed along the hedge, a blur of green on my right, squeak of twisting metal then crashing on to the road again and letting her go, the back end swaying wildly.

'We made it! We fucking made it! Ha-haaaa!' I roared, still struggling with the wheel. I glanced in the mirror and caught a glimpse of the Peugeot upside down in the hedge with the wheels still turning and broken glass winking on the wet tarmac. 'Are you all right?'

'I think so.' She opened her eyes gently. 'What happened to the other car?'

'We drove them round the bend,' I said. Then she smiled, then grinned, and I laughed, and then we were both laughing like idiots, exhausted, frightened, hunted idiots, wetting ourselves with laughter and just noticing the big yellow cross on the tarmac which marked the border as we sped across it.

'So where is the damn tape?'

'Well ... '

'For God's sake, surely you can tell me now?'

'No need to lose your temper.'

'I'm not ... all right. Sorry.'

'You're a bit of a madman, you know. I really thought we were dead back there.'

'Is that right? Well, I'll let you into a little secret. I thought we were dead, too.'

'What will we do with the tape, once we get it?'

'We'll get it to the papers, somehow. Make it public.'

'Do you think anyone will print it?'

'They'll print it. If I have to hold a gun to their head while they do it.'

'I'm glad you're on my side, you know.'

'I won't be for much longer if you don't tell me where the bloody tape is.'

'It's hidden in a derelict farmhouse. Not far from Castlewellan.'

'How did you decide on that?'

'I couldn't think of anywhere safe enough until I saw this place when I was out for a drive one day.

It's well out of the way. You can see it from the road but you have to walk about two miles across country to get to it, and it's surrounded by brambles. It seemed like a good place.'

'Why couldn't you have told me that this morning?'

'I didn't trust you then. Not really.'

'And you trust me now?'

'A little.'

'Thanks.'

'Sometimes it's not easy to trust, you know.'

'Yeah, I know.'


The rain began in earnest as we slipped through the outskirts of Newry, coming down heavy on the roof and bouncing off the bonnet as we drove, the windscreen wipers on fast and still not clearing it. The smashed rear window was letting in the cold, damp breeze and even with the heater on full the car was still freezing. Alison had pulled on the thick, woolly pullover I had left in the rucksack and now she sat curled up in the front seat, her face tired and drawn but her eyes bright. I wanted to sleep, yawning hugely as I drove. It was probably a reaction to the massive adrenalin surge when we tried to ram the Peugeot, isn't every day the body decides it's going to die and it takes a while to recover. Outside the day was grey and miserable through the rain, the wipers sweeping mournfully through the spattering drops. As we slowed to cross the ramps outside the police station I watched a woman hurrying past in a bright red anorak, head down against the weather and her wheeled tartan shopping bag bouncing along behind her. I wished I could change places with her; I would have given anything to be able to go home for a bath and a fire and a good night's sleep.

'It seems too easy,' Alison said after a while.

'I know what you mean,' I said. 'They've been giving it their all for the past few hours and now nothing. I didn't think we would lose them so easily.'

'Probably just can't trust our good fortune, that's all. We deserve a break, by now.'

'I never trust trust. Never.'

She giggled a little. 'Twit,' she said.

Out through Newry and right towards Rathfriland, the road winding and twisting through the gentle countryside, the Northern roads noticeably better and more signposts, too. Good to be home again. My eyes were beginning to droop now, how long was that without sleep? I tried to count the hours but got lost after thirty-six. The concussion didn't count. Far too long, and nothing to eat but biscuits, oh, you poor lad, nothing like feeling sorry for yourself. The hiss of the rain and the hum of the engine and the whirr of the heater, better turn that off, actually, because it dries out the eyes. I leaned forward for the switch and just then I saw the brake lights of the cars in front and the distant flicker of a bright red torch. My heart caught.

'Oh, shit!'

'What is it?'

'VCP. Checkpoint.'

The traffic slowed down as we drew near and I noticed the sentry in the ditch, the round silhouette of his helmet dark among the lighter grasses. Up ahead they had the two Landrovers well spaced in the shadow of a hedge and only two men standing on the road, one waving the red torch and the other checking the cars. The rest of the patrol would be scattered along the side of the road, watching.

'I don't suppose you've any ID, have you?' I asked weakly.

'They took it all.'

I tried to get my mind to work but it was like thinking in a deep bog. If we had really lost them then they couldn't be sure which way we'd go so they would have to organise a ring of checkpoints and this would be one of them. They would arrest us here and hand us over to Smith and his crowd and that would be that. We were screwed.

Nearly stopped now, the soldier leaning down to the driver two cars in front. I saw the driving licence held out, taken, examined. I noticed the airborne wings on the shoulders of their combat jackets, Parachute Regiment, bloody good soldiers which was why there were only two of them actually standing on the road making targets of themselves but, more importantly for us, Englishmen with no local axe to grind. We could expect no favours from these men.

'Looks like this is it,' I said quietly.

'Couldn't we make a break for it?'

'No.'

Well yes, technically, I suppose we could but these men were trained as soldiers and not as policemen and once they opened fire the devastation would be awesome and there was no way we could survive it. I watched the windscreen wipers thudding wearily to and fro across the glass, wondering what to say to the man when he leaned down to look in at us. So this was it. After all this way, after all the risks. I wondered how they would treat the shooting at the farmhouse because I had probably killed some of their people and injured others and it would all have to be explained somehow. Probably a series of fatal traffic accidents, terribly sorry Mrs Smith, your son was killed instantly, no, that's not a bullet wound in his forehead. I wondered if Clare had a family, if they really knew what she did for a living. There would be no question of legal action, in any case; there was too much potential embarrassment there, it would all be covered up. Maybe we would be covered up too. That would be the easy answer and they could be as neat as they liked, two lonely, unmarked graves in some desolate, windswept bog.

The queue shunted on a little. I didn't know what to say to Alison because I felt I should apologise to her in some way, and I was trying to think of words when I noticed the Para NCO reading the registration number of our car into his radio. I saw the recognition flicker across his face. Bad news that, son. If I was a terrorist and I noticed that I would be doing something about it by now. Never let it show. He called over the other soldier and spoke briefly to him. Both of them glanced towards our car, then the soldier turned back to the traffic and began to wave the other cars through. Wants to get to us in a hurry,

I thought. The NCO moved off a little to one side and continued to talk urgently into his radio mike. I let the car roll forward and slowed down for him but he was waving me on, waving me forward like the rest and I couldn't believe it at first but then I was accelerating slowly past the Landrovers, noticing a few other men watching from the verge and then away, on to open road and up through the gears again and hardly able to believe it. I forced my exhausted brain to work again, to examine and consider. My mind was fuzzy with sleep but something was ringing a bell in my head, something that wasn't quite right, that didn't fit.

'Why did they let us go?' Alison asked, incredulously.

'I don't know,' I said stupidly, and then I understood, all at once. Of course they didn't pick us up, they weren't after us, they were after the tape. We were only secondary targets. The Para NCO had been ordered to let us through and report in and now they would follow us until we picked up the tape. Bastards.

'They're on to us again, Alison,' I explained. 'Now they know where we are they can follow us again. They're hoping we'll lead them to the tape.'

'We'll have to get rid of the car, then.'

'Easier said than done. How far to this farmhouse of yours?'

She consulted the map. 'I'm not sure, really. I think we're about ten miles from it. I don't recognise these roads, I only ever came from the other direction.'

'Terrific.'

'I'd like to have seen you do better–'

'Yeah. Sorry. Tired.'

She smiled wearily. 'I know,' she said.

We made Castlewellan by lunchtime and I thought, to hell with it, I need to eat. I pulled in outside a chip shop in the main square. Alison looked at me as though I were mad.

'What are you stopping for?' she asked, her eyes wide.

'I want some grub,' I said.

'What about the tape?'

'It'll keep for an extra half hour.'

'But ... the police, the army ... '

'They would have arrested us at the checkpoint if they had wanted to. Obviously they didn't want to. So let's get something to eat. I've got a fiver here, what do you want?'

'Oh, God, I'd love a fish and chips!'

I ordered the fish and chips for her and a sausage supper for myself with a couple of cans of Coke for energy and a Mars bar each, which took up most of the fiver. When I handed the parcel to her she tore the paper unwrapping it.

'Hungry, are you?' I asked.

'Ravenous.'

'What did they feed you on, while they had you?'

'Chicken curry, mostly.'

'Lovely.'

'Mm,' she said, her mouth full of chips. She chewed and swallowed and coughed and then began to giggle uncontrollably, throwing her head back and holding her hand up to her mouth, her whole body shaking with it, Coke spilling out of the open can in her hand. I thought she had finally cracked and the concern must have shown on my face, for a quick glance over at me set her off in a fresh fit of mirth. I tried not to join in.

'All right,' I said seriously. 'What's so funny?'

'It's just ... it's just ... Oh, I'm sorry ... ' More laughter, loudly now, from the pit of her stomach. I munched sternly on my sausage. 'It's just that ... it seems so funny, I mean ... here we are, on the run ... We've just risked life and limb to escape, we've raced across the border, driven like maniacs and nearly killed ourselves in the process and now here we are having a bite to eat outside a chip shop. I just can't ... ' Then she was away again, tittering and laughing with her hand across her mouth.

'Sometimes, Alison, I don't think you treat our situation with the seriousness it deserves.'

More laughter. A woman passing by glanced in at us and smiled.

'I mean, we are in dire straits here.'

A fresh bout of guffaws. I was doing my damnedest not to join in but it was difficult.

'How is your fish, anyhow?'

That was the final straw and she was away, laughing with her soul, unwinding all her nerves and then I couldn't hold it any longer and I started, too, and we sat there like a pair of fools with the windows steaming up and the drizzle coming in through the smashed window in the back, guns

264

under the seat and MI5 no doubt watching us, tired and cold and frightened and laughing until our ribs ached.

'Oh Garrett,' she said at last, her eyes streaming. It was the first time she had ever used my name and it sounded odd, suddenly changing and charging the atmosphere. She rested her head on the headrest and looked across at me.

'Look,' she began, 'I want you to know ... '

'Save it.'

'But ... '

'We're not out of the woods yet. Whatever it is, it'll keep, all right?'

'All right.'

She stared at me with her eyes shining and the car was very quiet and it suddenly felt as though there was more between us than mere chance, as though something was joining us. Something unknown and unseen. Something ancient. I looked at her and I knew that she felt it too and I wished to God that we were somewhere else and not running for our lives.

'Well,' I said, clearing my throat after a long while. 'Are you going to finish that fish, or not?' I rolled my empty paper into a big, untidy ball and tossed it into the back seat. 'I mean, we don't want to keep the Secret Service waiting too long, do we?'

At about one o'clock I spotted the first car and it was purely by accident, the one time in a hundred when I happened to be looking the right way just when they made a mistake. It was a blue Sierra, parked in the entrance to a laneway about a hundred metres from the T-junction, obviously acting as a cut-off. When we appeared at the junction and turned out on to the main road they reversed hurriedly back up the laneway, very quick but not quite quick enough and I just caught the furtive movement. They would have us in a box, just as before, using maps and radios to follow us from junction to junction as long as we kept moving. I drove on round the next bend then pulled over sharply to the side of the road, bouncing over the verge.

'Your turn to drive,' I told Alison.

'OK.'

What they were doing was fine as long as the target was moving and you were sure it would continue to move, but the box would mean that the nearest cars would be at least half a mile away, maybe more; that gave us at least a square mile of ground to play with. If we stopped the car within that mile they wouldn't realise until we failed to show at the next junction. And if we hid the car well enough it might take them a few hours to find. And that was our ace.

'I know where I am now,' Alison said, adjusting the seat to her shorter legs. 'I can find the farmhouse from here.'

'Is it far?'

'I don't think so.'

'Right. Head for the farmhouse, but when we reach it just drive on past. Don't even slow down, I don't want these bastards to suspect anything. I'll have a good look at it, if I can, then we'll hammer out some sort of a plan. All right?'

'All right.'

The farmhouse was on a hill not far from the edge of a wood, a collapsing red-brick building with a rickety, tiled roof and some derelict outhouses, nearly hidden in a copse of grey, leafless trees. It was maybe a mile from the road but only a few hundred metres from the treeline and I looked carefully at it as we drove past, trying to take in every detail and memorise every line and curve and then we were between the trees again and I was staring into the gloom of the forest. I shifted the map around on my lap.

'This wood ... what's it called ... Trassey Forest ... it more or less butts on to Castlewellan Forest Park.

There's just a road between them. Now, if we were to drive into the forest park and leave the car there, we could walk to the farmhouse. It would take them quite a while to find the car. And once they do, there'd be no telling which way we'd gone. They could search for days.'

'Surely they'll be watching us more closely than that?'

'No, that's the beauty of it. They're waiting for us to stop somewhere, pick up the tape, then drive on. They don't realise that we're on to them, that we know we're being watched. And they don't know that the tape is so close. As far as they know, the tape could be anywhere in the Province, and they're just going to follow us around until they think we've picked it up.'

'Sounds like a good plan.'

'As good a plan as any.'

'Once we get the tape, what then?'

'We've got guns, we'll steal a car. We need to get to Belfast, I think; take the thing to the BBC or ITV or someone like that. The more people who hear the thing, the safer we are.'

'Steal a car? Is that wise?'

'What do we have to lose?'

I gave her directions to the entrance to the park and we slipped in through the gates and down the long drive towards the lake, tall fir trees towering over us on either side. The rain had eased off now and the smell of the forest was coming through the shattered window, fresh and open and clean. We took a right on to a service track, ignoring the sign which said no cars beyond this point. According to the map the track ran tight around the base of Slievenaslat before eventually curling back on itself and running back to the entrance. We bumped and ground along the gravel track for almost two kilometres before I stopped her.

'Pull up here.'

It was good to be in the clear mountain air, cold and damp with the smell of the pines. After the constant rumble of the engine the quiet was soft and numbing. All of our movements sounded loud.

'We'll leave her here,' I told her, crunching around to the boot and retrieving the rucksack. 'If there's anything you want to take, get it now.'

She shook her head.

'Right, then.' I tossed the rucksack on to the ground and jumped back into the car. I felt a moment of sadness, as at the loss of an old friend; the car had served us well over the past few hours. In that dull heap of metal and rubber we had gambled our lives, and won.

'What are you going to do?' Alison asked from the verge.

'Watch.'

A little way behind us there was a passing space where the track had been widened and beyond the opened-out part of the road a fire-break stretched down towards a small stream. I started the car and reversed it until I was facing the fire-break, then eased it forward gently to the edge of the gravel and then down the fire-break, slowly at first but gathering momentum and bouncing madly on the uneven ground, branches whipping at the windscreen and I began to worry a little as the speed increased and I was tossed around inside. I hung on to the wheel and stood on the brake and then the car reached the stream and bottomed out with a thud. I revved the engine and kept her moving and the car juddered and clanked along the stream-bed, rocks and stones clunking and scratching at the underside and the branches scrabbling across the roof. I eased the car about twenty metres up-stream then switched off the engine and let myself out. In the stream the car would be invisible from the track, unless you knew where to look. I tossed a few handfuls of dead pine-needles over the roof and bonnet to deaden the shine and pulled a broken branch across the rear window before scrabbling back up the slope to the girl.

'What do you think?' I asked, brushing the dirt from my hands.

'Very good. Definitely a born-again mountain man. Trapper Kearns and his trusty sidekick.'

'They'll never find it in there.'

I squinted down towards the car and could just make out the outline and a glimmer of reflected light from some smooth surface. 'OK,' I said. 'You know how to use a gun?' Her face paled and the humour drained out of her like someone had pulled a plug.

'I ... no.'

'You might as well learn.'

I gave her the Smith and Wesson which was the smaller of the two automatics and I showed her briefly how to load and fire it, making her practise it

270

a few times with the gun empty. She seemed to pick it up very quickly.

'I don't know if I could actually shoot someone,' she said quietly, weighing the heavy gun in her small hand.

'When they're coming at you and they want to kill you, believe me, you'll do it,' I told her. 'But if all goes according to plan, you won't have to use it. You're just carrying it for me, that's all.' I shrugged on the rucksack and slipped the Browning into my pocket. 'All right?'

'All right.'

'Then let's go.'

We moved out off the road and into the forest, keeping the bulk of Slievenaslat behind us as a marker, walking downhill on the soft bed of pine-needles. The space between the tall trees was remarkably peaceful. There was no sound except our breathing and the occasional swish of branches. I would retire here, I decided. I could live the rest of my days in this forest, with this peace. And perhaps with this woman.

Alison kept up with me, staying about two or three paces behind. Every few metres I would glance behind and she would smile bravely. She looked even more tired than usual, her pale face contrasting with the dark curls of her hair.

'Are you all right?' I asked.

'Of course I am!'

'Sorry. Only asking.'

We made the road in about half an hour, coming suddenly on to the high, dry-stone wall which marked the edge of the forest. Beyond the wall was the road and beyond the road was Trassey Forest which lay between us and the farmhouse, not more than a mile away. The ground across the road sloped gently upwards.

'Can you climb this wall, do you think?' I asked her.

'Of course I can, what do you take me for?'

'Only asked.'

'Well, don't just stand there, give me a leg up!'

I made a stirrup with my hands and she put her small foot into it and I pushed her up and on to the top of the wall, aware of the closeness of her and the warm, natural smell as her neat hips slid on to and over my shoulder. I turned and pulled myself up with less dignity, dislodging a stone with my stomach. We dropped on to the grass verge on the far side and the road was very quiet.

'Get across!' I told her. 'Quickly!'

'What–'

'Just do it!'

I sprinted across the tarmac, dropping down beside the far wall, glad of cover again after the naked open road. Alison tumbled down beside me.

'What's wrong?' she panted.

'Listen!'

There is something about hilly, forested country which distorts sound, so that loud noises in the next valley can be almost impossible to hear and it was like that with the helicopter; I had just recognised the quiet, monotonous drone which sounded like the thing was miles away then it appeared over the treetops, low and fast and heavy, a bulky green and black machine sliding over the road and disappearing over the trees again. The noise was sudden and ear-splittingly loud. We crouched down by the dry-stone wall, listening to the massive clatter over the forest.

'Do you think they saw us?' she asked.

'I don't know. Probably not.' Although it was amazing what you could see from a chopper, especially with those stabilised binoculars through which you could read the headline of a newspaper on the pavement. 'Let's get into cover, anyway.'

Over the wall and on to the soft floor of pine-needles again and the damp fragrance of them filling our nostrils and all our footsteps leaving dark brown smears in the pale, faded surface. The trees were closer together on this side and we had to bend more often, branches scratching and pulling at us. I could hear the chopper circling nearby, the dull clatter of it rising and falling. The helicopter was something I could have done without.

'How are you doing?'

'I told you, I'm all right!' she snapped. 'You think I'm delicate, or something?'

'Oh, no,' I replied. 'Not you, Alison, not delicate. Definitely not that.'

We were trudging around the side of the hill, rather than straight over the top of it, because the trees were sparser near the top and we would be more easily seen. The thing was, the helicopter meant that they knew we had stopped somewhere and were probably on foot. They had already started to search, and although they had a hell of an area to cover, it would only be a matter of time before they picked up the car. I had hidden it from ground view but a helicopter would be bound to pick it out after a while, and that would give them a centre for the search. And after that? I'll think about that one when I come to it, I decided.

On the far side of the hill the trees thinned out into a wide clearing, open on the lower side where the coarse grass ran down to a fence and a field where some bored sheep nuzzled at each other. Beyond the field the countryside stretched off towards the rolling crests of the Dromore hills, tough, scrubby country-side, hard to farm and still half wild, drenched in greys and greens. Near the centre of the clearing stood a single, upright stone, tall and bare and glistening from the drizzle. We paused for a moment in the treeline, gazing down past the stone at the silent, breathing landscape. I was glad of a few minutes' rest. The place was still and empty and there was a mystery about it which caught me deep inside, something about the space and the stillness and the smell of the damp grass and the sense that, under the heavens, all things are very small. It was a strangely comforting feeling. I wondered about the ancient people who had erected the stone; did they pick this place because of the eerie stillness? Or was it the other way around?

'You see that stone?' I said to Alison. 'Someone put that there maybe four thousand years ago. Maybe more.'

'So?'

I wanted to tell her about the mystery, about the stone and the forest and the things that lasted. I wanted to tell her not to worry, that the land was with us. That in thousands of years this stone had never fallen and that strength was ours, too. But you either feel these things or you don't, and any explanation would have sounded deranged.

'Oh, nothing,' I said. 'Just had a funny feeling, that's all.'

'What sort of feeling?'

'Lucky,' I said. 'I feel lucky.'

'You're weird, sometimes,' she said, smiling.

'It's a hobby.' I adjusted the straps of the rucksack and hoisted it up on my back. 'Let's get moving.'

From the edge of the forest the ground rose gently to the ruin, two hundred metres of rough and open grass. Too far to walk, we would have to sprint across, if we wanted to stay out of sight of the bloody chopper.

'Couldn't we work around it?' Alison asked. 'Maybe the trees are closer on the far side.'

'No. That's the road we drove along, down there, see? There isn't anything on the far side. Just more open land. We'll have to go from here.'

Or we could wait until the chopper used up his operational flying time and returned to Aldergrove to refuel, but that would give Smith time and time was our only ally. Besides which, they would probably have another one on standby. I stared out at the ruin. It was a little island of untidiness in the flat expanse of field, and it seemed to be miles away.

'I tell you what,' I said. 'Tell me where the thing is, I'll sprint across and get it. I'm not as tired as you.'

'Who says I'm tired?' She stuck her little chin out at me and I fought back an urge to smile.

'I do, you silly bitch. You've been locked up for almost a week. You've hardly eaten. Look at you, you're exhausted.'

'You're no oil-painting yourself,' she retaliated.

'I'm in better shape and there's an end to it.'

For a few seconds I thought she was going to argue the toss but she shrugged and let go of it.

'OK,' she said, primly. 'You do it. I could do with a rest, as it happens.'

'Right. Now we've got that out of the way, where's the tape?'

'In the main building, there's a downstairs room with a big fireplace. Just put your hand up the chimney a little and you'll feel a ledge. The tape is sitting on the ledge, pushed well into the back. You'll probably have to grope around a little.'

'You couldn't have thought of somewhere a bit more original, could you?'

'What's wrong with a chimney?'

'Everybody hides stuff in chimneys. It's the first place I'd have looked.' She pulled a face and looked away. 'But then, I did the Search Advisors' course, didn't I?.Right. You stay here. Don't move off to one side because I'll be coming straight back here, all right?'

'OK.'

'If you have any problems ... ' She had the Smith and Wesson and she could probably use it but if she fired on anyone they would fire back and kill her, and if it happened when I was in the house there was no way I could get back in time. I quickly ran various options through in my mind, what she could do if they surprised her, but none of them would work; if they found her, they could take her. 'Just don't have any problems, all right?'

'All right.'

'Main room?'

'Yes.'

'In the chimney?'

'Yes.'

'OK. Here I go.'

The throbbing beat of the helicopter engine had almost died away and I judged that they were over at the far side of the forest; I waited until the sound began to rise in volume before throwing myself over the rusty wire fence and racing across the open ground. The grass was rough and the ground pitted and difficult to run on and half-way across I tripped up and sprawled over on my back, knee scraped and painful and the grass soaking my trousers but I scrabbled back into a run again. Two hundred metres is a hell of a distance when you're tired and scared. I could hear the drone of the chopper rising gradually in volume as it swept low over the forest and I began to worry about getting caught out in the open when suddenly I was there, leaping through the clutching brambles and into the gaping doorway.

I stood leaning against the damp brickwork for a few seconds to get my breath back, gasping for air. The air inside the ruin smelt of dampness and decay.

It had once been a sizeable farmhouse with big rooms and tall windows but now the interior was filled with the thick smell of rotting wood and crumbled plaster. I tried to imagine family life going on in these rooms, cooking, washing, talking. On the walls, thin shreds of wallpaper still hung curling downwards. Silence. There was the sound of water dripping. My breathing sounded terribly loud and I pulled the Browning from my pocket which made me feel a little better.

There was no chance of moving silently with the rubble of dereliction all over the floor, old tiles, bricks, shards of wood, rusting metal, weeds. I checked the two downstairs rooms, one on each side of a central hall. Both about the same size and both with fireplaces. I clambered over the rubble to the first and stuck my hand up under the chimney breast. I could feel thick wads of damp soot. Most unpleasant, and no ledge. I withdrew my hand and wiped it over my jacket, shuddering a little. God knows what might have been up there.

Quickly through into the other room, making a bit of noise but speed was probably more important than stealth and my hand gently up into the chimney, thinking about what sort of a lonely place this must have been to live in and imagining long, desolate unspeaking nights around this fire and there it was, the ledge and something wrapped in plastic and pushed well back. I caught it in my fingers and dragged it out, shaking dirt and soot from the small package. So this was what it was all about. Well, I had expected elation of a sort but there was only sadness, deep and numbing sadness; to think that this small package had cost so many lives, what a senseless, bloody world. I weighed it in my hands for a few seconds and was about to turn when I heard it, the unmistakable metallic click of a safety catch being released and I knew they had a weapon trained on my back.

'Place the package on the ground. Place the weapon beside it. Move slowly.'

Bastards. The voice was English and cool and professional. They were behind me and I could try to use the Browning but they would kill me instantly and it would end here, in this stinking ruin, and I wanted a few minutes more of this sweet life. I bent slowly and placed the package on the ground, setting the pistol carefully beside it.

'Step forward, against the wall.'

If they had touched the girl I would kill them, so help me God I would tear them apart.

'Hands flat on the wall.'

Cold plaster and the tape being unwrapped and an unbearable urge to turn round, then rough hands frisking me, searching every pocket, the smell of nicotine from his clothes.

'Turn around, slowly.'

Two of them, standing by the door, one in a combat-jacket and one in a blue anorak, neat short hair, clean-shaven, nondescript. The type you'd never recognise again. Blue jacket with Heckler and Koch MP5 held in the shoulder and aimed at my chest which was professional, none of this fire-from-the-hip stuff. They looked clean and fresh and I was aware of my stubble and the smell of my sweat.

'We're going to move outside. You go first. Don't try anything or we'll kill you.'

'Fair enough,' I said. I moved to the door and they made way, combat-jacket going out backwards, in front of me, blue-jacket coming behind, well out of arm's reach. Part of my brain was whirring like a machine, frantically trying to work out a plan but the animal was quiet, accepting it. The man who has the gun makes the rules. It was over, they had the tape and they had me. The bastards had won. I stepped carefully over the debris of broken slates and fallen bricks, moving towards the brambles and the open field.

'Not that way. Over here.'

We emerged into what had been the yard, now just a square patch of land with dilapidated buildings on each side. Some big old farming machine was rusting in one corner, all bent steel rods and wheels, with the long grass growing up between its flaking ribs.

'On to the ground, face first. Spread your arms.'

The grass was wet. I put my cheek down on to it, looking to one side at my outstretched arm. They twisted my palms upwards so that I couldn't move without first flapping my hands around.

'How did you find us?' I asked.

'Shut up.'

'I suppose you're proud of what you do, are you?'

They said nothing. Bastards. It was over but at last I could sleep, at last I could sleep, that was all my brain could manage to dredge up, at last I could sleep. It was out of my hands now, I had no more control. They would kill me or they would not and there was nothing I could do. From a distance I could hear a car engine, coming closer and rising in volume until a blue Sierra bumped into the yard and came to a halt, the handbrake wrenched on with a loud creak. I could see it from where I was lying. Only one man, in the driver's seat, sandy hair and a calm, unflustered expression. Smith. Tired as I was, I could feel anger flaring in my chest.

'Did you get the tape?' he called over, stepping out on to the mud.

'Yeah, no problem,' drawled blue-jacket. Smith was coming towards me, looking casually down the way you would at a bag of rubbish dumped in the street.

'The girl?'

'In the woods. They're bringing her down now.'

'Good.'

I hadn't even dared to think about Alison in case these bastards practised telepathy. There had been no shooting so at least she would be alive. I watched Smith's cheap slip-on shoes as he walked around to my face and squatted down to look at me. I looked up at him like a fish on a slab. His face was calm and expressionless, perhaps a slight smile twitching at the side of his mouth.

'Got you at last, you bastard,' he said quietly. He waited for a moment, perhaps for me to speak.

'Three of my people are dead,' he went on after a moment. In my mind I saw Clare again, her hand moving and her mouth moving and the blood on the wall as she fell. 'I have another three in hospital.

You've managed to do us more damage in a few days than the IRA has done in years. And all you've really done is screw things up for yourself and the girl. You must be very pleased with yourself.'

The girl. Anger. If they touched her. I said nothing. He stared down at me for a long time, then straightened his legs suddenly and stood up. I expected him to give the order then, I almost felt it was time. Kill him, or something. Or maybe he wouldn't say it, maybe they had a sign, a hand signal or a nod of the head, to save them actually saying it. Must be hard to do, I thought, to shoot a man on the ground, who can't fight back, who can't escape, who can't do anything except wait to receive the bullet in his skull with as much dignity as–

'Stand him up. Over there, against the wall.'

Hands grabbing at me, lifting me up, so that was how it was to be, against the wall, maybe a blindfold but I wanted to see everything, every last moment of life, I wanted to see the bullet coming, I wonder can you see the thing anyway, in those last milliseconds, a small, dark bee boring towards your centre ... Pain as the hand cracked across my cheek.

'Wake up, damn you.'

There was a commotion and they were frog-marching the girl into the yard, holding her arms tight as she pulled and twisted and cursed and swore and tried to break free or bite their hands. Well done, Alison, I thought, just a little too late though.

'Miss Sharpe. Glad to have you back.'

'Let her go, Smith, or whatever your name is,' I said, my voice heavy with fatigue. 'You've got the tape, you don't need her now. I was the one who killed your people.'

He looked at me for a long moment and I noticed there was still a shiny pink mark on the bridge of his nose.

'Very commendable, Kearns. You should have thought about that before now.'

They pushed her up against the wall a little way down from me. I glanced to one side and smiled at her and she tried to smile back. I felt no fear at all, nor sadness, nor grief, and I found it very strange. There was guilt, guilt that I had not done better for the girl, made better choices, better decisions. But now it was all finished and they would kill us, either here or in another lonely place, and I hoped I could face it manfully and well, for the girl's sake.

'Clare was one of yours, wasn't she?' I asked him.

'Clare and Uel. Yes, they were ours; two of our best.'

'Certainly had me fooled.'

'We don't play games, you know.'

'You thought I knew where the tape was.'

He sighed heavily. 'I really don't go in much for all this confession business, you know. Much too melodramatic.'

One of them was at the car, talking quietly into a small radio, holding it close to his face. They were waiting for something.

'You thought I knew, and you thought I would lead you to it.'

'We had to cover every eventuality.'

'You tried to frame me.'

'Yes.'

'Don't you feel any guilt at all?'

'We're fighting a war, Kearns. I thought you would have understood, of all people. It's a war, and sometimes people get hurt, injured, for the common good. If you hadn't broken out of the police station you would have had about two years for manslaughter, and we would have had you out in ten months. But no, you had to play the hero.' He looked down at the ground, shaking his head slowly. 'Anyway, it's finished now.'

'You're not fighting a war, Smith,' I hissed at him. 'You're fighting for your neck.'

There was anger in his eyes for a second and I thought he would hit me again. He was the sort who would enjoy hitting a helpless man. If he hits me again I'll kill him, I thought, and to hell with it all, if I'm going to die anyway I might as well die fighting. He glanced around at the car and the man with the radio, glancing at his watch.

'What's keeping them?' he called.

'The van's stuck. Wheels in the mud.'

'Idiots. Take the Sierra and tow them out, for God's sake.'

So they had a van and presumably two or three men with it, that made about seven in all, or maybe eight. There wouldn't be more than four with the van because four men should be able to get a van out of ditch on their own. The animal was rearing up, shaking the sleep away and thinking of escape. I turned and winked at the girl.

'Are you all right?'

She nodded, chewing at her lip. For the first time since I had known her she looked really frightened.

'Did they get the tape?'

'Yes.'

'Shut up!' Smith snapped, spinning round towards us. I watched as combat-jacket stepped across to the car, placing the tape into his pocket. I carefully noted which pocket. He eased himself into the driver's seat and started the ignition.

'Are you going to kill us?' Alison asked, in a very small voice.

'We don't have much choice, do we?'

'You've got the tape. We can't do anything about that now, can we?'

Smith smiled, a thin, hay-stalk smile with cold eyes.

'For all I know you've got a copy stashed away somewhere. No, I'm afraid there's no option. I can't let you go, because Kearns is charged with murder. And we can't let him go to court now, with all that he knows. It really isn't anything personal, I'd like you to know that. It's business. That's all.'

The Sierra rocked and bounced back out of the yard. Blue-jacket held the Heckler and Koch steady at the hip, aimed in my direction. Smith was probably armed. Two of them. Against two of us. Tricky odds. I felt my heart beginning to pound a little harder. The girl was very pale.

'Will it ... will it hurt much?' she asked very softly. My heart wrenched for her. I began to cry. Tears burned around my eyes. I didn't want to die, I muttered and moaned. I don't want to die. The tears

285

came thicker, and my shoulders convulsed and shook in great, jerking sobs. I put my hands to my face and slid slowly down almost on to my knees. Smith was five feet away. There was a large stone by my knee. He was looking down at me, something like disgust on his face.

'Oh, please don't kill me,' I sobbed, bending over towards the damp ground. 'Please don't kill me, I want to live, I don't want to die, please, oh, God, Jesus' ... He looked over at blue-jacket as if to say, look at this pathetic bastard here and that was the moment I was waiting for and I swept up the stone and leapt outwards as hard as I could, grabbing for his legs and I caught them and pulled as I threw my weight against them, rolling on to the ground with him falling heavily on to his back and his head cracking on to the grass. I spun with him, keeping his body between me and blue-jacket and hoping that blue-jacket wouldn't shoot at his own boss, they were well trained but not that well trained, I hoped. Smith was scrabbling and kicking and trying to get his right hand inside his jacket and I could feel the hard line of his pistol, strapped to his side; both of us wanted it and the loser would die. For a fraction of a second we were locked together in a frantic contest of will and strength, two mating insects heaving for the final snap. He stank of tobacco and cheap aftershave. His breath was very close to mine. Blue-jacket was moving, he would be running round to get a clear shot at me but if he fired from that range the round would go through me and into Smith and he knew it. Smith made an immense effort and used all his strength to scrabble for my eyes, his right hand coming sharply round in a vicious clawing move but he left himself open and I still had the stone and I whacked it into his face with the weight of all my anger behind it.

Smith went limp in my grasp, his head dropping back and blood pouring and dropping from his injured face, smearing over my arms and chest. I reached for the pistol, in under the strange, personal warmth of his armpits and found the butt and tugged but the damn thing was strapped into the holster and I popped the catch, half aware of Alison suddenly running for the door of the house and blue-jacket not sure of who to watch and deciding on me but it was too late because I had the pistol out and aimed and I hoped the bastard carried it cocked because if he didn't I was dead but it worked, loud percussive crack and the empty case searing off to one side and blue-jacket suddenly dead and subsiding, lifeless, to the wet grass. My ears were ringing. I heaved Smith's body to one side and scrabbled up, snatching the Heckler from blue-jacket who was still twitching and jerking. He was only a man doing his job as best he could and now here he was, already lifeless but still flapping about like a dead fish. God grant me a more dignified death.

'Alison!' I roared, standing over the lifeless body.

'Over here!' she called back from the door of the ruin. Smith moaned. I had the pistol in my pocket and I was trying to figure out how to work the Heckler, otherwise I would have killed him. As it was I swung my boot into his kidneys on the way past and he moaned again, sharply.

The girl was standing in the doorway, shaking and crying, something inside her broken. She put her arms out to me and I pulled her in, holding her close to me, feeling her small frame shaking like a puppy. The machine-gun was awkward in my hands. A soft drizzle was beginning again.

'What was it all for?' she was sobbing, 'Oh, God, what was it all for?'

'Come on, now, be a brave girl,' I whispered to her. I wished there was something I could tell her. I was sure she could feel the fast drumming of my heart and sense my own desperation. There were five or six of them left, probably on their way up here now, although the sound of the shot might not have travelled all that far. All of them armed, presumably. I had to do something. I had to act.

'Get into the house, there,' I told her as brusquely as I could, trying to ignore the hurt in her eyes. It was important that she did as she was told. 'Stay there. Don't come out for any reason, no matter what. When it's over I'll come and get you, all right?'

'What are you going to do?' she asked, sniffing heavily.

'Never you mind. I'll be back for you, all right?'

She nodded, her eyes to the floor.

'Go on, then. Move it.'

I watched her until she disappeared into the main room then I ducked back out into the yard again. The drizzle had become quite heavy, hissing straight down into the long grass and misting over the outline of the distant trees. I ran over to blue-jacket and quickly patted his body, finding two magazines for the Heckler and a box of nine-millimetre rounds and I stuffed these into my own pockets. They certainly came well armed. Smith was still on his back, unconscious but moaning softly. I stood over him, the Heckler hanging loose but pointing at his chest and I thought about killing him, just the one pressure on the trigger and three rounds would judder into his body and he would die, just as easily as that. But it never is just as easy as that. I had killed and injured people who were trying to kill or injure me, and that was fair, somehow. It had been a contest, a trial of strength that I might easily have lost. Now I was contemplating the murder of a man who could not fight back and who could not escape and the civilised part of me was rattling the bars. There are some things you just cannot do.

'Fuck it,' I said under my breath, before turning and jogging out of the yard.

They had driven the Sierra over the grass and the wheels had flattened and disturbed it so that I could trace the twin trails down the field to an open gate at the roadside. From where I stood I could see the mud streaked on the tarmac. Further up the road I could see the white top of a van speeding along towards the gate, the roof just visible over the high hedges. I felt my stomach flip. Think, damn you, think! The ground was open and bare and there was nowhere to set the ambush. Not until they got to the farmhouse and I could do it there, just as they approached, if I hit them quickly. The van neared the gate, slowing down for it, and I backed into the cover of the bramble bushes, looking frantically around for a better place but there was nowhere, only the house. I jumped back into the yard and through to the farmhouse where the girl was hiding.

'Alison! Lie on the ground! Don't get up for anything, all right?'

'All right!'

Out into the rain again and round to the front of the complex, the magazines clattering in my pocket as I ran. They would have to pass along the side of the barn before turning into the yard and the back door of the barn would do at a pinch. I could rake them as they drove past, then slip back in and through to the yard if things went bad on me. The van was through the gate and labouring up the field, wheels spinning on the wet ground and the Sierra behind it. They were maybe two hundred metres away. At one end of the barn, the end farthest from the road, a clump of straggling weeds grew from an untidy pile of rubble where part of the wall had collapsed, a heap of bricks and slates and wood turned green by the rain. I could hit them from the doorway first of all, then fall back through the barn to the rubble and use it as a reserve position. Then back into the yard. And then ... and then it would be finished, and to hell with it all.

I slipped into the doorway, well back into the shadows. I could just see the van heaving up the grassy slope and I could hear the engine noise, harsh and racing. My head was aching. My chest was heaving. The stubby weapon was heavy in my hands. All

I wanted to do was sleep, lie down and rest for a while, out of the rain and the cold and the fear and far away from guns and death. I had to stop myself thinking about crisp, clean sheets and soft pillows.

They would probably use the same tracks on their way back and that would bring them across my front, a few metres from the doorway, right across my field of fire in a classic ambush position and if I did it right I could take out the whole van with the first burst. The car would be harder because they would deploy with the first contact and go to ground, spreading out to present a smaller target and heading for the ambush site to counter attack. At least, that was what I would have done, but then I was trained and anti-ambush drills were ingrained in me. Fifty metres to go. These men were civil servants, not soldiers, and I had to remember that; even though they had been trained in the use of weapons they would not be experts in fieldcraft and that would give me an edge. Thirty metres. Two men in the front seats, no side windows, standard Ford Transit. I was going to have to kill again and the thought saddened me for a moment. The sky was dark and grey and broody and low and it was a good sky to fight under, a wild, strong, Celtic sky, fit for contests between heroes. Swords and shields and the clatter of arms and strong and lovely women to tend the wounds. They were almost there and I stepped out a little with the butt in my shoulder and fired at the driver's side window as they lurched past me.

The first few rounds took out the glass and presumably killed the driver and I kept firing through the door, the gun hammering at my shoulder and a pattern of silver holes thumping into the white paintwork. The van began to slow down. The rear drew level with the doorway and the rear doors were open, someone trying to get out and I fired through the body of the van, aiming low because they would be crouching. A figure appeared, shoulders first, scrabbling madly to break his fall from the vehicle and I fired at him, hitting him in the head and chest as he slumped on to the grass. The van stalled and bounced to a halt.

The Sierra had slewed round with the first shots and was now broadsides on, all the doors opened, movement on the far side just glimpsed over the bonnet. I leaned out and fired the last few rounds from the magazine at them and ducked back in just as their bullets smacked into the old brickwork behind me, splattering dust and fragments all around me and leaving big, dry marks in the damp surface. The noise of ricochets in the barn like furious bees. Bastards. I stumbled up through the damp gloom to the hole in the wall and threw myself behind the rubble, staying well down behind the weeds, heart drumming madly in my chest, alarmingly fast. Change the magazine, old one out and toss it away, new one in. Weapon cocked and up into the aim. Watch for them, watch for them. Watch and shoot.

The car was behind the van and I could only see the rear half of it but I had a clear view of the gap between the car and the wall of the barn. If they tried to cross there they were dead. I could see a body in the van, slumped over the steering wheel, and the windscreen wipers were still sweeping sadly over the wet glass. Voices from the area of the car, they were calling to each other, probably trying to spot my position but I was hidden, well hidden, crouched low behind the weeds. Suddenly bullets were zipping past in the air and a round struck the rubble near me, a speck of brick dust stinging me on the cheek. I ducked involuntarily. They weren't shooting at me, just in my general direction, but even so it only took the one bullet and I kept my head a little lower, watching as more rounds hammered into the brickwork around the doorway.

Silence, sudden and shocking. I tried to quiet my own panting. They would be waiting now, crouched behind the car, trying to decide whether or not to make the mad dash for the shelter of the buildings, not knowing if I was alive or dead, not knowing exactly where I was, and I didn't envy them the decision. The first man to try it would die because I had the sights on the Heckler lined up on the centre of the gap and he would run into a three-round burst. Funny how easy it is to plan a murder, I reflected, once you were used to it.

A minute dragged by. Something was wrong, they were planning something, I could feel it in the air. Tension. It wasn't all going to go my way and then I saw it, arcing through the air over the top of the car, the sea-green cylinder with the plume of red smoke already beginning to spiral from the top of it, a smoke grenade, they were going to use smoke to cover their move. Just what I would have done, you bastards. The grenade rolled to a halt in the damp grass, hissing and spluttering a thick pink cloud over the car. I pulled the Heckler into my shoulder and fired a long burst of automatic at the gap, not much chance of hitting anything but it made me feel better, then I wriggled back down the rubble and into the barn, crunching on the debris, cutting my hand on something but my mind only on the girl because now they were in the building and they could get to the girl, the girl, if they touch her I'll kill them, so help me.

The smoke was drifting slowly through the rain, hanging around the derelict courtyard. I stumbled towards the main house, wanting to call to her but afraid of them hearing me, slamming into the wall just as the bullets spattered and buzzed into the grass beside me, Jesus that was close and already returning the fire at a sudden movement across the yard. I ducked into the house.

'Alison!'

'Over here!'

Not where I had told her to stay but then I suppose that was her, really, and I should have known. The house was full of warm, pink smoke. I stumbled into the other room and she fell on me, arms tight around me, head in close to my shoulder.

'Oh God,' she was sobbing. 'Oh God oh God oh God ... '

'Alison ... '

I heard him behind me and I spun round with the girl still hanging on to me and the Heckler held in one hand and the instinct switched in, trigger squeezed before my mind was even conscious of the nature of the threat. The heavy bullets slapped into and through him, holes in his chest pumping blood and his face jabbed with the pain. It was combat-jacket and he had the tape. The girl screamed. I pushed her to one of the windows. We had to get out of the room, the house was a deathtrap and if we stayed there we were dead.

'Out of the window! Move it!'

'But–'

I reached out and pushed her up on to the sill with one hand, still watching the doorway with the body stretched out on the rubble, wondering about his gun and if I had time to get it when she screamed again, and then my brain shifted and I was into that slow-motion effect again, my body heavy and hard to move, my mind small and hidden and separated from all events, watching and evaluating and giving orders to the lumbering creature as it resisted death.

Smith was outside the window, his hair plastered on to his forehead by the rain, struggling with the girl. I took in all the details at once; mud on his sleeve, grass stains from our fight, still a tiny red mark on his nose and blood spattered over his chest. Mad, staring eyes, a man out of his world. Hatred and anger boiled up in me almost instantaneously, although it seemed to take long dragging seconds. Whereas the fight with the men from the Sierra was a technical, professional thing, a manic dance per-formed out of necessity with no other thought than survival, now Smith had appeared and there was hate; I wanted to kill him, I wanted to destroy him, this man who had destroyed my life.

Another man, too, stepping into the room behind me and glancing down at the body of his colleague sprawled across the floor, a pistol held in both hands in the alert position, pale beige zipper jacket and a day's growth of beard, a rip in one of his training shoes, my mind whirling all the details together and everything slow, so slow, each movement lasting forever. The threat was from the man with the pistol and I turned to face him, raising the Heckler to aim as he turned to meet me, our eyes meeting across the room and quick acknowledgement of the fact of it; death was fluttering down for one of us, and for one of us there were only seconds of life left. Rain outside, hissing. My feet missing their grip and crunching on a broken tile. His eyes. Nothing personal, they said. Nothing personal.

Two shots booming together, his pistol cracking as my weapon jerked once and was still. Stoppage, I thought, only one round away and the damn thing jams, perhaps this will be my last thought. But he had missed and my one round had found his neck, tearing a long, gashed track along his throat. He dropped his pistol and was gagging, both hands clutching at the dreadful wound, his eyes full of the realisation that it was him and not me, his last few seconds and not mine. He had lost and I had won. I stood, watching him, appalled. He fell to his knees. His eyes clouded, lost their shine, life left him and his remains collapsed into a final bundle of nothing. Dear God, is this where I have come to?

There was commotion outside. I felt tired beyond hope. I tossed the Heckler to one side without

296

bothering to clear the jam and drew Smith's pistol from my pocket, jerking myself into movement. The girl was screaming. I threw myself from the window and landed on the two of them, aware of nothing but Smith and my hatred, vicious, flailing hatred, he had brought me to this and now I was a killer and by God he would pay.

The rain was damp and clean on my neck. I pushed the girl to one side and noticed that he had a knife and part of my mind registered his plan, he was going to use her as a hostage for safe conduct but it was beyond that now and if he had been any sort of a man he would have known it. He was frightened, I could smell it, feel it. I felt his hands scrabbling at me. He was a civil servant, a thinker, not a fighter, a Saxon rather than a Celt and he was out of his depth, knowing fear and not recognising it. I smashed the pistol across his face. Blood sneezed from his nose. He swung at my eyes and I ducked it and punched him in the side, once, twice, losing my grip on him as he wriggled away and I followed him and grabbed at his thighs. He swung his heel at my face and it connected, cheekbone impact and the pain and I rolled away, feeling blood on my face mixing with the rain.

He was wriggling away towards the house, crawling on the soaking grass, sobbing as he crawled. The girl was huddled across the yard, crying as she watched the two of us fight. Her hair was soaking, plastered flat to her head. I sat back and took a firm grip on the pistol, then heaved myself up and walked after him. He crawled on. I walked on, two steps behind him. He was crying, weeping, knowing I would kill him and knowing there was no escape. I searched and scrabbled in my heart for pity but there was none for him; he had chosen to play with fire. Now he would be burned. I pulled the slide back and cocked the weapon, letting it slam forward hard so he would hear it. He sobbed more loudly. I aimed it at the back of his head, following it as he crawled, aware of the mud and the grass stains on his clothes and the hole in the sole of one of his shoes and the pathetic way he was choosing to go. He had no honour.

'No! Don't do it!' Alison had risen to her knees, arms tight across her chest, her face white and rainwashed. 'Garrett, no, don't do it, don't kill him!'

I glanced at her, then back at Smith. For me he had lost all human identity. He was a target, nothing more.

'Garrett, please, please, don't do it!' she was sobbing. For God's sake, I thought.

'Alison, he was going to kill us!' I roared back at her.

'Don't kill him, Garrett, please don't kill him!'

To hell with you, you stupid bitch, this man is a killer, this man is nothing more than an insect, he will do anything that his reasons allow, let me finish him and the world will be a cleaner place. But somewhere deep inside the little, half-forgotten voice was calling, screaming to be heard. 'Give me one reason,' I demanded, shouting, almost crying myself now, wanting to do it but not wanting to do it. 'Just one good reason, that's all!'

She wiped the back of her hand across her mouth and nose and sniffed heavily before tossing her head back and shouting at me; 'Because you're a better man than he is!'

And that was the crux of it and if I was better than he was then how could I kill him, lowering myself to the level of rats and insects, I was better than him yet he deserved death and it was all fighting inside me. I felt tears streaming down my cheeks, the rain on my hair, pain in my head.

'Aren't you?' she was screaming, 'Aren't you?' and I had him in my sights and one jerk of the trigger would have finished it, there in the rain and the mud but the little voice had won and I lowered the pistol, slowly, until it was pointing at the ground. In a fit of sudden anger and temper I emptied the magazine into the ground by my feet, pulling the trigger deliberately for each shot, whipping up damp earth against my legs, pulling and pulling and pulling until it was empty and the thing was over. Smith was lying on his side, open-mouthed, panting, watching me with terrified eyes. I threw the empty pistol at him.

'Fuck you, Smith,' I said loudly to the rain. 'Fuck you anyway.'


'What about the tape?' she said, as if just remembering.

'The tape is gone.'

'What?'

'The tape is gone. The man in the farmhouse had it in his pocket, the one with the combat-jacket.'

'Well, what do you mean, it's gone?'

'When I killed him, one of the bullets went through his pocket, through the cassette. It's gone.' When I had pulled it from the pocket, smeared and bloody, the tape had been tangled and pushed into the wound and there was no way I was going to pull it all out.

'So that's it then,' she said. Her voice was very flat.

'That's it. The tape is destroyed.'

'It's what they wanted all along.'

'It is.'

'And they're going to get away with it.'

'Look, Alison. We did our best. We couldn't do any more. So they get away with it, so what? Smith is finished. He'll never work for them again. Besides, what does it all matter in the end, anyway?'

'What does anything matter, in that case?'

'We're alive, you and me, and a lot of other people are dead. I think that matters. I think that's important.' I slipped into third gear for a bad bend.

'I just wish we had the tape, that's all.'

'No one would have published it. They would have slapped a "D" notice on it and no one would dare to even look at it, and even if someone did publish it, it would be just another article, and who believes what they read in the papers, anyway? Besides, there are a thousand cans of worms. We just opened one of them.'

The car bumped and jolted over a patch of uneven tarmac. At last the rain was easing.

'We've restored an equilibrium,' I told her. 'We're back where we started, more or less, and we can pick it up and go on from there. We're the lucky ones. Remember that. All right?'

I looked across at her and smiled. She smiled back, weakly. She looked tired and sad and beautiful.

'All right,' she whispered.

'Good,' I said. 'Now let's get to a police station and you can do some explaining.'

# A Selected List of Fiction Available from Mandarin

While every effort is made to keep prices low, it is sometimes necessary to increase prices at short notice. Mandarin Paperbacks reserves the right to show new retail prices on covers which may differ from those previously advertised in the text or elsewhere.

The prices shown below were correct at the time of going to press.

| | | | | |
|---|---|---|---|---|
| ☐ | 7493 0576 2 | **Tandia** | Bryce Courtenay | £4.99 |
| ☐ | 7493 0122 8 | **Power of One** | Bryce Courtenay | £4.99 |
| ☐ | 7493 0581 9 | **Daddy's Girls** | Zoe Fairbairns | £4.99 |
| ☐ | 7493 0942 3 | **Silence of the Lambs** | Thomas Harris | £4.99 |
| ☐ | 7493 0530 4 | **Armalite Maiden** | Jonathan Kebbe | £4.99 |
| ☐ | 7493 0134 1 | **To Kill a Mockingbird** | Harper Lee | £3.99 |
| ☐ | 7493 1017 0 | **War in 2020** | Ralph Peters | £4.99 |
| ☐ | 7493 0946 6 | **Godfather** | Mario Puzo | £4.99 |
| ☐ | 7493 0381 6 | **Loves & Journeys of Revolving Jones** | Leslie Thomas | £4.99 |
| ☐ | 7493 0381 6 | **Rush** | Kim Wozencraft | £4.99 |

All these books are available at your bookshop or newsagent, or can be ordered direct from the publisher. Just tick the titles you want and fill in the form below.

**Mandarin Paperbacks**, Cash Sales Department, PO Box 11, Falmouth, Cornwall TR10 9EN.

Please send cheque or postal order, no currency, for purchase price quoted and allow the following for postage and packing:

UK including BFPO
£1.00 for the first book, 50p for the second and 30p for each additional book ordered to a maximum charge of £3.00.

Overseas including Eire
£2 for the first book, £1.00 for the second and 50p for each additional book thereafter.

NAME (Block letters) ............................................................................................................................

ADDRESS...............................................................................................................................................

............................................................................................................................................................

☐ I enclose my remittance for ...........................

☐ I wish to pay by Access/Visa Card Number ☐☐☐☐☐☐☐☐☐☐☐☐☐☐

Expiry Date ☐☐☐☐